Eric Archer was thinking about Christmas.

Dad had said he'd pick him up for Christmas and they'd have a great time. Dad had also said he'd like it here at school. He didn't. He hated it. This was a dumb school.

He didn't want to spend Christmas with Dad. He sure wasn't going to have a great time in that stuffy apartment in New York City or in some hotel in one of those other cities Dad was always visiting. Spending Christmas with Uncle Dave would be a *lot* better....

But what he *really* wanted...he couldn't have. He wanted things to be the way they were before Gramps and Grandma got on that awful plane that crashed. Then he'd still be with them and not stuck in this school. And probably he and Gramps would be riding all over Kentucky looking for the horse Gramps was giving him for Christmas.

It was *suppo*   is life. Only now it w

"Eric! Eric Arc

It was some t   er was calling his nan

Eric was silent. The other kids snickered and Miss Johnson glared but he didn't care.

"Eric Archer, I can see you haven't been paying any attention. *Again.* I'm sending you to see Miss Powell."

He didn't care about that, either. He didn't care about anything. Not even Christmas.

ABOUT THE AUTHOR

Eva Rutland began writing when her four children, now all successful professionals, were growing up. She became a regular—and very popular—contributor to Harlequin's Romance and Regency series. (Several of her titles have been reissued in Harlequin's By Request anthologies.) She's well-known for the warmth, sincerity and charm of her writing. *A Child's Christmas* is Eva's first long romance novel—and we're delighted to introduce her to Superromance readers.

Eva lives in California with her husband, Bill, who actively supports and encourages her writing.

Books by Eva Rutland

HARLEQUIN ROMANCE
2897—TO LOVE THEM ALL
2944—AT FIRST SIGHT
3064—NO ACCOUNTING FOR LOVE
3240—ALWAYS CHRISTMAS
3283—FOREIGN AFFAIR
3412—PRIVATE DANCER
3439—MARRIAGE BAIT

HARLEQUIN REGENCY ROMANCE
 1—MATCHED PAIR
20—THE VICAR'S DAUGHTER
28—ENTERPRISING LADY
45—THE WILLFUL LADY
89—GRETNA BRIDE

A CHILD'S CHRISTMAS
Eva Rutland

Harlequin Books

TORONTO • NEW YORK • LONDON
AMSTERDAM • PARIS • SYDNEY • HAMBURG
STOCKHOLM • ATHENS • TOKYO • MILAN
MADRID • WARSAW • BUDAPEST • AUCKLAND

ISBN 0-373-70769-X

A CHILD'S CHRISTMAS

Copyright © 1997 by Eva Rutland.

Printed in U.S.A.

A CHILD'S
CHRISTMAS

PROLOGUE

ERIC ARCHER sat in the fifth-grade classroom and stared at his teacher. A frilly sleeve would fall back from her plump arm as she made hard jabs on the blackboard like she was mad at it. Then she'd tap the figures lightly with the pointer as she talked to the class. Eric watched her little round mouth open and close, open and close, but he wasn't listening.

He was thinking about Christmas.

Dad had said he'd pick him up for Christmas and they'd have a great time.

But Dad had also said he'd like it here at this school. He didn't. He hated it. This was a dumb school. Living in a dorm with a whole bunch of boys he didn't even know, boys who were always mouthing off or giggling at something stupid, was a real pain. And all those bells! Get up, go to sleep, time to eat, go to class. Dumb. And Matron, always saying, don't do this, do that, room inspection!

He didn't want to spend Christmas with Dad. He sure wasn't going to have a great time in that stuffy apartment in New York City or in some hotel in one of those cities Dad was always visiting.

He wanted...what he couldn't have. His eyes stared at the teacher, but his mind reeled backward, willing things to be the way they were before. Before Gramps and Grandma got on that awful airplane that crashed. If they hadn't, he'd still be with them at Greenlea Stables and not stuck in this dumb boarding school. And probably he and Gramps would be riding all over Kentucky's bluegrass country looking for the horse Gramps was giving him for Christmas.

"I don't think he'll fit in Santa's sleigh," Gramps had said with a teasing wink, because he knew Eric knew about Santa Claus. Anyway, Gramps said if Eric was big enough to help train a prize stallion, he was big enough to pick him out.

So they'd probably be looking now. Long before Christmas. Long before he and Gramps cut the tree and trimmed it, and the house was filled with Christmas decorations and lots of presents and the smell of Rosella's special Christmas cooking, his stallion would be pawing in the paddock, waiting for him to ride.

It was supposed to be the best Christmas he'd had in his whole life. Only now it wouldn't be.

"Eric, can you answer that question? Eric! Eric Archer!"

It was some time before Eric realized that the little round mouth was calling his name. And then he didn't know what the question was he was supposed to answer.

Miss Johnson glared at him, waiting for him to speak.

Eric was silent. The other kids snickered, but he didn't care.

"Eric Archer, I can see you haven't been paying the least bit of attention. *Again.* I believe I've had quite enough of this. I'm sending you to the counselor."

He didn't care about that, either. He didn't care about anything. Not even Christmas.

CHAPTER ONE

"MR. ARCHER, this is Monica Powell."

"Yes?" Dave pressed the phone closer to his ear. As if that would help. Who was Monica Powell? Somebody's secretary or someone he'd met at the club. No! Business or pleasure, he'd remember that voice. Low and melodious, with a husky undertone. Seductive. He leaned against the wall, drinking in the sound.

"Do you think you could possibly arrange a time, Mr. Archer?"

He straightened, startled out of his stupor. "Er... why, I...I suppose I might be able to do that," he said uncertainly. Time for what? Why did she sound irritated? He'd been so intrigued with the voice he hadn't attended to the words.

"Thank you. It *is* important. I'd like to set up a meeting now, if you don't mind. This week, if possible. I'm here at the school from ten to four o'clock, Monday through Friday."

"School?" Then Dave understood. She was calling from the academy and had the wrong Mr. Archer. She wanted Lyndon, Eric's father and Dave's older brother. Dave was immediately alert.

"What's wrong? Has something happened to Eric?"

"No, no! Don't be alarmed, Mr. Archer. Eric is fine," she said.

Dave felt immense relief at hearing that. He'd intended to go over there to see the kid before now, but he'd been so damn busy. The woman began to talk about the boy's academic progress, and he was about to tell her that he wasn't Eric's father, that Lyn, who was, had flown to London, England, for a few days on business; but instead, he found himself just listening, completely absorbed in the seductive tones. He could listen to that voice forever....

"My office is on the second floor of the library building," she was saying now. "When would be convenient for you?"

"Tomorrow, three o'clock?" he said, feeling his senses quicken. He'd never forgive himself if, in Lyn's absence, something had gone wrong. He *had* promised Lyn that he'd be there for the kid. But she did say Eric was fine. So why a meeting?

Oh, well, at least he'd get to see who was behind that voice. A woman with a voice like that was no ordinary woman.

MONICA POWELL marked the time on her calendar and again studied the notes on Eric Archer before setting aside his file. She had, at least, managed to contact the boy's elusive father, but she honestly wondered if it would do any good. He hadn't bothered to return her previous call, nor had he answered her note. Obviously he was not concerned about his ten-year-old son. Too busy at the helm of the vast Archer empire.

Hardly. Judging from what she'd read about him in the papers, more likely his racehorses and his women were the distraction. There was a wry twist to Monica's mouth as she cleared her desk. When she'd left Central High, an inner-city school in Philadelphia, to move to Pueblo Beach, California, this past summer, she'd felt as if she was deserting really needy kids.

But as counselor at the prestigious Joel E. Smith Academy, she was finding that rich kids had problems, too. Day classes at the private school, grades one through twelve, included girls, as well as boys, but boarding facilities were available for boys only.

Monica had been saddened to learn that at least half the boarders were elementary students. Boys that young should live at home. They should never be dumped in a boarding school, no matter how fancy! Perhaps, she thought now, she was needed here as much as she'd been needed in Philadelphia.

Anyway, she had no choice. Dad needed her, and she'd been lucky to get any job at all, much less in Pueblo Beach, an expensive resort town and a playground for the idle rich!

Bite your tongue! she chastized herself and then chuckled. Dad's house was here and they were darn lucky to have it. It wasn't one of those mansions set on five acres, complete with stables, swimming pool and tennis court. Just a two-bedroom cottage on the edge of the ritzy area, but nestled in the quiet little seaside town of Pueblo, with its wide shaded streets and quaint shops, and far enough from San Diego not to be filled with traffic and crowds.

An ideal place for her parents to settle, Monica had thought three years ago when the company that employed her father closed down and forced him into early retirement. But one blow followed another. Her mother's long battle with cancer exhausted their savings and her father's strength. He'd had a stroke only one month after his wife's funeral. He was out of the hospital now and slowly recovering.

Too slowly. As if he really didn't care. Dad. Who had always been the most enthusiastic man alive, whether coaching her summer volleyball team, playing Scrabble or managing Temper Food's most successful sales district. If the company hadn't sold out…if her mother hadn't died…

No. She wouldn't look back. Dad was alive. He would be himself again. It just took time.

Monica glanced at her watch. She'd better hurry. She wanted to stop at the grocery story for fresh vegetables. She picked up the three books she'd selected from the school library and made her way downstairs.

It was like being in another world, she thought, as she walked through the spacious tree-shaded campus to the parking lot. So different from Central High's bleak corridors and pitted pavement, where students shouted obscenities and took shots at the netless basketball hoop against one grimy concrete wall.

Here at Joel E. Smith Academy, there was a kind of serenity at day's end when classes were over. The campus was relatively quiet. She encountered only a few students drifting to or from the dormitories or library, music hall or tennis courts. As she neared the soccer field, she heard a whistle and a few shouts. The parking lot, which was just to the left of the gym, was bordered by lush shrubbery.

As she started toward her car, a boy burst through the shrubbery, a small scruffy dog leaping at his heels. The boy was laughing, but when he saw her, the laughter died on his lips.

Monica was sorry. It was the first time she'd ever heard Eric Archer laugh, and the sound was a pleasure to hear. Now he was silent, his blond hair ruffled, his freckles standing out against his thin pale face, his blue eyes wary. He was obviously trying to pretend there was no dog cavorting at his feet, snapping at the cuffs of his jeans.

This was the dog, she realized, that had gotten Eric in trouble with the school. Pets were not permitted, yet Eric had been found more than once with the animal in his room. She wanted to say, *Don't be scared. I'm not going to tell*, but all that emerged was a gentle "Hello, Eric."

"Hello, Miss Powell." As polite and uncommitted as when she'd chided him about his schoolwork.

She paused, but for the life of her couldn't think

of anything to say. Or if she could, couldn't say it. *"What a darling dog!"* would mean she'd seen it. Surely Eric knew he couldn't hide his frisky pet for long. Despite those sketchy grades, Eric Archer was no dummy. No, she thought, just desperately lonely. If he wasn't, he'd be on the tennis court or soccer field or horsing around with some of the other boys.

Poor guy, she thought as she climbed into her car and switched on the ignition. It was hard being the new kid on the block. Or the new fifth grader whose classmates had lived together for four years. Glancing through her rearview mirror, she saw Eric toss a stick, watched the dog race after it. The little tableau plucked at her heartstrings. If Eric lived at home, he'd probably be permitted to keep a dog.

Once again she wondered why the boy was a boarding student when his father lived practically next door to the school. She felt a rush of anger toward the uncaring father.

AT TWENTY MINUTES to three the next day Dave Archer climbed into his Jaguar and drove reluctantly to the academy. The effect of the voice had worn off. Besides, it was doubtful the woman on the other end of the wire would live up to it. Now he only wondered about Eric.

I should have checked on him before now. Lyn placed Eric in this school only because I live nearby.

The Pueblo Beach house was just one of the residences his family owned, and currently it was being shared by Dave and his three-times-divorced older brother. Lyn, however, was seldom in Pueblo, for he'd taken to the business end of Archer Enterprises like a duck to water and, since Dad had retired, was running the show. He much preferred New York and London, the hub of their commercial world. He declared that "wheeling and dealing in international finance is an exciting game."

It didn't excite Dave. The only prize there was money, and what was the point when you already had more of that than you could use? Dave preferred the game of baseball, which was why his main residence was the beach house at Pueblo. Isolated, but only an hour's drive from San Diego, home of the Demons, the baseball team of which he was prime owner. He'd be in San Diego now were it not for Lyn's son.

As he turned into the academy gates, he wondered again what was up. He knew practically nothing about the boy. Neither did Lyn, for that matter. Except for brief vacation visits, Eric had lived for the past eight years exclusively with his maternal grandparents, who'd died in an airplane crash in June. Tough for the kid. After one month, Lyn's ex, Marion, too busy being an actress to be a mother, had shipped Eric to Lyn.

Lyn, with his bachelor quarters in New York and London and widespread business affairs, was totally unprepared. But acting with his usual dispatch, he'd taken the boy with him during his summer travels while he checked out boarding schools. The highly recommended Joel E. Smith Academy seemed to be the best and was conveniently located in Pueblo, where he could keep in touch.

Where I can keep in touch, Dave thought irritably as he entered the school library and mounted the stairs to the counselor's office. He wondered what sort of devilment the boy had gotten up to that required a conference with a parent. Perhaps he should explain that Eric had been through a lot of changes recently.

He knocked on her office door, heard a brief "Come in!" and swinging wide the door, opened his mouth to tell her he was Eric's uncle. But he was thrown again by the voice. She'd stood up and come around her desk, extending a hand.

"Mr. Archer? Good afternoon."

Not only the voice. The woman herself. He didn't know why. He was not immune to female charms, had had his share of relationships in his thirty-six years, but unlike Lyn, was not prone to go berserk over a woman's looks.

But this time...well, what was it? That hint of something indefinable and exciting beneath the austere image she projected? He could tell by the glasses perched on top of her head and the way her bronze-gold hair was pulled tight and held by a large barrette at the nape of her neck that she was striving for a professional look. Her outfit, a primly buttoned tailored silk blouse tucked into a gabardine skirt of matching tan, was certainly correct, but served only to emphasize the delicate curves of her figure. She was slender and of medium height.

"Please, do have a seat." She took the glasses from her head and waved them toward a chair. Yes, maybe the glasses *were* only for effect, he thought. Nothing myopic about those clear hazel eyes, which at the moment were regarding him intently. "I'm glad to finally have this opportunity to speak with you, Mr. Archer. I'm very concerned about Eric."

"Oh?" His eyes focused on the cleft in her chin. It made her seem vulnerable, the full curved mouth more kissable—

"I assume you're also concerned?"

Dear Lord, what had he been thinking? "Er... yes," he replied in a rather stumbling fashion. "Of course. What has the boy been doing to upset you?"

"Nothing."

"Nothing?"

The kissable mouth tightened. "*Absolutely* nothing, Mr. Archer. Take a look for yourself." She opened a folder and extracted some papers. "These are reports from his teacher."

He scanned them, conscious that she was watching him. "...consistently fails to complete assignments...no participation in class discussions... inattentive...."

The comments accompanied a deplorable progress report. "I see what you mean," he said at last, raising his head.

The hazel eyes focused on him, an assessing look that made him decidedly uncomfortable. "I'm sure

one of the reasons you chose Smith Academy for
your son is our high academic standards."

"Actually I had no part in it. You see, I'm not—"

She cut him off. "Then it was Eric's choice?"
she asked, looking surprised.

"Yes, at least partially," he said slowly, thinking
about it. He seemed to remember that Lyn had taken
the boy over to inspect the place before enrolling
him.

"Then we may safely assume the choice was not
made on academic grounds," she said, smiling. The
smile illuminated her whole face, and he became
quite lost in the radiance. "His transcript from his
school in Kentucky indicates excellent achieve-
ment." She hesitated. "That is not the case here. In
fact—" she hesitated again "—Miss Johnson, his
teacher, is convinced that Eric is rather...slow."

"That's impossible," he said. "Eric is a bright
child." At least he'd seemed so when... How many
times had he seen him? And what did he know about
Eric's schoolwork? Not much, he answered himself.

She was nodding. "I get that impression, too, but
I've only had one twenty-minute conference with
him. It's the residence matron and his teacher who
see him on a daily basis."

"Look, Miss Powell, Eric has been through a lot
this summer. I think he needs time to...to get ad-
justed."

"Yes." She was regarding him intently. "You
think the move from Kentucky has caused some

emotional disturbance and might have affected his work habits?''

"Perhaps. But there's more," he said, thinking of the drastic changes Eric had had to cope with in just a few months. Tough for a ten-year-old. Tough for anyone.

He bent toward the counselor, willing her to understand. "He's still dealing with the shock of losing the two people closest to him. You see," he said, "his grandparents were killed in an airplane crash this year. And he had...well, they were more like parents than grandparents."

She gasped. "How dreadful for him!"

"Yes. He'd lived with them from the time he was two."

"Poor kid. What he must be going through..." It came out in a whisper. She *did* understand. She stared at Dave as if in shock. "And we weren't notified of this?"

He stared back. "Notified? The school, you mean? But it only happened last June, you see. Lyn...that is, we weren't sure Eric would be coming here." He swallowed. "By the time he was registered, it was a little late to notify you."

"I'm sorry. 'Alerted' is perhaps the better word. Had we been aware of the circumstances, we might have been able to help—or at least to understand. Poor kid," she said again and for a moment looked as if she might cry. "And he holds it all in. No wonder he can't concentrate on his schoolwork."

She met Dave's gaze directly. "And he came to you immediately after the accident?"

"Oh, no! He was with his mother until August. She's—"

"I know. Marion Holiday, the actress."

"Yes. She has a very busy schedule, you see, and thought it best for him to be...here."

Dave wasn't sure why he had yet to explain that he was only the boy's uncle. After all, Eric was Lyn's son, Lyn's problem, not his.

"I see," she murmured, her gaze even more assessing now.

He was about to tell her she was judging the wrong person when she leaned forward, an earnest expression on her face.

"Mr. Archer, may I speak openly with you?"

"Please do."

She paused as if trying to decide how to put what she wanted to say. Or was it how she thought he'd be affected? She swallowed, and he saw the muscles in her throat working. At last she said, "You put it mildly when you said Eric needs time to adjust. The trauma of his grandparents' death, the move to his mother's, then to you... So many changes in such a short time can be devastating to a child."

"I know. We thought perhaps living at school with children his own age, might...well, help lift his spirits." He and Lyn had talked it over. They'd both been in boarding school when they were young. They'd made great friendships there, had even looked forward to seeing their pals again after the summer breaks.

"An excellent motive, but...well, things don't always work out as you plan." A sad smile played about her lips, and he was moved by the compassion in her voice. "I'm afraid that Eric feels like an outsider."

"An outsider?" The image disturbed him. "How's that?"

Now her smile was wistful. "Children can be cruel, Mr. Archer. They tend to form cliques. These cliques become quite strong after four years of living together and—" she spread her hands "—well, often firmly closed against someone new."

"I see." He felt a surge of guilt. He and Lyn had just dumped Eric, really, leaving him to cope on his own. Lyn should have— Lyn wasn't here. *He was.* He sat up straighter. "How can I...I mean, is there anything that would help?" What did one do to bring ten-year-olds together, to help form friendships? Hire a bus and take the whole class to a baseball game?

She looked directly at him. "I notice that in the almost two months Eric's been here, he hasn't spent any weekends at home."

"Well, no." Lyn hadn't been here, that was why. He'd been involved in some big deal. Still was. *I was involved in a big deal, too,* he thought. His team had made it to the World Series, and he'd been running like a rabbit between San Diego and Detroit. Seven games, lost by a thread when Duke, their star pitcher, had developed muscle cramps in his arm. They'd given Detroit a run, though, and it had been exciting. He was aware that the counselor was watching him, waiting for some explanation. "I was mostly out of town this month."

He felt a rush of guilt. He should've thought of the boy. Taken him to a couple of games.

"I understand, Mr. Archer. I know you're busy. But Eric... Please forgive me. I have no right to interfere in your affairs or tell you how to rear your son." She hesitated, but then plunged right in. "I'm really concerned about Eric. I'm not sure how his life has been in the past, but I do know that he is very unhappy and lonely now and that you as a parent ought to—" She stopped, bit her lip. "This is an extremely difficult time for Eric. He needs the emotional support of a father, an assurance that he is worthy and...and..." She seemed at a loss as to how to finish.

"Loved?" Dave said, and watched the color stain her cheeks.

"Yes." She faced him defiantly, then gave what appeared to be a forced smile. "Eric is so uncertain of...of everything. He may have doubts about what he should take for granted." She paused. "I guess what I'm trying to say is, if you could have him home more often, talk with him, feel him out and..." She heaved an exasperated sigh. "Oh, you must know what I mean."

She cared, Dave thought. Really cared. She wasn't just a school counselor doing her duty, talking to a parent about a student's problems. She had feelings for his nephew, itched to help him.

And suddenly Dave knew what intrigued him about her, what was behind that sultry voice and pretty face. A warm loving compassionate woman. A woman he wanted to know. If she knew he wasn't Eric's father, would she—

His beeper sounded, startling both of them.

"Excuse me," he said. The board meeting. They must be waiting for him. "I need to make a quick call. Do you mind?"

"Not at all," she said, gesturing toward the phone on her desk.

"Sorry, Val," he said into the phone. "I know I'm late, but... No. I'm still in Pueblo. Can't you...? Oh. OK. I'll get there right away." He broke the connection, irritated. Surely the situation wasn't anything Val couldn't handle. But... He brightened. A convenient interruption. As good an excuse as any.

"Miss Powell, something's come up and I need to get to San Diego as soon as possible," he said, turning to her. "I'm sorry to have to end our discussion so abruptly. The circumstances are such that I've not had much practice being a parent, and I'd really value your input." He would explain the misunderstanding later, he thought. "I'd like to continue this discussion as soon as possible."

"Of course. I'm always available between—"

"No." Dammit, he didn't want to see her in this formal office setting with this desk between them.

He wanted... He didn't know what he wanted, only that he had to see her again. "My schedule is very tight," he lied. "My daytime hours are crammed, and there are constant disruptions."

He touched his beeper. "Could we discuss this sometime after hours? For dinner, perhaps. I'd really appreciate it if I could see you during an evening when neither of us would be in a rush. And as soon as possible—tomorrow, if you can. I know it's crucial for Eric."

She was right. The boy needed someone. With Lyn away, he would stand in.

CHAPTER TWO

ADA JOHNSON shook her head as she made her way across the faculty lounge to the coffee urn. "That Archer kid is a moron."

"Come on now, Ada." Monica tried to keep her cool. Something else she'd learned—insensitive teachers invaded exclusive private schools, as well as cash-poor inner-city ones. "That's an awful thing to say."

"Maybe, but it's true!" The older woman ran a hand through her short gray hair. "He just sits and stares into space, no matter what's happening in class. Totally out of it. A real moron, I tell you."

Monica set down her mug so hard coffee splashed on the table. She tried not to dislike Ada, but her way of labeling kids made her skin crawl. "Staring into space doesn't make a kid a moron," she said evenly.

"Oh, there are other symptoms and, believe me, I know them all." Ada filled her mug and came to sit facing Monica across the table. "I've been teaching for twenty years and I can read a kid like a book."

"Amazing."

Oblivious to the sarcasm, Ada tapped her head significantly. "Eric Archer is not all there."

"That's a serious accusation, Ada, and I don't think it's one you're qualified to—" Monica broke off. *Cool it,* she warned herself. Ada was Eric's primary teacher. She needed to feel the woman out about the boy. More to go on when she saw his father tonight.

"There's no evidence of mental deficiency in his transcript," Monica said. "His records from Kentucky show excellent grades. No mention of—"

"I've thought about that." Ada pursed her thin lips with firm conviction. "Probably one of those borderline cases."

"Borderline?"

"A thin line, you know, between genius and—"

"Oh, don't be ridiculous!" Monica snapped. "Eric Archer is a perfectly healthy normal boy who's been through a very trying time."

"Poor, poor baby who was sent to the counselor's office. What did he do? Burst into tears or something for you?"

"No. He did nothing of the kind. He simply stared—" She stopped, swallowed. "He regarded me solemnly as if—"

"Hello, hello, hello!" Lisa Hamilton burst into the room, looking so fresh and vibrant that Monica felt a pang of envy. How great to work outdoors almost every day, as Lisa did as gym teacher. Much easier than wrestling with muddled minds, teachers', as well as pupils'!

Lisa headed straight for the fridge. She filled a tumbler with orange juice and drank thirstily. "Mmm, delicious," she declared when the tumbler was empty. "Nothing like a tough game on the tennis court to work up a good thirst."

"You should have gotten changed before coming up here to the staff lounge!" Ada gazed pointedly at Lisa's short tennis skirt and bare legs, which were, to her credit, long and shapely.

The winsome gym teacher grinned. "Stopped by in my working clothes, just like you did. Shouldn't think that would bother you."

Ada bristled. "Not me. The men use the lounge, too, you know."

As if to prove her point the door opened again to admit James Atwood, the head of the history department.

Lisa struck a pose. "Are you intimidated by my attire, Dr. Atwood?"

The gray-haired professor smiled. "Not at all. I'm covered."

"Covered?"

"Sexual-harassment insurance."

Lisa's eyes widened in mock surprise. "Haven't heard about that before."

"It's called the aging process, my dear," he said dryly as he sat on the sofa and unfolded his newspaper.

Lisa giggled and Monica smiled. She was glad of the interruption, for it had kept her from lashing out at Ada Johnson. She'd seen Ada's quick nod when she'd inadvertently said that Eric had "stared." But it wasn't, as Ada thought, a moronic stare. Eric's expression was listless, uncaring, like...yes, exactly like Dad's! As if all the savor, all the joy, had gone out of life and nothing meant anything to him anymore.

She was familiar with the feeling herself. She'd weathered quite a few changes—her father's loss of employment, her mother's death only last Christmas, her father's stroke. Not to mention her total change of environment.

But she was a grown woman, twenty-eight years old. Eric was just a little boy, and for him, everything had gone all at once. *Zap!* The two people who'd been closest to him, given him a home, all the security of his young life. Then his mother had quickly discarded him, passing him on to a father who, in a way, had discarded him long ago. What was it he'd said? *Not much practice being a parent,* and *You know Eric better than I.* What kind of father was that?

"Back to Eric," Ada said, turning her attention from Lisa who, complacently munching an apple, had joined them at the table. "He should be removed from here and placed in a special school."

"Watch it, Ada!" Lisa cautioned with a mischievous grin. "I don't know who you're talking about, but every kid here means big bucks that the administration does not take kindly to losing."

Ignoring Lisa, Ada spoke directly to Monica. "I mentioned this to the dean, and he says such a recommendation should come from the counselor's office.''

"Then you may as well forget it, because the only recommendation I'm going to make is—'' Monica hesitated, engulfed by rage ''—that he be given special attention.'' And transferred to another class with another teacher! One who'd encourage him, not label him.

"But that's just what I'm saying. He should be where he can receive special attention. Not where he disrupts a class of normal children.''

"How can he disrupt a class,'' Monica said through gritted teeth, ''if, as you say, he's totally out of it? It's not like he's throwing spitballs.''

"That staring is worse. It gives me the creeps.''

"It has nothing to do with you. The boy has been shifted around so many times during the past three months that he feels lost. I had a long talk with his father yesterday and—''

Ada sat up. "You mean the *great* Lyndon Archer has finally surfaced? Why didn't you tell me?''

Lisa almost choked on her apple. "Are you talking about *the* Lyndon Archer? The one with all those racehorses and all that money?'' Understanding dawned in her expression. ''Oh, I see. Archer. Eric Archer. He's a new student here, isn't he?'' It was more a statement than a question.

"Yes, I'm talking about his father, and he's quite concerned about him.'' Monica hoped this was true.

"Monica Powell, I can't believe you had a conference with Eric's father and did not include me, his primary teacher." Ada's tone was one of disappointment, as well as disapproval. "I should have been the one to explain Eric's condition. Did you tell him what I said?"

"Of course," Monica replied, aware that "rather slow"—which was what she'd told Archer—was not exactly the phrase Ada had used.

"And what did he say? Did he agree that Eric should be placed in a special school?"

"He, uh, he'd like further discussion. I...I'm to meet with him again."

"When?" Ada asked. "I should be in on this."

Monica colored, feeling cornered. But why should she? She had nothing to hide. "He...his schedule is very full, and he wanted to take time to go more thoroughly into Eric's problem. I...I agreed to have dinner with him tonight."

Long pause. "Oh. I see." Ada drew out the last word.

Lisa was more direct. "You mean you have a date with *the* Lyndon Archer?"

"It's not a date! It's a conference. And I wish you'd stop calling him *the* Lyndon Archer!"

"But all those horses! All that money!"

"All those women," Ada said darkly.

"Yes, be careful, Monica," Lisa cautioned, her apple forgotten. "He *is* one handsome guy!"

Monica shrugged, annoyed. "I suppose." Strong chiseled features came to mind. Dark deep-set eyes that held a friendly warmth, the skin around them crinkling when he smiled. Dark reddish brown hair and—

"Oh, he's handsome all right, and he's rich." Ada gave Monica a significant glance. "Arrogant and unpredictable, too. And if you can believe the tabloids, a real womanizer. He dumps women as fast as he picks them up."

"He doesn't come across as arrogant," Monica said, thinking how Ada's labels were not limited to students. "Anyway, Ada, I'm not interested in Lyndon Archer, nor his women. Just his son."

"And that's why you're going out on this date with him, I presume," Ada muttered.

"Like I said, be careful." Lisa stood and gave Monica a pat on the shoulder before heading out. "Gotta run."

Monica glared at Ada. "Presume as much as you please, Ada. I'm seeing Mr. Archer because I'm concerned about Eric, and that's the truth. The poor kid's been moved three times in the past three months, after losing his grandparents, the two people who brought him up. He hardly knows his father."

"And you plan to introduce them?"

"Oh, Ada!"

"That's your excuse for this little excursion, isn't it?"

"Excuse?" Monica had to fight hard to control her temper.

"Oh, yes." Ada's voice was sweetly sarcastic. "But don't get carried away with this parental-involvement ploy! You're wasting your time trying to get Eric Archer's father interested in you.''

"I resent that!'' Monica felt her pulses soar, but the rustle of Dr. Atwood's newspaper made her lower her voice. "I am a counselor, professionally engaged in a conference with a parent about his child.''

"Over dinner?''

"When and wherever convenient.'' She'd survived conferences in Philly's dangerous tenements, hadn't she? What was dinner with a handsome man, regardless of his reputation? Good grief, she wasn't some starry-eyed ingenue!

She knew she'd better get out of here before she really blew her top. "I have an appointment," she lied, gathering up her papers to leave.

Unfortunately she didn't miss Ada's parting shot. "Extremely unprofessional, I'd say. Having a consultation outside the office!''

Back in her office, Monica slammed the folders on her desk. Damn! Damn! Damn! She shouldn't have mentioned the meeting. Why had she opened her big mouth? But then, why be secretive? It was a professional meeting and she didn't give a hoot what Ada thought.

Maybe she should call him and cancel.

No! That boy needed help. And the first thing she was going to do was help him get transferred to a different class.

But how? Only one fifth-grade class, and Ada was primary teacher. Furthermore the woman wasn't going anywhere; she had several more years to sit on her damn tenure, pasting labels on kids and making them stick. The thought of Eric's being under her for a whole year made Monica feel ill. Was there nothing she could do about it?

The problem plagued her as she went about her various duties, and it wasn't until lunchtime that a solution occurred. A chuckle erupted when she thought of it, for Ada herself had given the cue. A borderline case. Well, maybe Eric wasn't a genius, but the excellent grades on his transcript might have some influence. She could suggest that fifth-grade subjects lacked challenge for Eric and recommend that he be promoted to sixth—under the tutelage of the cheerful and understanding Josie Spencer.

Would Ada oppose her? A new counselor's recommendation would carry little weight against that of a long-tenured teacher. But, with the support of a rich parent... Big bucks, Lisa had termed it.

Yes, she would definitely keep her appointment with Lyndon Archer. She would leave early so that she could fix Dad's dinner and get him settled before Archer arrived to pick her up.

MONICA'S HEART ached every time she returned home and found her father sitting just where she'd left him in the morning. In the big easy chair where he could stare—look out the window. Had he eaten the lunch she left? Turned on the TV? Opened a book?

She felt for him. Herb Powell had been so strong

and vital it was hard now for him to accept his weakness. The stroke had left him more emotionally than physically crippled.

"Hi." She tossed her purse on the coffee table and went over to kiss him on the forehead, rumple his thinning gray hair.

"Hi, honey," he said, turning to look at her. "Did you have a good day?"

"Hectic. Come on into the kitchen with me and I'll tell you all about it." She willed herself not to help him. She knew he found the walker awkward, but the doctor said that the more he did for himself, the sooner he'd recover.

In the kitchen she peered into the refrigerator. Oh, no. Only half the sandwich she'd left for him had been eaten, and none of the soup, which he could've just popped into the microwave.

"Dad, I think I've just realized something today." She pulled out a chair from the table, watching him make his slow progress across the floor.

"What, honey?" he asked as he settled himself into it.

"Some teachers don't like children."

"Quite possibly," he said. "They're notoriously underpaid. And you know what they say...."

"Yes, I know. Those who can do, and those who can't, teach." She shook her head.

"But that's not true," she protested as she washed five small red-skin potatoes and put them on to boil. "Many, I'd say the majority, teach because they *want* to. They love children and are dedicated to helping them.''

"Like you?'' he said, smiling.

"Well, maybe, but nothing like Alice Watkins.'' She went on to tell him about Alice, an English teacher at Central High who held after-school classes to show students how to make out a résumé and fill out job applications, to explain about work habits and correct attire. "She even took them through mock job interviews. Practical things they would have to know in order to earn a living, things she didn't have time to teach in class. And she didn't get an extra penny for it.''

"Did you?''

"What?''

"I expect you helped.''

She grinned. "Okay, yes, several of us did. She couldn't do it all by herself! But she did the bulk of the work, and she had the idea, too. An excellent one, I think.''

"I agree.''

"In that school the only students who got the personal touch were the jocks—the coaches took care of them!'' She chopped viciously at a stalk of celery as she thought of Robert. She didn't know whether she was angry at him or herself.

Robert had persuaded her to tutor Zero—not that she'd needed much persuading. She'd been proud as punch that Robert had selected *her* out of all the women who were pursuing him. Maybe, she thought wryly, because she was the only woman in their little academic circle who was *not* pursuing him! Of course that was because she'd been brainwashed by Mom, who'd drummed into her head such old-fashioned ideas as, *A man likes to do the chasing; he's not interested in a woman who chases him!* Still, she'd been bowled over like all the other female staff members at the sight of the handsome new football coach with his tall muscular body, captivating smile and obvious virility. She'd been quite beside herself when he'd chosen to date her, and she'd enjoyed their brief affair as much as he had.

So of course when he said that Zero, his most valuable running back, would not be eligible to play the next fall unless he brought his grades up, she'd agreed to tutor the boy over the summer.

But it wasn't just because of the football coach's "Without Zero, we can forget the championship." She really liked Zero. She also found he was not the dummy his dreadful grades implied. In truth he was quite bright, and she made him work, grooming him for college.

He didn't make college. He was the bright star that carried Central to the championship and himself into the Chicago Rebels at a salary so high it boggled the mind. His good fortune didn't last. Two years later, addicted to drugs, he was suspended from the team. He'd since disappeared from the limelight, and she was not sure what had happened to him. But it still haunted her. She'd helped push him into fame and fortune he was not capable of handling.

The championship had also propelled Robert into fortune, as running-back coach for the Pittsburgh Vikings. However, this was not what had propelled him out of her life. It was when she discovered that he played the field with women, as well as the field in football. She'd been devastated. She did not easily enter intimate relationships. She'd tried to tell herself it was only her pride that was hurt, but there was no denying that the hurt went deeper than that.

She returned her attention to her father. No need to dwell on the past. She kept talking, trying to find something to interest her father, make him come alive. He did perk up a little when she told him about her own activities and problems.

It wasn't until she set his dinner before him that she got around to Eric Archer. Her dad seemed only mildly interested. There was a time, she thought, when she talked up a blue streak, that he would have focused on the problem, given practical advice on what to do. How she longed for the vital man her father had been.

"Where's *your* plate?" he asked. "Aren't you eating?"

"Later. I'm going out."

"Oh? School meeting?"

"No. Mr. Archer is taking me out to dinner."

"Good. It's time you went out and had some fun. Who's the lucky guy? Archer, did you say?"

"Dad! You haven't been listening. I was telling you about Eric Archer, the man's son. The parents have been divorced for ages, and now the boy is suddenly in the charge of his father. The man seems somewhat at a loss. He asked me to have dinner with him to discuss the boy's problems.''

"I see. But—'' he hesitated and his lips quirked "—isn't that usually done at the office?''

"Oh, Dad, now you're sounding like Ada and Lisa with all those stupid innuendoes.''

"Oh?''

"Like I've got designs on the father because he's rich and famous!''

"*Is* he rich and famous?''

"Every parent at that school is rich!''

"And famous?''

"'Notorious' would better describe Lyndon Archer.''

"That bad, huh?'' He chuckled and Monica smiled, glad to see a glimmer of her father's old humor.

"Oh, I don't know that you'd call it bad,'' she said. "He just seems to be loaded with racehorses and women.''

"Not much room for one small boy?''

"Something like that. Only…'' She paused and watched her father eat. Good. He was showing an appetite. "The boy's arrival, I take it, was unexpected and sudden. Possibly rather overwhelming for the busy Mr. Archer. Still, he does seem concerned,'' she said, thinking of the warm dark eyes. The compassion he'd shown when she spoke of Eric's rejection by the other students, his loneliness.

"I think he just doesn't know how to reach out to the boy."

"Then he's picked the right person to tell him how."

"Oh, Dad, I'm afraid you're prejudiced!" she said, laughing.

Later, as she turned down the bed for her father—he was in the habit of retiring early and watching TV or reading a book in bed—the conversation with Ada and Lisa continued to prick at her.

"Maybe meeting with Mr. Archer out of the office isn't a good idea," she said, helping her father into bed.

"Why?" Herb asked.

"Oh, you know how people can misconstrue things. They might get the impression I'm interested in the father and not the boy."

"Then they're wrong." He gave her hand a loving pat. "Anyway, it doesn't matter what they think. We know better. With you, honey, nothing and nobody comes before a mixed-up kid."

She warmed to his words. This was her old dad. Always loving and supportive, giving her confidence. Did this signal a return to his old confident self? Perhaps, if she continued to involve him...

She handed him the remote control to the television. "Isn't there a game tonight?"

"Not tonight."

"Too bad." Dad loved all sports, but baseball was his game. He'd gotten really involved in the

World Series, which had ended only days ago. She was sorry it was over. "Well, maybe there's a good movie on," she said as she started out.

"Maybe. And, honey..." he called. She turned. "Nothing wrong with mixing a little pleasure with business."

"What do you mean?"

"I mean it's been a long time since you went out to enjoy yourself. This past year you've been bogged down with your mother, me and work. You deserve some relaxation. Enjoy the evening, honey."

She felt a little shaken as she left him. Goodness, did he, too, sense that more than business was afoot?

Her cheeks grew hot as she remembered how at one point she'd glanced up and encountered Archer's steady gaze. There'd been something *there,* something appreciative, and she had, for a moment at least, been flattered by it.

Oh, for goodness' sake! That was probably the way he looked at all those women who'd made fools of themselves over him. She was not one of them. She was interested in Eric, not his father!

CHAPTER THREE

"WE'LL GO to the Beach House," he'd said. "It's usually quiet there during the week."

Monica knew the Beach House was a private club-restaurant, a hangout for the horse-racing set, where trainers, jockeys and owners gathered to talk about whatever racing people talked about.

"Casual elegance" was probably the dress code, she thought as she slipped on her lavender jumpsuit. Not very elegant, but okay.

Very okay, signaled his admiring glance when she opened the door to him at seven-thirty. What he said was, "How about that? We match." It was true. The cardigan sweater he wore with his designer jeans was a deep lavender shade that blended well with her jumpsuit. The color gave his dark eyes a luminous sheen, and again she felt that strange magnetic pull. She tore her glance away.

"Be with you in a moment. I'll just go tell Dad I'm leaving."

Minutes later, as they drove, he said, "It's good of you to spare this time for me."

"For Eric," she said, determined to make that point very clear.

He inclined his head and gave her a quick smile.

"All right. We *both* appreciate it." He changed the subject. "Have you been with the academy long?"

"Just since September."

"So Pueblo is new for you?"

"Not so new. I've been in and out for the past three years, and I moved here at the beginning of the summer."

"Strange—I've never seen you around."

Not strange, she thought. They moved in rather different circles. "I don't get around very much," she said.

"Well," he said. "We'll have to see about changing that."

She darted him a glance, again feeling compelled to remind him of the reason she was here with him now. "The changes affecting Eric are our chief concern. The depth of his loss, coupled with being plunged into an entirely new environment, must be devastating."

Her words pricked Dave like a knife. How could he and his brother have so neglected Eric? He vowed it wouldn't happen anymore. After his talk with Monica Powell yesterday, he'd gone directly to the dorm to see Eric. The boy had been totally unresponsive, and little wonder! He'd bring him around, though, once he got him out to the house on weekends. He'd also called Lyn and given him holy hell. After all, he was the father. *And I'd better get my own relationship straight right now*, he thought, and glanced at the woman beside him.

"Wait. Before you go on, I must explain about Eric. I regret the misunderstanding, but—"

"I regret it, too," she interrupted. "We should have been informed about the situation as soon as he registered. Any boy who's been through what he has needs special attention. I think—"

"Uh-oh, I goofed," he said, as he pulled into a crowded parking lot. "Did I say the Beach House was quiet during the week? Seems I was wrong."

It should have been called the Ranch House, was Monica's first thought as they entered the restaurant. The motif was definitely Old West—rustic furnishings, artifacts and pictures of horses lining the walls. Through an arched doorway, they could see into the bar where a girl in cowboy attire was strumming a guitar. And she'd been right about casual elegance, she realized as she viewed the array of expensive riding habits, silk shirts and fine leather boots. Several people they met called a friendly greeting to Archer.

"Spillover from the horse show at the Mosley Ranch," the maître d' explained. "Would you mind a five-minute wait, Mr. Archer? A table should be ready by then."

"No problem," Archer said, and apologized to Monica as the maître d' hurried away. "I'm sorry about the crowd, but it's too late to go anywhere else."

She nodded, thinking this was definitely a bad beginning. Certainly no place to discuss a child's problems.

"No need to wait." A heavyset man in a fancy Western shirt and tight-fitting jeans clapped Archer on the back. "You and your friend are welcome to join us."

"Thanks, Al, but I think not. Miss Powell and I have some business to discuss."

"Now that sounds downright dull," said the man, turning to Monica. "Miss Powell, is it? Sure you wouldn't rather adorn our table?"

"Yes, this is Miss Powell. And this pushy guy is Al Freeman," Archer said to Monica, who smiled and extended her hand. "And no, you wouldn't care to adorn his table."

"That's too bad," Freeman said, laughing. He turned and sauntered back to his companions.

At last Monica and Archer were ushered to a corner table in a room full of happy convivial people, all of whom, including Archer, seemed to know everyone else. Jokes and laughter mingled with the clink of silver and china during a continuous round of table-hopping.

Their waiter came right over, took their drinks order—both had a glass of Chablis—then advised, "The salmon is delicious, Mr. Archer."

Archer grinned at him. "Are you telling me that's all you have left after this mob?"

"Oh, no, sir. Just the best selection."

Archer looked at Monica. "Okay for you?"

She nodded. Anything, she thought, distracted by the joyous revelry around her. How long since she'd been at a party?

The table across from them seemed to be the most popular spot in the room. Several people paused to chat with the four occupants, but attention centered mainly on one man, very tall, very black and very handsome. However, it was his companion who caught Monica's rapt attention. Her coffee-colored skin, gleaming black hair and exquisitely chiseled features combined to make her stunningly attractive.

But it was not her beauty, rather her expression that interested Monica. Something haunting and remote in her dark eyes. As if, like Monica, she didn't belong here. No. That wasn't right. She was smiling, talking, very much a part of the group. But she looked...well, as if she'd rather be somewhere else.

Monica was so busy analyzing her that she didn't realize the other woman at the table was staring at her. When at last she did become aware of the blond woman's curious gaze, the woman quickly looked away. Then she leaned across the other man, fortyish and freckled, to beckon to Archer. He answered her I-need-to-speak-to-you gesture with a smiling nod and waved a cordial greeting to the others in the group.

"That's my business partner, Val Langstrom. The guy with her, Ted Mosley, owns a stable, and they're sitting with Duke Lucas and his wife, Vicky," he said, nodding toward the black couple.

"Oh." The name Duke Lucas sounded familiar, but—

"He's our top pitcher."

"Oh, yes!" Now she remembered. "My dad's one of his fans."

"But you're not?"

"It's just...well, I don't follow the game."

"You don't like baseball?" He put down his fork and looked at her as if it really mattered.

"Actually I like the game itself," she said. "It's just..." She flushed slightly under his steady gaze. Why did she find it so unnerving? "Well, I have a few reservations about professional sports."

"Really," he said. "That's interesting. May I ask why?"

"It's just...oh, so much influence over so many young lives, and not always good." She stopped. How to explain? Athletics versus academia. Too little schooling versus too much money too soon. "Well, a couple of my boys have been hurt."

"Your boys?"

"My boys at Central High," she clarified. "It's an inner-city school in Philadelphia."

"I see. That's where you were before coming here?"

She nodded. "Those kids are terribly vulnerable. Most are poor and underprivileged, and the emphasis on sports has a heavy impact, not always good." She shook her head and smiled thinly. "But, Mr. Archer, we didn't come here to talk about sports."

"No, we didn't." He took a bite of his salmon, swallowed, looked at her again. "You must find the academy a breeze after such a school."

"Not really. Just different kids with similar problems. I'm sure Eric feels his abandonment as keenly as any newly orphaned kid living in a ghetto."

"Ouch!" He held up a hand as if to ward off attack. "All right. I get the point. But a berth at the Joel E. Smith Academy can hardly be called abandonment. I spent most of my life at such schools."

"You did?"

"Since third grade. My father...well, it's heavy-duty being the head of a big corporation. He was always on the road and my mother liked to be with him."

Since third grade! So he'd been just as abandoned as Eric. "That must have been difficult for you. A boarding school at that age can be—"

"Can be a lot more fun than a houseful of stuffy servants," he finished. "After a session at home I could hardly wait to get back to school."

So that was the pattern. "Like father, like son?" she asked.

"What?"

"I hear what you're telling me, Mr. Archer. You, like your father before you, are weighted with many responsibilities and—" she hesitated "—as a single parent with the full care of your son suddenly thrust on you—"

"It's not like that. Let me explain." He looked so uneasy, guilty even, that she reached out to touch his hand.

"Don't misunderstand. I'm not criticizing. But we must face facts."

"I know. But the fact is—" He broke off and

stood to greet the blond woman who'd beckoned at him.

Monica looked at her with interest. She was truly elegant, so perfectly attired that Monica experienced a momentary pang of envy. The translucent perfection of her pale skin was accentuated by the wide collar of the beige silk blouse, and she looked as if she might have been poured into the matching suede pants.

"Naughty, naughty." The woman tossed her mane of hair and shook her finger at Archer. "You missed yesterday's meeting."

"Oh, I knew you could handle everything," he said, smiling.

"And I knew *you* must be goofing off down here. But I was sure I'd catch you at the horse show," she said. Monica detected accusation in her tone.

"Nope. Missed it. Val, this is Miss Powell. Valerie Langstrom, Miss Powell." Both women acknowledged the introduction, but the blonde gave Monica a keen who-are-you inspection and said, "I'm sure we must have met before...."

"I doubt it," Monica replied. "I'm relatively new to this area." *And certainly to this crowd.*

"Miss Powell is a counselor at Smith Academy," Dave explained.

"Oh, I see." This seemed to give the woman a strange kind of satisfaction, and she immediately returned her attention to Archer. "Something came up that we need to talk about. As soon as possible."

"I'll be in San Diego tomorrow," he said. "I'm driving there in the morning."

"Good. I'll ride with you," she said decisively. "I'm staying at the Towers. Call me. Nice to meet you, Miss Powell."

The green eyes seemed to flash with a sort of challenge, and Monica felt a surge of annoyance. She was hardly in competition for Lyndon Archer! She stabbed viciously at her salmon.

"We, at Joel E. Smith," she said as soon as the woman moved away and Archer resumed his seat, "are interested in the whole child, not just how he does academically. As Eric's counselor, I strongly feel that first we should focus on his emotional state."

She went on in her most professional voice to make certain recommendations. "Perhaps a change of teachers might be a good idea," she finally said. "But I think that suggestion should come from you."

"Wouldn't that be yet another change for him?"

"Yes. But, I believe, one for the better." How could she explain? She couldn't say that Ada Johnson was a critical shortsighted bitch who'd labeled Eric a moron. "It's just that some personalities clash. And, well, I just don't think Ms. Johnson is the right sort of teacher for him."

"I don't know." Archer looked thoughtful. "We can't always regulate his environment. Eric needs to learn to adjust, especially to teachers. He's got to deal with a hell of a lot of them in the coming years.

When I was twelve, I had a math teacher I couldn't stand, and I remember my father told me—''

"You're not Eric," she interrupted with a frown. "You don't seem to realize how traumatic the changes are he's suffered."

"Of course I do. I just don't think changing a teacher will solve anything."

"Maybe not, but it might soften the blow. And certainly there's more than a teacher involved here. His needs at this moment are so great." She looked across at Archer, willing him to understand. "He needs someone to help him hurdle these changes. He needs…" *A home. A loving teacher or parent. Not a father too busy with horses, women and business to bother.* She swallowed. "Eric is terribly lonely. He hasn't yet managed to relate to his new classmates—kids can be cruel, and they sort of close ranks on someone new. And he's withdrawn from his teacher. I suppose that's why he became so attached to that dog he sneaked into the dorm."

"A dog? Sneaked? When?"

She explained, hardly believing he hadn't been told of the incident. "He's been warned," she finished. "But he's still hiding the dog, probably taking him scraps of food. I saw him near the parking lot the other day playing with the dog. It's the only time I've ever heard Eric laugh." She sighed. "He's headed for trouble if he keeps hiding him. It's just that he's so lonely."

"I know. And I plan to fix that. I've already discussed this with his father and he faxed—''

Monica choked on her wine and went into a fit of coughing.

He leaned over, concerned. "Are you all right?" he asked.

She nodded, her cough subsiding, and stared at him. She finally managed a strangled whisper. "Did you say…his father? Aren't you…?"

Dave winced as he again took his seat. That had been one hell of a way to reveal his identity. "No, I'm not Eric's father. I've been trying to tell you."

"Really."

"Yes, really." He sounded defiant, as if resenting her sarcasm. "I haven't had a chance. This crowd and so many interruptions all evening…"

"All evening?" The hazel eyes flamed with accusation. "What about two days ago when you came to my office? Really, Mr. Archer—or is that your name?"

"It is. I'm Dave Archer, Lyndon's brother. Eric's uncle," he added unnecessarily.

She regarded him, as dazed as she was angry. "I can't believe it. All this time I've been talking with you, trying to resolve Eric's problems, thinking you were concerned. And all this time you—"

"I was…*am* concerned. Miss Powell, please. Just listen. Eric's father is in London and not likely to be home for two months—and then not for any length of time."

He talked rapidly, as if she might take off before he could get it all in. "I live here, at least most of the time. And when you called saying Eric was in trouble, well…'' He spread his hands. "I'm his uncle. Why shouldn't I stand in for his father?''

"Okay, but what's wrong with *saying* so? I mean, that you're the uncle, not the father.''

"At first I didn't understand who you were. When you phoned—''

"That's another thing. When I phoned. Why didn't you tell me then who you were?''

"You didn't ask.''

"I certainly did. I requested to speak to Eric's father.''

He shook his head. "Oh, no. Only 'Mr. Archer.' We were deep in conversation before I realized who you were or what it was all about.''

"And then?''

"Too late.''

"Too late?''

"Your voice.''

"My… What on earth has my voice to do with anything?''

"Aren't you aware of how beautiful your voice is?'' There was a warm teasing glint in his dark eyes. She straightened and pushed back her chair. He leaned forward, seized her hand. "I had to meet you.''

"And Eric was a handy excuse!'' She snatched her hand away, more upset with herself than with him. She'd been sitting here all evening, enjoying herself, while he—

"No. I told you. I *am* concerned about him. I want, *intend*, to help him.''

"I don't appreciate your tactics, Mr. Archer."

"Come on now, don't be angry. Don't blame me just because I wanted, still want, to know you better."

"Then you'd better know I don't play games with a child's life."

"Neither do I. I wouldn't—"

"You used Eric. You deliberately deceived me, led me to believe... Oh, never mind! Thank you for dinner." She put down her napkin, stood and strode to the door, not knowing nor caring if he followed.

VAL LANGSTROM viewed the abrupt departure with some satisfaction. "Well. Something's made *her* angry."

"Seems so," Vicky Lucas replied, knowing the remark was addressed to her, since the men were discussing horses and hadn't even looked up.

"Stormed out right after our little talk. Guess she didn't like Dave being so chummy with me."

"Maybe," Vicky said, going along with the game. Val was too smart to delude herself. She knew that *she* had been the one chummy with *him*, not the other way around.

"Women!" Val set her wineglass down so hard a little of the ruby liquid splashed over the rim. "She's a counselor at the school where Lyn's son is, and I bet she's using him to see Dave. Any excuse to latch on to a man who's rich and famous. I tell Dave it's hard on me, too. I know you have the same problem with Duke."

Vicky blushed. She knew she'd been called a jealous bitch. But she hated the way women fawned over Duke. Hated his liking it. But she was Duke's wife, while Val was only Dave's business partner. Well, she *was* a little more than that, Vicky knew, but not as personally intimate as Val made it appear. Or as Val would *like* it to be.

Vicky scolded herself for being catty and changed the subject. "I hope Ted's not trying to sell Duke another horse."

"Me, too," Val said, giving Ted a playful jab in the ribs. "Lay off Duke, Ted. If you're peddling a racehorse, I can offer a better investment. As for any other kind...well, I'm putting it in his contract. He's to stay off any horse's back."

Vicky laughed with her, but couldn't be sure she was joking. The feeling was that Duke's sprained arm, the result of a fall from a horse, had cost the Demons the World Series.

"Now, wait a minute," Duke protested with a grin. "Don't go messing with my pursuit of happiness and all that jazz. If it makes me happy to ride—"

"And if it makes me unhappy?" Vicky reached over to squeeze her husband's hand. "Put it in the contract, Val. My sentiments are with you."

She knew they wouldn't put it in his contract, though, and she knew he wouldn't stop riding. As if he had to prove his excellence in this as he had in all sports, football and basketball, as well as baseball. But riding wasn't his thing. Moreover, it was another expense. Like their big house and fancy parties, it was a way to prove to himself that he was part of it all, this exclusive community, the rich horse owners, the in crowd. She wished he wouldn't try so hard.

IN THE LOBBY Dave Archer took Monica's hand and propelled her toward the door and out to the parking lot. "No need to call a cab. I always see my dates home."

"I am *not* your date," she said through clenched teeth, "so it's not necessary for you to see me home."

"Common courtesy to a stranded pedestrian, then."

"I am *not* stranded!" But he still held tight to her hand, and she was forced to stumble along after his rapid stride.

"Also, Miss Powell, we haven't concluded our business."

"Oh, yes, we have. My business isn't with you. It's with Eric's father."

"You're going to abandon Eric, are you?" He unlocked the car with his remote, then pulled open the door. "Come on. Get in and we'll talk this over."

She slid into the passenger seat. Silly to stand and squabble in a parking lot. But, once home, she planned never to see Dave Archer again.

"I don't see why you're so steamed up, anyway," he said as he started the car.

"I'm steamed up, as you put it, because you used Eric. You pretended to be concerned about him, when you...you...had an entirely different agenda. You don't care about him at all."

"That's not true. We're talking about two things—my being attracted to you and my concern for Eric, neither of which has any bearing on the other."

"You're mistaken. Had it not been for Eric, we would never have met."

"Right. Nevertheless, one has nothing to do with the other. My attraction to you... Oh, for God's sake, I'm sounding like a stuffed shirt. Okay, your voice turned me on, and then when I saw you... Hell, I like you. Is that a crime?"

"No, but you didn't have to pretend you were Eric's father and you were concerned about him."

"Like I said, I *am* concerned about him. When you called—"

"Oh, yes, when I called saying Eric was in trouble. But before that... Oh, for goodness' sake, Eric has been here almost two months, and in all that time, no one, not you or his father, has inquired about how he is or had him for the weekend. Even though you live practically next door."

"Guilty." He'd pulled to a stop at a red light, and she could see the muscles in his face tense. "Look, I hardly know the boy. His folks divorced when he was two. I've seen him maybe three times since then. When his dad brought him here, I was on the road. I'd forgotten he was at the academy. But now...well, talking to you has made me see he needs help, and I'm willing to do all I can."

"I appreciate that, Mr. Archer. But you aren't his father and have no authority. I prefer to deal with Mr. *Lyndon* Archer."

"Like I also said, Lyn is not here. I am. And I do have authority. I was about to tell you before you bolted that I had a long talk with Lyn by phone. I think you'll have a fax from him when you arrive at your office in the morning."

"And?"

"It states that, during his absence, all matters concerning Eric are to be referred to me. So, Miss Powell, if you are concerned about the boy, I'm afraid you'll have to deal with me."

CHAPTER FOUR

VICKY LUCAS climbed into the sleek two-seated Porsche, tying a scarf over her head to protect her hair from the damp sea air. The top of the sports car was down as usual. Duke liked it that way, the big showoff. He'd been in his element tonight. All these horse-owning high-muck-a-mucks gathered around him like he was some kind of god. All that praise for his big pennant win, sympathy and excuses for the World Series bummer. He ate it up.

He was so damn cocky. Her fists clenched, then relaxed. That was what she liked about him, wasn't it? His wide-open "everybody loves me, I'm on top of the world" grin. That was what had attracted her to him in the first place, when they'd met two years ago. He'd walked into the Atlanta television station, tall and vital, his eyes alight with a no-hit World Series victory, as full of himself then as he was now. She was not into baseball, so her coanchor had taken the lead in the interview. She'd simply stared, fascinated by the man with the smooth dark skin and incredible grin. Six weeks later they were married.

He slid into the seat beside her and she ran a hand over his thigh, exulting in the feel of the hard taut muscles, in the knowledge that he belonged to her.

She hated these bucket seats with the barrier between them. She wanted to be close to him, her head on his shoulder, his arm around her.

"Can't wait, huh?" he teased.

"Oh, you!" She slapped his leg. He knew what he did to her.

He leaned over to kiss her, his full lips clinging, his tongue tasting, probing, fanning the fire smoldering within her. She reached up to caress his face, her fingers tugging the lobe of one ear.

"Yeah, me, too, honey. Never mind. I'll have us home in three minutes." He put the car in gear and tore out of the parking lot.

"Slow down!" she cautioned. "You already have one speeding ticket." It was no use. The man thrived on thrills. Which reminded her... "You're not going to buy another horse, are you?"

"Just thinking about it. That little filly at the show tonight. You know the one that—"

"We don't need another horse. Just because the house came with a paddock is no reason to fill it up."

"This one's for you, Vicky. You could take some riding lessons and—"

"Not me! I was scared silly that time you put me up on Timber. I don't like being so high up on a big animal."

"Oh, once you got used to it, you'd like it."

"I don't *plan* to get used to it. I don't like your riding, either. Neither does Val."

"Maybe not," he said, chuckling. "But she can't put it in my contract."

"She would if she could. She was really upset about losing the series."

"Hell, I'm not the whole team. Anyway, if they're so pissed off, why is Dave talking about upping my stake?"

"Dave likes you. Val likes what you deliver. For Val, baseball is strictly business."

"Big business, honey. Pays pretty good."

"I know."

"Anyway, what've you got against Val? She's been a friend, as well. Found that house for us, introduced us around, making sure we got to know everybody. She's kept us happy."

Kept *herself* happy was more like it, Vicky thought. Using Duke to wedge herself into what she considered the hallowed social circle. "Duke Lucas, our star pitcher, you know..." Which allowed Val to also be surrounded by the hero worshipers, something she seemed to savor as much as Duke. "She wants to hold on to the best pitcher in the National league," was all Vicky said.

He laughed. "That's business, baby! She *is* a broker."

"And you're an investment."

"Right. So what's wrong with that?"

"Nothing," she said, trying to reason with herself.

"So why do you resent Val?"

"She thinks she owns you."

"She does, in a way. So does Dave. You don't resent *him.*"

"He's different."

"How so?"

He wasn't a user, she thought. "He'd still be your friend if you never played another game or went to another team or lost your skill or whatever. He's into baseball for the game. To win, but not for the money. And he's not trying to...to get somewhere."

"Maybe because he's always been there."

"Huh?"

"Not like Val. She's really had to scratch to get where she is. Did she ever tell you about her childhood? Her folks were tenant farmers and really had it hard. One time they were on welfare."

"No, she didn't tell me." Val always played the grand lady for her. Why had she told Duke? Then Vicky smiled. Because, she knew, everybody told Duke everything. He was that kind of guy.

"What are you grinning at?" he asked when he halted at a stop sign.

"Just trying to figure out why I love you," she said, touching his cheek.

"It's mutual, baby." He kissed her fingers before making the turn toward their house.

"I guess that's what makes the difference," she mused, almost to herself.

"Difference?"

"Between Dave and Val. Old money and new."

"Money is money," Duke said, "and shame on you if you ain't got it." His money was new, but it spent like everybody else's, didn't it? He wished he could spend some of it on his mother.

Memories of her were dim, but some things stuck. Like that sad lonely time between twilight and dark when he would sit on the corner waiting for her to come home from cleaning other folks' houses. When she saw him, her eyes would light up. She'd hug him, and the sad feeling would go away. She explained about work, too. "Gotta work hard for what you want," she'd say. "Nothing comes for free."

And so he'd worked for the baseball mitt he wanted when he was eight, running errands for Mr. Sims. Until Mom had stopped him. She said that what Mr. Sims was doing wasn't lawful. Still, she was glad he had the mitt. She wanted him to play baseball and took him to the Little League field herself that first time. "Life ain't no fun unless you know how to play," she'd said.

Now his work was play. Wouldn't Mom have liked *that!*

He'd been almost eleven that morning he couldn't wake her up. He'd been terrified. But Mom must have sensed his fear, for suddenly she opened her eyes and reached for his hand. "Never you mind, son. I be with you when I go. You won't see me, but I be watching over your shoulder, wherever you are, whatever you do."

That had scared him even more. Sometimes a guy did things he wouldn't want anybody seeing.

Mom had seemed to sense what he was thinking, for she gripped his hand harder. "Don't you worry none 'bout my being there, son. Whatever makes you happy makes me happy. One thing, son—'' her eyes bored into his, seeing past the tears and through to his very soul ''—you gotta watch out for things that just make you feel happy, like that stuff Mr. Sims sells. And like that whiskey that destroyed your dad. Promise me, son. You won't touch them things.''

''No, I won't, Mom,'' he promised, not quite sure what he was promising.

''Don't matter,'' she said, seeming to find some kind of peace. ''I'll be there, watching. I'll knock that bottle right outta your hand.'' Her smile had turned mischievous like it always did when she was teasing him. It made him feel that everything was going to be all right.

It wasn't. Minutes later she'd stopped breathing, and so began his life of being shunted from one squalid abusive foster home to another. He didn't seem to fit in with the kids where he lived, and he was shunned by schoolmates at the school where he was bussed. He'd never felt so alone in his life.

But Mom must have been with him the day he hid in the school john and begged the janitor to take him home with him. The janitor said he couldn't; runaways had to be reported. It might have been luck that the janitor couldn't find whoever it was he was supposed to report him to. Luck that the frustrated janitor took him along to his night job. Luck that the night job was at the Demons' clubhouse and that the club's owner just happened to be there. But Duke didn't think so.

"Why are *you* smiling?" Vicky asked.

"Just thinking about Mom." Yeah, his angel mother had guided him to that spot. To Dave Archer. To baseball.

Yeah, Dave and baseball had been pretty good to him, he thought as he rounded the driveway and drove into the underground garage.

HARD TO GET ACCUSTOMED to one beautiful day after another, Monica thought as she walked through the campus the next morning, feeling the warm sun on her back and the soft breeze tickling her nose. Today didn't fit her mood. One of Philly's blizzards would have been a better match. Might have even helped to blow out the anger and frustration.

How could she have been taken in by a playboy like Dave Archer? And now that the lying so-and-so had owned up to who he was, he was taking over like his was the last word. *No, I don't think it wise for Eric to switch teachers in midstream.* What the hell did *he* know? Or care? she asked herself as she entered the teachers' lounge.

"Hi, there!" Lisa greeted. "Kinda early, aren't you?"

"Coffee. I need to wake up," Monica said, glad Lisa was the only person around.

"Rough night?"

"I'll say." Monica let out a deep sigh as she sat beside Lisa. "Want to share my croissant?"

"No, thanks. I'll stick to my juice and yogurt."
Lisa gave Monica a keen look. "Sounds as if your
conference last night didn't go too well."

"Didn't go at all. Wrong man."

"What?"

"Eric's father is in London, England. I met with
his uncle," she said, deciding to skip the details.

"Oh. *Dave* Archer."

"You know him?"

"Hardly. But I've seen him. Being in sports is the
reason. I had a prime seat at all the home games
during the World Series. You know they lost by a
thread when—"

"Wait a minute. What are you talking about?"

"About his team—the Demons. Dave Archer was
sitting nearby watching every pitch. And right beside him, as close as she could get, was his alter
ego, Val Langstrom."

"Ah, yes. I met her. Very blond, very chic."

"You got it. Very rich, too, according to the media. She's part owner of the Demons."

"Right. She's his business partner." Monica took
a bite of croissant as she digested the information.
More than a business partner, judging from that possessive keep-your-hands-off-him glare.

"Everybody's still moaning over the series," Lisa
said. "I'm surprised he didn't mention it."

Didn't even mention who he is, Monica thought.
But then, that guy at the next table—didn't Dave
say *our* star pitcher? And the way he looked when
she got on the subject of sports. Did he think she

was criticizing him? Oh, well, Dave Archer was not her concern.

"Lisa," she said, deliberately changing the subject, "you have the Archer boy in gym. I know he's new, but why do you think it's taking so long for him to...well, get in with the other kids?"

"Because he's new at being a kid."

"What do you mean?"

"I mean, he doesn't know beans about soccer or any of the games kids play today. A kind of grandparent-isolation syndrome." Lisa went on to explain further despite interruptions as other staff members drifted in. She said Eric's grandparents had owned a famous racing stable in Kentucky, and it seemed his only contact with other kids had been during school hours. "He's more familiar with horses than children," she finished as they headed out of the staff lounge. "He can ride like the wind. Which reminds me—I want to put Eric in the spring horse show, and I have to have parental consent for that. So if you ever do catch up with Lyndon Archer, let me know."

"I certainly will," Monica promised. She meant to catch up with him. She certainly had no intention of dealing with his brother!

DAVE WASN'T THINKING about the weather as he drove toward San Diego that morning. He was thinking about Monica Powell.

"Dave! You're not listening to me." Val Langstrom's voice rose, sharp, above the hum of freeway traffic, the low music on the car radio.

"Sorry. Something on my mind." *Monica Powell. Spitting mad.* He grinned. Wide hazel eyes, dazzling even as they shot arrows at him. That cleft in her chin, giving her an impish look. The woman, provocative even in anger.

"What is it?"

"Pardon?" Dave pulled out to pass a long truck loaded with sports cars.

"What's on your mind?"

"Nothing important." Why had he said that? Two days ago he hadn't even known Monica Powell, but now she was damn important. How was he going to get through to her?

"Then will you please forget it and listen to me?" Val gave his jacket sleeve a tug. "This owners' meeting about free agency in Vegas next week—I made reservations for us at the Palace."

One room, she meant. Reservations together had somehow become routine. But now for some reason, he wanted no part of it. "For you, Val, not me."

"Oh, come on, Dave. We need a break together."

"That's no break. Just a big to-do about money. Your alley."

"But I like having you by my side. You know that." She laid a hand affectionately on his thigh. "Maybe I'm getting too dependent on you, Dave."

"It's mutual." He kept his eyes glued to the road and tried not to shift his position. "I sure depend on you."

He liked Val, admired her. She was a self-made woman. Starting as a clerk in a brokerage firm, she'd worked her way up. Now, not yet even thirty-five, she was head of her own firm. When Archer Enterprises decided to go public with the Demons ownership, Val bought thirty percent of the holdings, which gave her a big say-so. Dave's share was fifty-two percent, which meant control and veto power. He'd been glad when it was revealed that Langstrom and Company was really just Val. She was not only damn good-looking, but she had a business head second to none.

And, yes, they did enjoy a personal, as well as professional, relationship. Mutually satisfying, but not binding, the way they both wanted it. "You're a great partner," he said.

"Yes. We do go well together, don't we?" Her hand began a rhythmic caress of his knee. "You're spoiling me, Dave."

"Nonsense. You just say that because I let you handle the numbers." He was as happy with Val handling the business end of the team as he was to have Lyndon run Archer Enterprises. He had long conceded that his forte was the integrity of the game and the people in it. That done, the numbers would always come out right.

"I'm beginning to like being spoiled. Maybe I'd better marry you." Val laughed when she said it, but Dave wasn't fooled. Their no-commitment understanding, which she herself had suggested, was the bond that held their long-standing relationship together. But now it was wearing thin. Of late he'd gotten the distinct impression she wanted more, that she'd marry him in a flash. But would probably discard him as quickly as she had her first husband if things didn't go her way.

But he didn't want to play the Ping-Pong marriage game. He'd watched Lyndon suffer through bad marriages and a string of the wrong women, and had long ago decided that if and when he married, it would be forever and to the *right* woman. Val Langstrom, beautiful and smart as she was, was not that woman.

His musings returned to Monica Powell. Something about her. Not just her voice or the way she looked, though both were very appealing, he thought with a grin. No. There was also something steady and solid, down-to-earth about her. Dedicated teacher type—he'd sensed that immediately. But last night he'd sensed something else. A certain need. It was like she'd been plodding along, chained to duty, and suddenly was released to enjoy herself. Of course, all that had ended when he'd dropped his identity bomb. But before that...

She'd liked being there. She'd had a sparkle in her eyes, taking in the revelry of the crowd, as if vicariously becoming a part of it all. As if...yes, that was it. As if she hadn't had much fun in her life. Not lately, anyway, from what she'd told him. Not for a long time, if she'd been worrying about those kids she talked about. She needed to have some fun and he was the guy to show her how.

"Dave! You're not listening," Val snapped.

"Of course I am."

"Okay. What did I just say?"

What the devil *had* she said? "Well, now...I...er..." he stammered.

"I *knew* you weren't listening." She stared at him suspiciously. "That woman with you last night. Who is she?"

"Monica Powell. I told you. She's a counselor at the academy. Eric, Lyndon's son, is having some problems adjusting."

"And you had to take her out to dinner to discuss it?"

Dave's mouth quirked. "I was trying to make it convenient for both of us."

"Her suggestion, I bet. Any excuse for contact with you." She smirked. "Not that it'll do her any good."

He glanced at her. "What do you mean?"

"I mean, Dave Archer, that when it comes to fending off women who chase you, you're a master at the game!" The teasing note held an undercurrent of anger.

"Come on, Val."

"Come on, yourself. Tell me how you manage to turn them off and keep them drooling at the same time."

"You're asking *me*? You're the expert at turning admirers off." And what he'd like to know, he thought, was how to turn a certain woman on. She'd turned off the moment he told her who he was. He hadn't been able to get a word out of her all the way to her house. Hell, you'd think he'd committed a crime.

And dammit, he wasn't playing a game. Not with Eric. Not with a child's life. True, he hadn't thought about his nephew, or if he had, he'd at least thought he was okay. The boy had come on the scene during the middle of the baseball season, his busiest time. Besides, he'd been with his father, and Dave hadn't seen much of him, either. But now he *was* thinking about the boy. He knew how he'd followed Lyn from city to city, hotel room to hotel room, waiting while Lyn conducted his business. Eric must have been as lonely then as he was now.

Okay, so they'd both goofed, he and Lyn.

But hadn't he rushed right over when she'd called from the school?

And it hadn't been just because of her voice. With Lyn in London...

Suddenly he realized how much Lyndon was like their father. Either at home or away, involved in business. And Mother with him. He and Lyn had been left pretty much on their own. He thought of what Monica Powell had said. That Eric was so lonely he'd become attached to a dog, one that furthermore had gotten him in trouble with the staff.

He and Lyn had never had a dog. Horses, though. Plenty of those. That had satisfied Lyn, but Dave had never taken much to the big animals.

"Dave!" Val intruded on his thoughts again. "Come on! Where *is* your mind this morning?"

"I was thinking of horses," he said.

"Horses, huh! Not you, Dave Archer. And I've been talking and talking and all I get from you is a grunt."

"Sorry. I'm a little worried about Lyn's kid."

"Seems to me Lyndon's kid is Lyndon's problem, not yours."

"He's not here. I am."

"So am I, Dave. Right here beside you. And I wish you'd take your mind off Lyn's kid and horses and come out of the clouds to concentrate on me. At least you might be interested in what happened at the board meeting yesterday."

"So shoot. I'm all yours," Dave said. For the rest of the trip he tried to concentrate on Val and what she was saying, how she'd handled things at the meeting. But his errant mind kept wandering to Monica Powell, and he was glad when eventually they reached Val's condo.

"Lunch?" Val asked.

"No," he said. "Better not. Al's waiting for me at the clubhouse, and I need to get back to Pueblo as soon as possible."

To see Eric. And the dog he'd befriended.

CHAPTER FIVE

ERIC SHUFFLED into the visitors' room and stood looking up at his uncle. He remembered what Dad had said when he'd brought him to this dumb place. *Dave'll see to you. He lives here. Most of the time, anyway.*

Eric wished his uncle didn't live here, wouldn't see to him. Because maybe they'd let him go back home. He shook his head. No, they wouldn't. Gramps and Grandma weren't there anymore. But his uncle...

Dave sensed his nephew's rejection. Ignored it. "So how are you, Eric?"

"Fine."

"Well, that's not what I hear—" Dave checked himself. *Jerk! Gonna jump on the boy about schoolwork right off? That's no way to reach him.* "How are things going here?"

"Okay." Eric stuffed his hands into his pockets, shifted to his other foot.

Dave studied his young nephew. Not a strong resemblance to Lyn. Same thick blond hair, narrow face and big blue eyes as Marion. But *his* eyes held misery in their depths. "Just okay?"

Eric shrugged.

"Come on. You can tell me anything." Dave laid a hand on his shoulder and barely suppressed a gasp. So thin! Not much more than a frame. How could Marion just dump her child? How could Lyn? *Dammit, how could I?* He drew Eric close, felt him stiffen. "Hey, let's sit over here and talk." He steered the reluctant boy toward the conversational grouping near the window, two small sofas facing each other, a table between them. "Pretty tough starting at a new school, isn't it?" he asked when they were seated side by side on one of the sofas.

"Guess so." The thin shoulders lifted, drooped again.

"I know. I landed in boarding school when I was eight."

"You did?" The eyes flashed, for the first time looking directly at Dave.

"Sure did. I was in third grade."

"Did you like it?" The first direct question the child had asked.

"Not at the beginning." Dave had to be honest. "But later it got to be fun. You just have to give it time. Right now, I know—" He stopped. He *did* know. He could all but feel the boy's desolation. But he wasn't going to do the "Miss your grandparents?" bit. He'd keep the conversation on the here and now. And let the boy know he had somebody in his corner. "Look, your dad and I are not always around, but you know we care about you, don't you?"

Eric nodded.

"The truth is, both of us are on the go a lot. And, anyway, well, it's like my dad told me, Eric. There comes a time when a guy has to learn to look after himself. Understand?"

The blue eyes focused on him again, revealing nothing.

"He said a boarding school was just about the best place to do that. Not easy, I know," he added, giving the bony shoulder a squeeze. "But you can still have fun. Lots of things to do, lots of other kids." He saw Eric wince and remembered Monica Powell's words: *Children can be cruel, and they close ranks on someone new.* "It takes time to get to know everybody. But when you do, it'll be fun, I promise." He'd make damn sure Eric got accepted if he had to drag every damn kid in school out to the house!

"My dad, too?"

"Pardon?" Hadn't the kid heard anything he'd said?

"Was my dad at that school, too? The one where you went?"

"Yup, your dad, too. He was your age." Dave thought about that. At least he and Lyn had had each other. He took one of Eric's small hands in his. "Tell you what. Come out to the house this weekend, and I'll tell you all about it. Maybe we could—"

"I don't think so." Eric shook his head, his eyes on the camellias on the table. "I'm pretty busy."

"Oh?" For a moment Dave had thought the boy

was opening up, but now he was back in his shell. "Well, how about the next weekend? What about... Who's your roommate?"

"Tommy Atkins."

"You could ask him to come along. We could..." Eric was shaking his head vigorously now.

"All right. Just you. Oh, by the way, I understand you have a dog."

Eric's heart lurched. Somebody'd snitched. "He's not mine." A stray, Matron had said. "He's just a dog."

"I know. But I thought we could find him, and—" The phone in Dave's pocket sounded. He talked into it, cursed, turned back to Eric. "I've got to get back to San Diego now. We'll talk about this later. Okay?"

Eric nodded. He didn't want to talk about this at all. And he sure didn't want to look for the dog. Matron had security looking for him so he could be taken to the animal shelter. Probably that was what Dave would do, too. Then, if nobody wanted him, they'd kill him.

"Meanwhile," Dave was saying, "here's my card. I've written in my private number. I'll be in touch again soon. But if you need me before then, call, anytime for anything. Okay?"

"Okay." Eric stuffed the card in his jeans pocket. But he knew he wouldn't call. He didn't need Dave. He didn't need him for anything. He wished he would just go away and leave him alone.

MONICA WENT ABOUT her regular duties at her usual clip, but Eric Archer stayed on her mind the whole while. She had to do something about him. What she wanted to do was call him in, wrap her arms around him and let him cry his heart out. Poor kid. Not a shoulder to cry on. Certainly not the shoulder of his game-playing uncle whose guardianship authorization was now, just as he'd said, on her desk.

Guardian indeed! He'd not taken the time, even once, to visit the boy during the two months he'd been here. Probably wouldn't even now. Anyway, he didn't seem to approve of her idea of changing Eric's teacher, which she definitely meant to do.

She tapped a pencil against her chin, thinking. Did she dare contact the father by phone in London— "I thought I should have your input for this," she could say. Or maybe she could tackle Ada herself.

But even as she concocted ways to circumvent Dave Archer, she couldn't get the man out of her mind. The easy relaxed manner that made her feel so...well, comfortable, dammit! The warm genial smile that teased and beckoned...

Her mouth twisted wryly. It was called charisma. And it was something she had better watch out for. Made her forget to think.

She found the plant on her stoop when she returned home that afternoon. A plant so exquisitely lovely she caught her breath. An orchid. At least a dozen pale pink blossoms on a stem that curved upward from a foliage of flat glossy leaves. She lifted the basket that contained it and carried it into the house.

"I saw the boy coming up the walk with it. I had him open it and leave it there," her father said. "So I wouldn't have to get to the door."

"Yeah, that's fine, Dad. I'm sure it didn't suffer. Not on this glorious day." She set the basket on the table, still gazing at the blossoms, so delicate, so perfectly etched. This is an orchid, you know," she said softly. "I've never seen one before, except in a corsage. Never growing like this. Oh, I wish I had Mom's green thumb." She wanted to keep these delicate yet sturdy blossoms alive forever.

"Who's it from?" Herb asked.

She had a pretty good idea. Although she'd have pegged Dave Archer the long-stem-roses type. She reached for the card, and her hand struck something hooked onto the basket—a fine gold chain, from which dangled a disreputable-looking tiny gold shoe. Her fingers closed around it as she read the card. "Sorry I got off on the wrong foot. Can't we take another walk?"

There was no signature, but of course one was hardly needed. What a funny ridiculous absolutely clever way to apologize!

"From Mr. Archer," she said managing to sound steady and matter-of-fact. "Thanking me, I guess, for the consultation."

But it was more than a thank-you, and she felt anything but matter-of-fact as she hurried to the privacy of her room. She opened her hand and for a moment was caught by the sheer beauty of the dainty bracelet. It glittered in the afternoon sun pouring through the window. Slender gold chain, intricately designed shoe, lopsided, laces loose, as delicate, as perfectly etched as an orchid. Sad, funny and so exquisitely beautiful a lump rose in her throat.

And it was pure gold, she could tell. Hooked onto the basket like some inexpensive bauble.

Which it probably was to him. Dammit, it wasn't fair! All that charisma and all that money, too!

Not fair to make her feel...what? Special?

Silly. As giddy as a schoolgirl with an unexpected gift from the football captain. And ashamed for feeling that way. *You're losing it, Monica.*

Of course she couldn't keep the jewelry, she thought as she fastened it on her wrist, watched the shoe dangle. She laughed. It *was* a funny gift.

Abruptly she took the thing off, put it away. She'd return it when she saw him.

She had to see him—about Eric of course. But the next conference would be in her office, not over dinner at some fancy restaurant. She would make that clear when he phoned.

HE DIDN'T PHONE. He just dropped in. Without notice, dressed in a pullover that looked as if it had seen better days and faded jeans. Just a casual neighborly visit. Like they'd parted the best of friends, instead of...the way they had.

She and her father had been watching a video on

the TV in the living room. When Dave Archer arrived, she switched it off and introduced him. "This is Mr. Archer, Dad," she said. "He came to talk to me about Eric."

Herb Powell politely acknowledged the introduction, then reached for his walker. "I'll just leave you alone, then."

"No, please," Dave said quickly. "I don't want to disturb you. Perhaps Miss Powell would come for a drive with me?"

"Good idea," she agreed. She didn't want her dad disturbed, either. She'd been delighted to find his interest perked by the old movie of *Gone with the Wind* she'd picked up at the video store. She switched the movie back on and assured him she wouldn't be long.

Once outside with Dave Archer, she insisted they walk, instead, believing a walk was less intimate than a ride in his car. Still...why did a twenty-eight-year-old professional woman having a professional consultation feel like a sixteen-year-old on a date with the football captain?

Maybe, she thought with a grimace, because she *looked* like a sixteen-year-old, an unkempt teenager in torn jeans and long hair hanging loose. And again, the wrong setting—balmy night, full moon, soft lights glowing through windows of the houses. A walk along these silent uncrowded streets was far more intimate than a ride in his car.

She cleared her throat and spoke in her best professional tone. "I did receive a fax from Eric's father, and—"

"Good. He said he'd get it right off."

"Yes. Well, I—" Suddenly she stumbled over a large stone.

"Watch it!" He caught her hand and stopped her from pitching forward.

"Thanks." She swallowed, feeling her heart race as his hand continued to hold hers in a steadying companionable grip. It wasn't the setting, she thought, it was the man. *And never mind the charisma, lady. Watch the chemistry!*

She had to say something, anything, to break the silence, to counteract the strange current that was spiraling through her. All she could think about was his gift. "Thank you for the orchid," she said politely. Then added sincerely, "I've never had an orchid before. It's absolutely lovely."

"Glad you like it. So I'm forgiven?"

"Forgiven? Oh, yes," she said, then chuckled. It not only lightened her mood but, we thank goodness, slowed her pulse. "How could I refuse, after such a clever apology? But you know I can't keep the bracelet."

"Why not?"

"It's much too..." Too what? Expensive? Personal? "It's...inappropriate."

"Very appropriate, I'd say. A souvenir of our first date."

"It wasn't a date!"

"The first of many," he said, and she could tell,

even just in moonlight, that the genial smile was no longer teasing. Before she could absorb the implication, he was steering her onto a side street. "Let's go down to the beach."

She started to protest, but found herself almost running to keep up with him. By the time they reached the end of the street and climbed over a low wall to the sandy beach, she no longer wanted to protest. The beach was deserted except for them, the only sound the roar of the ocean, rolling in, rolling out.

She leaned against the wall and drew a deep breath of the salty air. "It's nice out here," she said. "So peaceful. Like all is right with the world."

"Let's take off our shoes and walk barefoot," he suggested, pulling off his socks and running shoes.

"All right." Quickly she shed her socks and loafers, leaving them with his by the wall.

She wriggled her tocs as they walked, loving the feel of the cool sand squeezing between them. How long since she'd walked on the beach? On any beach? She couldn't remember. Mom, Dad, work. But she should take the time, and so she made a solemn vow to do so. Often. *Just the sand, the sea and me,* she thought, suddenly possessed by a deep longing. For what?

She was startled when he spoke.

"So all is not well with your little world?"

She smiled. "Oh, well enough, I suppose."

"Your father lives with you?"

"Yes. Only I should say I live with him. He and Mom moved here about three years ago."

"I see. Your mother's here, also?"

"No. My mother—" hard to say, even now "—she died last...last December." Her voice faded as she relived the overwhelming loss. The strong familiar scent of the sturdy pine tree, brilliantly arrayed with the old familiar Christmas tokens of the past. The bells she'd fashioned from the tops of orange-juice cartons when she was a Brownie, the little white birds Mom so loved, the angel that was always on top, the gaily wrapped packages beneath. It had been Christmas Eve when Mom had died. Tears burned in Monica's eyes.

He took her hand, seeming to sense her grief. "I'm sorry. It must be hard to lose a parent."

"Yes, it is." She would never love Christmas again.

"Difficult for your father, too."

"Doubly so. They'd been together so long and..." There'd been genuine sympathy in Dave Archer's voice, and she found herself telling him about her mother's illness, her father's stroke, her move from Philadelphia.

"Is your father's stroke so debilitating?" he asked. "Sometimes a good physical therapist can do wonders."

"That's what the doctor suggested. He says the kind of stroke Dad had appears more destructive than it really is. He thinks Dad could regain his normal functions with a series of treatments."

"So, is he getting them?"

She frowned. "I'm waiting until he's ready. There's an excellent therapist at Ocean Villa, but Dad would have to move in, and he won't." She gave a rueful chuckle. "He says he doesn't want to be around those old folks. The truth is, he misses Mom and, for the time being, he's just clinging to home and me."

"I see. So all the burden of his care is on you."

"Oh, no! Not at all!" She almost lost her balance as she turned quickly to face him. "I mean, it's no burden. Dad is such good company, always has been. I like having him around. And to tell the truth, I think he needs me—emotionally. Everything that's happened has taken the starch out of him, and he needs me to bolster him up, to—"

"I know," he interrupted, taking her by the shoulders, shaking her gently. "You're all he needs, and you love having him. Right?"

"Right," she agreed rather dubiously. If Dad could have her and the therapy, too...

"Did you regret leaving Philadelphia?" he asked, taking her hand and beginning to walk again.

"Well..." She tried to adjust to the change of subject. "Yes, a little. Some things were...unfinished," she said, a sad note in her voice.

He stopped, again turned her toward him. "Something unfinished? A man?" He sounded so serious she laughed.

"No. Nothing like that." The episode with Robert

was long over. It had taken some time, but now she hardly thought of him at all. "I was thinking of some of the students. Like Debbie Sands. She's just sixteen. Much too young for the load on her shoulders."

"Debbie had problems?" he asked as they began to walk again.

"An alcoholic mother and three younger children virtually in Debbie's care when her father died."

He gave a low whistle. "A heavy load. With no help at all?"

"A little—financially. Her father had worked, so there was some social security, which we managed to get administered by Debbie, even though she was still a minor. Otherwise it would have all gone for whiskey."

"And I suppose you counseled her on how to manage?"

"Some. But Debbie was a pretty smart kid who grew up fast. What she needed most was encouragement to keep going, get her diploma." Monica sighed. "Actually she was better off than many others. There was—" She broke off. "But I am not going to burden you with the problems of those poor kids."

"As *you've* been burdened," he said, sounding thoughtful.

"What?"

He released her hand and stopped, turning to face her. "You know something, Miss... No. Monica. I like that. You must know, Monica, that there's always going to be something not quite right in your little world.''

''What are you getting at?''

She tilted her face, trying to read his expression, but it was too dark.

''I'm saying that if things aren't right for one of your students or someone you care about, then things aren't right for you. If it's raining on someone, you feel you have to hold an umbrella over their head. That it's up to you.''

''So?''

''Well, much as you'd like to, you can't hold up *all* the umbrellas.''

''Are you saying I take on other people's burdens too readily?''

''Monica, you are a warm loving compassionate person who cares too much.'' He ran a knuckle along her cheek. ''You want to fix everything for everybody. That means they don't get much practice fixing things for themselves.''

All she could think of at that moment was the gentle way he caressed her cheek, a caress that sent spirals of delight through her body.

''And you don't get time to smell the flowers or walk on a beach or...''

Now his hand was cupping her chin, lifting her face, and he was kissing her. Just a light kiss, but so warm and tender. And so magnetic that when he drew away, her arms wound about his neck and she stood on tiptoe to capture his lips again, to drink in the feeling.

As if sensing her need, he responded. He drew her close and deepened the kiss. She felt his hands caressing her neck, her back, felt his tongue, probing and demanding, felt a deep erotic yearning explode within her.

She clung to him, the sea breeze whipping her hair around her head and his as if to bind them. Her heart pounded against his as waves of pleasure washed over and through her. She wanted it to last forever. She wanted—

"Hey, we'd better go," he said, pulling his lips away and gently unclasping her hands from around his neck.

Go? Didn't he want what she wanted? Didn't he—

"It's starting to rain."

"Oh!" she gasped, coming out of her stupor. Indeed the moon had disappeared, and raindrops were falling on her head and shoulders.

He grabbed her hand and they raced back down the beach to their shoes. Stupid, she thought, almost giggling. Not her heart, but the pounding of the sea. Not waves of passion but honest-to-goodness rain!

Good Lord! Had it been so long since she'd been kissed?

She laughed at herself as they ran back to her house like a couple of kids playing in the rain.

CHAPTER SIX

ERIC LAY IN BED listening to the sound of rain beating against the window. It didn't drown out the sounds that came through the thin wall from the room next door. He could hear Bert bragging as usual, and he could hear Tommy's giggle. Tommy always laughed and the other kids did, too, at whatever dumb unfunny thing Bert said. Sucking up to him because he was the biggest guy in the class, and a big bully, too.

I don't laugh. Not scared, neither. Gramps said the bigger they are, the harder they fall, and the guys you better watch were the ones like Runt. They'd called him Runt because he was little and skinny, didn't hardly weigh anything, but Gramps said he was the best trainer he had, wasn't a horse on the place he couldn't control.

That empty feeling was stealing over Eric now as it always did when he thought about Gramps and Runt and Pete, and the other guys at the stable. Then he thought about the horse Gramps had been going to get him for Christmas.

Now he didn't even want Christmas to come.

There was a great thump and a loud burst of laughter from the other room. Those guys had better keep it down. They knew they weren't supposed to sneak into one another's rooms in the middle of the night. They weren't supposed to have food in their rooms, either, even if it *was* somebody's dumb birthday—as it was Bert's now. But Matron was on the first floor, and Jake, their floor monitor, was a heavy sleeper and his room was on the other end. Probably all the guys at this end were in Bert's room, so there was nobody to hear but Eric. And he didn't care.

He blocked out the smothered talk and laughter and listened to the rain, the first since he'd moved to California. It rained a lot in Kentucky, even in summer, sometimes big storms. Grandma didn't like storms, but he did. He liked the huge claps of thunder that shook the house, the jagged flashes of lightning. He would snuggle up close to Grandma and tell her not to be scared.

He wished Grandma and Grandpa weren't dead, and he was back in Kentucky.

He got out of bed and opened the window so he could smell the rain. He sat on the floor, his chin on the windowsill, and sniffed the damp air. It didn't smell like in Kentucky. He thought about Jumbo. Kind of a stupid name for such a little dog, maybe, but he'd named the dog after the first horse Grandpa had given him. Jumbo probably didn't have anywhere to go when it rained and was probably getting soaking wet. Maybe he should bring him in here with him where he could be warm and dry and would snuggle up to him like with Grandma. Nobody would know, just like nobody knew about that dumb party next door.

It was easy to push back the screen and shimmy down the tree right outside his window. Easy to steal across the campus between the trees and under cover of the rain. When he got to the gym, Jumbo ran right out from behind it, then ran back with him across the campus, not barking even once. It wasn't easy to climb back up the tree with the dog in his arms. But Eric made it.

Back in his room both he and Jumbo were wringing wet, dripping all over the place.

"You're okay now, Jumbo," he whispered. "We'll go down to the showers and get all dry with the towels. Then you'll be nice and warm in my bed." He'd sneak him out early in the morning.

That was the plan. If the dog hadn't smelled the cold cuts and leaped out of Eric's arms just as they passed Bert's room... If Jumbo hadn't scratched on the door... If Bert hadn't cracked the door open... If the dog hadn't rushed through and landed in the middle of the cold cuts...

"Get that stinking dog out of here!" Bert shouted.

That was what he was trying to do. But Bert kicked Jumbo, sending the little dog flying across the room, yelping in pain.

Eric saw red. "You didn't have to do that!" he yelled, ramming his shoulder hard into Bert's stomach.

The surprised Bert landed in the middle of his

birthday cake, but bounced right back, both fists flying. Eric was ready for him, and they went at it,
hard and fast.

If the other boys hadn't made so much noise, hol-
lering and trying to pull them apart, and if Jumbo
hadn't kept barking, maybe Matron wouldn't have
heard. But she did and was up there in a second.

Even Jake, their sound-sleeping floor monitor,
heard. He was there in those dumb pajamas he wore,
trying to get the mess cleaned up and the boys back
in their rooms. And Matron was wiping Bert's
bloody nose and asking why they couldn't act like
gentlemen, why they didn't obey the rules. They
knew there was to be no food in the rooms, no dog
in the dorm, no midnight parties. And, above all, no
fighting! Both Eric and Bert would be reported to
the dean.

Eric didn't care. Maybe the dean would expel
him. He hoped so.

Matron turned to Jake. "Take this mutt to the
basement, then straight to the animal shelter first
thing in the morning."

"No!" Eric flew at Jake just as he had at Bert.
"You can't take him to no animal shelter."

"Eric, behave yourself!" Matron said. "I told
you before. We cannot have dogs in the dormitory.
The animal shelter is the place for strays, and—"

"He's not a stray. He's mine. I'm taking him to
my uncle's house."

"Did your uncle say you could?"

"He...he... Yes!" Eric said desperately. Dave

hadn't said he couldn't. "You can ask him." He remembered Dave had said to call him anytime for anything. "Wait. I'll call him right now."

He ran into his room. Where was that card! He searched in his jeans, found it. "I'll call him right now."

"Jake, take that dog out of here," Matron said.

"No!" Eric reached for the squirming dog, but Jake held on. Eric turned to Matron. "Please. Let me call my uncle. He'll take him. Please."

"Eric, it's after midnight. Your uncle—"

"He said I could call him anytime! *Please.*" Eric couldn't hold back the tears any longer. "He said I was to call if I needed him."

Matron's eyes softened. "Oh, all right. If he said you could. I'll have to do so in the morning, anyway."

DAVE LINGERED in the shower, letting the hot water sluice over him. He'd advised Monica to do the same when he'd left her at her door. Both of them had been thoroughly drenched in that run from the beach.

But it had been worth every drop!

He grinned. He'd been right about Miss Prim and Proper. Tied up in a knot. And carrying a heavy load, all the burdens of every child she'd ever counseled. Quite a weight if many were like the girl Carol she'd mentioned. Which was probably the case back at that school in Philly.

And now there was her father. Did she think she

could get him well just by talking to him and holding his hand? The only reason she had gone out with him tonight was so her father wouldn't be disturbed.

Well, he ought to be grateful for that. Because it got her out of the house, and once the barriers were down...*wow!* He hadn't even noticed the clouds gathering. And when he'd kissed her...

No! When *she'd* kissed *him!* If that rain hadn't hit him full in the face, the two of them would still be— Damn! The phone. Who the hell was calling him at this time of night? It was past midnight.

He stepped out of the shower to answer the ringing phone. Listened to the gasping, choking, almost incoherent words that poured from Eric's throat.

"Dave, you know that dog? The one you said we should look for only you didn't have time? Well, I found him. It was raining so hard and I knew he was wet and so I...I... He got in Bert's room and... Dave, can you come over here right away?"

"You mean now? Eric, stop babbling. Calm down and tell me exactly what's going on."

"I got in a fight with Bert 'cause he kicked Jumbo and he didn't have to do that and now...now they're gonna send him to...to...you know, where he'll be killed and I...don't...don't... Dave, you said if I needed you... You said anytime!" The words dissolved into choking sobs.

Then a woman's voice came over the wire. "Mr. Archer, this is Mrs. Moody, the matron, I'm sorry we disturbed you at such an hour. But Eric insisted that he call you. This is just a little altercation that we can easily handle. Perhaps if you could stop by in the morning—"

"I'll come now if you don't mind," he said. "I think Eric needs me." *Needs me badly*, he thought. *He's come out of his shell at last.* "I'll be there in ten minutes."

MONICA HAD SPENT a restless night. How could what had seemed such a delightful exhilarating experience at the moment become a shameful episode in retrospect?

It had been nothing, really. A walk on the beach, a kiss. What bothered her was the way she'd reacted. *Over*reacted, rather.

She was making too much of the incident, she decided as she drove to work the next morning. Maybe Dave Archer was so used to eager women throwing themselves at him that he hardly noticed how *she* had.

And maybe he was laughing his head off!

Forget it, she told herself. *Treat it as a learning experience and stay away from the man.*

She found it hard to settle down to the day's business and was quite upset when Dean Simmons informed her of the episode in the dormitory the night before.

"I'm afraid the Archer boy is getting to be a real problem," he said gravely. "This is the second time, after a severe warning, that he's brought an animal into the dormitory."

The boy was lonely. The rush of compassion

combined with the sting of guilt. She and his uncle had been cavorting on the beach!

"You know he's going through a very difficult time," she said. "His grandparents' death and—"

"Yes, yes, so you told me." Dean Simmons, a stickler for the rules, had not been as touched by the boy's history as Mrs. Moody had been. "A very sad circumstance to be sure, and I'm sorry. Nevertheless, any student attending this school must adhere to the rules. Mrs. Johnson reports that his schoolwork is poor and his attitude belligerent."

"Oh, no. He's not belligerent. It just appears that way because he's so withdrawn."

"He wasn't withdrawn last night. Apparently it was he who started the fight, burst into McAfee's room and tore into him. That kind of behavior cannot be tolerated."

"Of course not," she said, thinking that anyone who bloodied the nose of Bertram Ashley McAfee III was in deep trouble.

"McAfee is not exempt, either," he added as if sensing her thought. "He also broke the rules. It was, however, his birthday, and if it hadn't been for the ruckus, the infraction might have been overlooked. But I'm meting out the same punishment to both boys. Confinement to campus for two weeks and two hours' work duty each day. Still, I am worried about this Archer kid. I understand you've talked with his father?"

"His father is in London. I've been in contact with his uncle—he's acting as guardian." She hoped the hot flush on her cheeks didn't show. Eric had not been mentioned last night. Not once.

"Oh, yes, the uncle. He came over last night as soon as he was summoned."

"Summoned? Last night?"

"The boy insisted. Seems he was out of control, almost hysterical. He calmed down after Mr. Archer talked with him and collected the dog. Perhaps you'd better maintain close contact with this uncle—he appears to have some influence on the boy."

The dean switched gears. "Now, have you received a transcript about a Lewis Simpson? His parents are seeking admittance for him for the spring quarter...."

They launched into a discussion about the Simpson transcript and other matters. When she finally left the dean's office, Monica was relieved. For her mind remained on Dave Archer, who appeared "to have some influence on the boy." How was that, she wondered, when he'd never even visited him?

No matter. He'd come last night when the poor little guy had needed him. In all that rain, after he'd left her. He'd calmed the boy down. She could picture Dave Archer, his dark head bent, his eyes warm and understanding, quietly listening.

Like he'd listened to her last night. Good Lord, what had come over her? She'd babbled like a house on fire. She hardly remembered now what she'd said, only that it had felt good, as if a weight had been lifted.

Now why was that? He really hadn't said anything. Something about rain falling on people's heads and not holding up all the umbrellas.

And then…well, whatever he'd said then had been blocked out when he touched her cheek. And followed it up with a kiss.

Just a friendly kiss, but good Lord, what *had* come over her? She'd gone completely out of control.

Thank God for the rain!

And now this incident with Eric. Too bad he'd been confined to campus at the very moment he'd made contact with his uncle, who, surprisingly *did* seem to care.

Her phone rang and she picked up the receiver. "Monica Powell," she said.

"Good morning, Monica." It was Dave Archer. She felt a peculiar thrill shimmy along her spine. "Have you recovered?" he asked.

"Recovered?" *No!* The shame of it still burned her cheeks. The way she'd clung to him, so brazen, as if she was starved for—

"From last night's drenching? Did you take a hot shower like I suggested?"

"Oh. Oh, yes. I…I'm fine."

"Good. I thought I should see you. Something has come up. Eric—"

"Yes, I know. I've just spoken with Dean Simmons and I planned to call you. As I told you, my office hours are ten to four, Monday through Friday.

Just let me know when it's convenient for you to come in.''

One thing she promised herself. The close contact with Dave Archer that the dean had recommended would be a professional one and confined to her office!

CHAPTER SEVEN

IT WASN'T the mucking out he minded, Eric thought as he finished his two-hour stint at the stable. He'd often helped the guys at home. But he'd done it then because he wanted to. Not, like now, because he had to!

It wasn't his fault, either. If stupid Bert hadn't kicked Jumbo, he could've got him out quiet as anything. And their dumb party wouldn't have been busted up and he wouldn't have been mucking out and Bert wouldn't have been on kitchen duty. He grinned, thinking about Mister Bad Bert scrubbing pots.

Okay, so he didn't really mind working at the stable. But he sure wished he had Jumbo with him. They could go behind the gym and he could carry on with the dog's training. Jumbo was learning fast, even if he wasn't a pedigree like Silver.

Thinking about Silver, his pet collie, made him think about home. He'd had so much fun training Silver. Runt, who knew as much about dogs as he did about horses, had shown him how. Runt was keeping the dog for him, and they were both still at Greenlea where all the horses and hands were staying till Gramps's will was pro...pro something. Eric didn't see why he couldn't stay there, too, at least till that pro thing happened.

Oh, well, at least Runt was keeping Silver until he got settled—whenever and wherever that'd be. Silver wouldn't like it in Dad's New York apartment, he was certain, and they didn't allow dogs anywhere near this dumb school. He was sure glad Dave had taken Jumbo.

Dave wasn't such a bad guy. He'd said Eric could come and visit Jumbo on holidays and weekends after he got off detention. But right now, well, he didn't have Silver or Jumbo, and so didn't have anyone to talk to.

Jeez, he wished he was at Greenlea, riding around with Gramps, looking for a horse and talking about Christmas....

"DUKE. GOOD. I thought you'd be here."

Duke, stretched out on his stomach on a table, shifted his head to see Dave striding across the therapy room. "Where else would I be! Damn, Art! Take it easy!"

The therapist, to whom the last remark was addressed, grinned and continued to manipulate Duke's shoulder muscle. "Just relax. Let me handle it."

Duke groaned as the excruciating pain shot through him. "How's it coming, Art?" Dave asked.

"Pretty good, Mr. Archer. Pretty good."

"Pretty good, hell!" Duke said, breathing hard. "The guy's trying to kill me, Dave."

"Just trying to get you back in shape," Art said. "Your fault. I didn't tell you to get on that horse. Okay. Sit up."

"Art, please. Don't you start," Duke said, obediently swinging his legs down and sitting up. "I get enough flack from Dave and company. If I hear, 'Stay off a horse!' one more time, I'll—"

"Not me," Dave said. "As a matter of fact, I came to ask you to get back on one."

"Back on a horse?" Duke said, his suspicions aroused. He felt the therapist's hand still for a moment, echoing his surprise.

"Right. Remember I told you my nephew is at the Joel E. Smith Academy?"

"Yeah. Lyn's kid. How old's he now?"

"Eric's ten."

"Dammit, Art!" Duke tried to jerk his shoulder away, winced as the therapist held on. "He must have been about three that time Lyn brought him down here. I haven't seen him since."

"Haven't seen much of him myself. That's the problem."

"Oh?"

"Yeah, he's having a bit of trouble adjusting and difficulty relating to me. Just when I thought I might be reaching him, he got grounded, and…well, when I go to visit him, try to talk, he just clams up."

"Tough," Duke said, wondering what all this had to do with him getting on a horse.

"So I thought maybe you could go. Now, listen," Dave said as Duke's eyes widened in surprise. "Let me explain. I thought I'd ask Eric to do me a favor and give you riding lessons. I could arrange it at the school stable, and he's really pretty good at—''

"Wait just a cotton-picking minute! If you think I'm gonna let some half-pint kid tell me how to ride a horse, you got another think coming!"

"You owe me one, Duke."

"Damn!" Duke appealed to the therapist. "Art, this guy's been giving me that line ever since he gave me a leg up." He frowned at Dave. "I guess I owe you my life, huh?"

"You got it." Dave smiled. "But I'm doing you a favor this time. I know you're the greatest and all that, but this kid's been riding practically since he was born. You might learn something."

Duke shot him a furious look. He, the great Duke Lucas, had anything to learn? "Just a damn minute!" he snarled. "I—"

"Wait, wait, hear me out." Dave said, making an effort to soothe his friend. "The riding lessons are just a gambit. A way to get you two together. I really want *you* to help *Eric*. I think you're the one to do it. I know you've been volunteering at the group home, working with the boys."

"Have to. Mandy's worse than you about what we ol' used-to-be's owe."

"The thing is, Mandy says you're especially good at showing the boys how to get along with each other. That's what Eric needs. He hasn't got a friend in the whole school."

"I ain't no magician, Dave. But I'll give it a try."

"That's all I ask. Thanks, pal."

"YOU OWE ME ONE," his uncle Dave had said. "If I can keep your dog, you can give this friend of mine some tips on riding a horse."

Some tips? The guy didn't know beans about riding, Eric thought as he sat on the corral fence, watching Duke going round and round on Citro.

Gramps said some people didn't take naturally to horses, and if you didn't, the horse knew it. He said a horse could sense what was in the mind of whoever was on his back. If you were calm and in control, the horse would easily follow your command. If you were the least bit jittery, you'd never get control of the horse.

Citro was the gentlest horse in the stable. The guy must've thought he was the wildest, the way he was riding, sitting too straight, arms wide, feet hanging like he might jump off any minute. Dumb.

Eric stood on a rail and shouted at him. "In! In!"

Crazy kid! Duke thought. *He's gonna scare the horse, and I'm having enough trouble keeping my balance as it is.*

The boy shouted louder. "Turn your feet in! And lean in closer."

Okay, I know that, Duke remembered as he tried to comply. He really didn't appreciate taking instruction from some puny kid, even if he was Dave's nephew.

He didn't need any damn lessons. Riding was a sport, wasn't it? He was a natural at any sport, baseball, basketball, football, you name it. He was great, in fact, especially at baseball. On that mound, he was in control.

When he was on a horse, though, it was like the horse took control, dammit!

Maybe Vicky was right. When he told her Dave wanted him to take lessons from a ten-year-old kid, she'd said, "Good! You need lessons from somebody if you're not gonna break your fool neck!"

And maybe Dave was right. The boy looked proud as a peacock, sitting on that fence, playing coach. Downright cocky!

Well, he'd play it up. "How'd I do, Coach?" he asked as he climbed down from the horse.

"Okay. Good boy, Citro," Eric said, stroking the horse's neck before handing him over to Frank Cello, the stable manager.

Paying the horse more attention than he's paying me, Duke thought. "Just okay? That's not telling me anything."

"Not much to tell," Eric said, turning his head away.

"What kinda coaching is that? Come on over here where we can talk." Duke propelled the boy back to the fence. "If you can sit here and shout at me while I'm riding, you can sit here and discuss my technique. What did I do wrong?"

Eric giggled. "You got on a horse."

"Hey, wise guy! That's a real putdown. You're supposed to be coaching me."

"I'm not... Okay, I'm coaching you. But Gramps

said—'' Eric burst into another fit of giggling "—some people don't take naturally to horses. I...I think you're one of them.''

"Oh, yeah? And I guess you're an expert.''

"I am.''

"Oh, yeah?''

"Yeah. I even trained racehorses. Don't look at me like that. I did. At least, I helped. And that's what I'm gonna be when I grow up. A trainer, 'cause Gramps said I was gonna be too big to be a jockey. And I was gonna get to pick out my own horse for Christmas and was gonna get to train him myself, only...only...'' The soliloquy ended on a choke, and Eric looked away.

Duke swallowed. The boy had been talking up a blue streak like he needed to tell somebody. Like he'd been holding it in for a long time, Duke thought. *Like me after Mom died.*

Dave had said Eric's grandparents had been more like parents to him.

Duke remembered how it was. He'd been just about this kid's age when the only person who loved him was no longer there.

"So what happened?'' he prompted. He knew what had happened, but he also knew how you needed to spill your guts to somebody. Anybody.

Bit by bit he drew the whole story from Eric.

A hell of a lot different from his own story, he thought with a touch of irony. Beverly Hills with his mom, a New York penthouse with his dad, excursions to London and Paris. Then here. Gee. Tough.

Still. If *he'd* had those things, would it have made up for losing Mom?

Never. *Things* couldn't replace love, couldn't banish loneliness. He looked at Eric beside him and knew at once what he needed. A base. Something to hold on to.

"So you don't like it here?" he asked.

"I hate it."

"Better start liking it."

"Huh?"

"You got a place to sleep?"

"Yeah. We all got our own bed, a desk, and—"

"Anybody beating you?"

"Huh? 'Course not. Nobody—"

"You need to know this, Eric, my boy. There's nothing more certain in life than change. And when change lands you in a place like this...well, you oughtta kiss the ground. You sure got no cause to complain."

"*You* don't know," Eric said, scowling. "You're not a kid and nobody's telling you what you have to do. You're a grown-up and you can do what you want to." Then he smiled. "'Cept maybe ride a horse."

"Okay, that's enough!" Duke gave the boy a push, knocking him off the fence.

Eric landed on his feet and climbed back up, still smiling. "You don't even know how to *sit* on a horse!"

"Cut it! At least I know when I'm well off. Something a know-it-all like you hasn't figured out yet."

"Whaddaya mean?"

"I mean, when I was a kid like you, I never had enough to eat. I was so hungry I felt like my stomach was sticking to my backbone. I used to rummage in other folks' garbage pails hoping to find food." God, it hurt to remember.

"You didn't have a mom or a dad or anybody?"

"I sure didn't have an Uncle Dave and a fancy school to live in. Nope. When my mom died, I lived in foster homes where I got more beatings than bread. And the only reason I'm telling you this, Eric, is so you can know you're much better off than most."

But Eric was still into Duke's past.

"That's called child abuse," he said. "I've seen it on television. You could've gone to the police."

Or to the social worker who came every other month or so, Duke thought. *But if a drunken slob three times your size said he'd kill you if you opened your mouth, you tended to keep it shut.* "I was just a kid. And not a smart kid like you who knows all the answers."

Eric didn't seem to take offense. "So what did you do?" he asked, wide-eyed.

"I hid in the school john. You see, I figured I could stay there all night, maybe sneak into the cafeteria and find some food, then turn up at school the next morning like I just got there." He paused. He'd been pretty naive.

Eric nodded. "That was a good idea."

"Not so good. The janitor found me."

"What did he do?"

"He said runaways had to be reported. But everybody was gone, so he couldn't do that. I guess he felt sorry for me, because he did get me something to eat."

"And let you go?"

"No. He said he had to keep me until I was reported, else he'd lose his job at the school. So he took me with him to his other job, which was pretty lucky for me."

"Why? What happened?"

Duke sighed and gave the boy a grin. "His other job was at the Demons' clubhouse, and your uncle Dave was there. He's an all-right guy."

Eric nodded. "I know. He took my dog home."

"Took me home, too," Duke said, and started laughing. Dogs and nig— Blacks, he amended. Vicky didn't like his using the n-word even in jest, so he'd better stop thinking it, too.

"What's so funny?"

"Your uncle," Duke managed between chuckles. "He was at the club, see? Working on some papers or something. And he asked Shad, the janitor, what was I doing there. And when Shad told him I had to be reported, he said, 'Let's get him cleaned up first. He's stinking up the whole place.' Then he gave Shad some money and told him to buy me some clothes while he stuck me in the shower."

I'm talking up a storm now, Duke thought, but couldn't seem to stop. "It was when he took off my shirt that he saw the bruises and...well, I guess that made him mad. He told Shad I wasn't going back to wherever I'd come from, and nobody was going to report me. And Shad kept yapping about the law, and Dave told him to cool it—he'd take the responsibility. He'd say he found me hiding in the clubhouse. And he took me home with him.''

"Oh. So you lived with Dave?''

"No. He couldn't keep me." Duke stopped. No use telling the boy all the legal complications. "But he promised me that nobody was going to hurt me again, and I wasn't going to go hungry again, either. He kept that promise. He got me into a good home with Mandy and Jim Ross, and...well, it wasn't Mom, but pretty close.''

Duke pulled himself out of his reverie and back to the present. "Now I play on his baseball team.''

"You do? I hope you play better than you ride a horse.''

Duke barked a laugh. This kid was something. "I'm a pitcher." And maybe Vicky was right. Maybe he ought to stay off horses.

"Why don't you like it here?" he asked Eric.

"Everybody's so mean. None of the kids like me." He scowled fiercely. "But I don't care. I hate them.''

"Hate's a bad word. That's what my mom told me. She said, 'Don't hate. Love.'''

He didn't often quote his mother, as if her sayings were gifts left only for him. But this kid was hurting and he needed them. "She said if you remember to love, you ain't never going to harm anybody.''

Eric looked wary. "Like I hurt Bert. I busted him in the nose and made it bleed."

"Yeah. Like that. She said something else, too. She said love, like measles, was catching."

"That's dumb."

"No, it isn't. What you give, you get back. Pressed down and running over. Says so in the good book."

"Well," said Eric, "you can't love somebody you hate."

"Yes, you can."

The boy looked confused. "How?"

"You start out by being nice to them. Do something for them or tell them something they'd like to hear. Like what a good play they made or how well they ride a horse."

Eric looked incredulous. "Even if they don't?"

"Oh, heck, everybody does something well. Talk about whatever that is."

"Okay. But suppose they don't like you?"

"Then you have to be even nicer. It's like a gift they didn't expect, see? Throws 'em every time."

Eric thought about that. "I don't suck up to anybody."

"Big difference between sucking up and finding something good to say. That's better than always putting somebody down."

Eric was still thinking about that when Duke gave him a friendly thump on the back and jumped down from the fence. "I'm gonna do you like the farmer did the potato."

"Huh? What's that?"

"Gonna plant you now and dig you up later," Duke said as he sauntered off.

Eric hated to see him go. "Hey!" he called. "You coming back?"

Duke turned. "What was that crack about some people not taking naturally to horses?"

Eric flushed. "Maybe you could learn."

Duke grinned. "See you next Saturday."

MONICA AND LISA walked together toward the parking lot. Neither had stayed for the social coffee hour after the faculty meeting.

"I have to go home to check on Dad," Monica had said.

"And my folks are waiting for my weekly phone call," Lisa said. Her parents lived in Laramie, Wyoming, where she would also live, Lisa had once confided, if she could have found a job there that paid as well as this one.

"Did you ever get in touch with Lyndon Archer?" Lisa asked.

"No, I didn't." *Maybe I should,* Monica thought, *especially if I keep avoiding his brother.* She sighed. "His boy's in a bit of trouble."

"I know."

"You heard about it?"

"I got the work-duty assignment." Lisa chuckled. "Which was like throwing the rabbit into the brier patch. Eric's as familiar with horses and stables as I am."

"Really?"

"Sure. His grandparents owned Greenlea Stables, which is a famous Kentucky training and stud farm. Folly was one of theirs."

"Folly?"

"You know—winner of the Kentucky Derby last year."

"Oh." Monica didn't know. But now she'd learned a bit more about Eric and what he was missing.

"Eric's a natural for my spring horse show. I need to contact his father so I can get an okay for Eric to ride in it and start training. Do you have his address?"

"Yes, but his uncle, Dave Archer, is here in town. He has guardianship. I've been meaning to see him myself again, but his schedule is so full..."

"And you're reluctant to expose yourself to his lethal charm?" They'd reached the parking lot now, and Lisa leaned against her ancient station wagon, a perceptive twinkle in her eyes.

"His lethal charm?"

"I've seen Dave Archer in action." Lisa smiled. "Right in front of his so-called business partner, Val Langstrom, who's trying desperately to hang on."

"Oh." She blushed, realizing she'd seen it, too. At the Beach House, Dave's giving the woman his attention, Val Langstrom anxious and possessive.

"Lured you out on a dinner date, didn't he? Somehow forgetting to tell you he wasn't the man you thought he was."

"Yes, but...well, he did apologize." Monica smiled, remembering the orchid—and the funny little shoe. Which she must return! "It's just that...oh, he does seem to have a sense of humor."

"Sure. The Archer men are reputed to be loaded with humor, charm and sex appeal, not to mention money and whatever else it takes to make them irresistible to women."

Irresistible. Monica was glad Lisa didn't know about the night on the beach. But she'd sure hit the nail on the head. It was she, not Dave, who'd been the aggressor.

"Thanks for the words of wisdom," she said, trying to laugh. "I'll keep those women in mind and leave Dave Archer to you."

"Unfortunately it's the brother I've got to tackle," Lisa said. "When it comes to the horse-riding program, everything has to be channeled through the actual parent."

"Then you *are* in trouble. Isn't he worse? I hear he's been married three times already."

"Don't worry about me. I'm immune to womanizers."

"Immune?" Monica wondered about the bitterness.

"Overexposure." Lisa opened her door with a jerk.

"Wait a minute," Monica said, wanting to ease the pain she detected in her friend. "Why don't you come over to the house and have dinner with Dad and me?"

"Thanks, but not tonight. Gotta call the folks, remember? And then I've got my discussion group...."

Monica watched her drive away, wondering. Some man had really done a number on her.

CHAPTER EIGHT

"GO SEE THE COUNSELOR?" Eric frowned at Dave. "What'd I do?"

"Nothing. You're okay, fine. This isn't school stuff. Just a social visit."

"Why?" Nobody visited a counselor unless he had to.

"Just to let her know you're doing all right. That you're off detention and visiting me."

"She knows that. They pass papers around like crazy at that school, telling everything a kid does and— Down, Jumbo, down! Sit." Eric pointed a commanding finger at the dog who continued his jumping and gleeful barking. "He's not minding. He forgot everything. I'm gonna have to start all over again."

"Okay, okay. When we get back, you can do all the training you want to."

"But I don't want to go anywhere, Dave. Me and Jumbo are gonna—"

"Jumbo and I. And whatever you and Jumbo are planning will have to wait until after we visit Miss Powell."

"I don't *want* to visit Miss Powell."

"I do. Hey, you, quiet!" Dave gave a resounding clap, and the dog settled quietly at Eric's heels.

"Wow!" Eric exclaimed. "He obeyed you and that wasn't even the right command. Runt said—"

"Whatever works," Dave muttered. "Come on. Let's go."

"Jeez, I don't want—"

Dave turned. "Didn't I hear you express a desire to have yet another mutt boarded at this residence?"

"He's not a mutt. He's a pedigreed collie. And you said I could if I paid Mr. Jones out of my allowance to take care of him when I'm at school. You *said* so."

"You're right. I did. Because I like to please you. And you like to please me, don't you?"

"Yeah."

"And that's why you're going with me to visit Miss Powell, isn't it?"

Eric sighed. "Okay. Can we bring Jumbo?"

"We cannot."

"How come?"

"Never mind. Let's go."

MONICA WAS in the kitchen up to her elbows in cookie dough. Dad could usually be tempted with sweets if they were the homemade kind Mom had always baked. She'd just put the last batch in the oven when the doorbell rang. She hurried to the door.

"Good afternoon," Dave Archer said. "We were

passing this way and Eric thought, er, that you might like to know how well he's doing.''

She knew he was lying, and her first impulse was to tell him that. But she was so pleased to see Eric looking complacent, well, almost happy, that she did what she wanted to do. She gave him a big hug. "Oh, Eric, I'm so glad to see you!" At school, touching wasn't allowed. But they weren't at school now.

"I'm glad to see you, too," Eric said. To his surprise he meant it. It felt good to be hugged like Grandma always hugged him. And Miss Powell smelled sugary and spicy like Rosella. Or maybe it was the house smelling like Rosella's kitchen when she was doing the holiday baking. It wasn't so bad visiting a counselor, and it was easy to do what Dave said. "Smile like you're having one hell of a good time!"

Dave said again that they were just passing by and he happened to mention that she lived here, which wasn't the way it was at all, and Eric could tell Miss Powell didn't believe him. She was being all polite and everything, but she kept talking to him and not to Dave. Anyway, she asked how he was doing, as if she really wanted to know.

And he was just telling her that he wasn't going to be in any more trouble with Jumbo, because Dave was letting him stay at his house, when she said, "Oh, my goodness!" and bolted.

Dave followed her, so he did, too. Her kitchen was smaller, but it looked just like Rosella's when she baked Christmas cookies. All messy with flour and stuff, and bowls and that rolling thing. He liked kitchens like that.

He liked Miss Powell, too. She didn't look the way she did at school. She had flour all over her shirt and jeans, and her hair was tied back in a ponytail like a little girl's. But even though she was all messy, she sure was pretty. He could tell Dave thought so, too.

Dave rushed to clear a place when she opened the oven and took out the cookies. They weren't burned, after all, and smelled yummy.

Tasted yummy, too. "Thank you," Eric said as he finished the one she gave him. "That was good."

"Look. Why don't you take this platter for me," she said, "and we'll go to the patio out back and join Dad." She put some glasses on a tray and handed it to Dave. Then she took a carton of milk out of the fridge and shooed the two males out ahead of her.

Eric almost forgot the cookies when he saw her dad. He felt a great lump in his throat. It was like he was seeing Gramps all over again. That was crazy. This man's hair was brown, not red and gray and thick like Gramps's. And he wasn't big and tall like Gramps. Well, almost as tall, he guessed, though he couldn't tell because the man was sitting down. But he looked...sad like Gramps had when he first got sick, and right beside him was a walker just like Gramps's.

"Did you have a stroke?" he asked bluntly.

The man nodded. He looked like he didn't want to talk.

But Eric kept talking, anyway. "That's all right. Having a stroke, I mean. You'll get better like my gramps did. He had a stroke and he had a walker. But he said he didn't like the darn thing and he was going to get rid of it. He did, too. Are you gonna get rid of yours?"

"Here you are, Eric," Miss Powell said, handing him a glass of milk and a napkin. "Help yourself to the cookies. Dad, this is Eric Archer."

"Hello, Eric." Herb Powell inclined his head, but gave his daughter a look. Was this the silent withdrawn boy she'd told him about?

"Eric, this is my father, Mr. Powell."

"Hi." Eric gazed earnestly at Herb. "I'm sorry you had a stroke."

"Kinda sorry about that myself," Herb said, a rueful smile curving his lips.

"Yeah, Gramps said it's awful not being able to do what you always did. Gramps trained racehorses. What did you do? Before the stroke, I mean? Ouch!" he exclaimed, feeling a sharp kick in his shins.

"Sorry," Dave said.

Eric ignored him. He was still looking at Mr. Powell. "What did you used to do?"

"Nothing so fancy as training racehorses," Herb said. "But I could walk."

"You still can. Gramps got back to walking real

quick. A man came out to massage him and help him to do exercises. Do you—"

"Eric," Dave broke in. "I'm sure Mr. Powell would like to talk about something else."

And so the four of them sat there for a while having a really dull conversation, Eric thought, about the weather. At last Miss Powell got up to take things back to the kitchen. Dave followed her, offering to help her clean up, and that left Eric with Mr. Powell. He started telling him about Gramps's exercises.

"He was sure glad to get rid of his walker. He hated it. I used it more than he did. I could ride it like this, see?"

Eric hopped onto the walker and sailed across the patio. Right into something that toppled with a resounding crash. He looked up in dismay at Monica and Dave, who'd rushed out from the kitchen.

Monica's gaze shifted from the broken pieces of the jardiniere, which had held Mom's prize cactus, to her father. He was laughing!

"I see," Herb said. "Looks as if you can't handle a walker any better than I can."

Eric's eyes were on Dave. "I didn't mean to do it. I just... Look, I'll pay for it out of my allowance."

"Some things can't be replaced with money," Dave said. "You shouldn't have—" He broke off when he felt Monica grip his arm.

"It's all right, Eric. Accidents happen, so don't worry about it."

"*We* certainly won't," her father said. "Why don't you two go back to whatever you were doing? Eric and I will take care of this. Bring me that walker, Eric. We'll go down to the shed and find another pot."

Dave started to say something, but again Monica stopped him, this time with a sharp glance. She watched her father grip the walker and make his way toward the shed with Eric following. The boy was looking up at him, talking a mile a minute and Dad was still smiling.

"I'm really sorry," Dave was saying. "I can tell that's no ordinary jardiniere and—"

"Please, not to worry," Monica said. "Children are more precious than things. And—" there was a catch in her voice "—so are fathers. It's been a long time since I've heard him laugh like that."

And she'd never seen him using the walker like that. Awkward, but not self-conscious. As if his mind was on something else.

Dave also watched the boy and Herb. "They do seem to get along pretty well together."

"Yes. So I forgive you."

"Forgive me? For what?"

"For using Eric!"

"I didn't—"

"Oh, yes, you did." She looked up at him, her eyes dancing. "That was your excuse for dropping by."

He grinned. "Whatever works."

"I told you I prefer that conferences be conducted in my office."

"And I told you that I had another agenda, preferably conducted elsewhere." He bent close to her, and the look in his eyes sent a tremor through her, a vivid reminder of how it felt to be in his arms. The rush of feeling battled with Lisa's warning about the Archer men being loaded with whatever it was that makes a man irresistible to women.

Not this woman! she promised herself. She drew away from him. "You can have the coffee I promised, but we'll stick to the main agenda—Eric."

"Eric's doing fine," Dave said, following her back into the kitchen. "Can't you tell?"

"He's doing fine here. But what about school?" She filled the pot with water, measured out coffee. If she kept busy, didn't look at him...

"School?" He dropped onto a stool at the breakfast bar and sat there watching her. "Well, he's off detention and not likely to get into any more trouble now that I've got the dog. He'll adjust."

"Not in Miss Johnson's class. I want him out of there." She switched the percolator on and tried not to notice that Dave was watching her.

"Why?"

"She says he doesn't even try to participate. He's withdrawn, silent." How dared that woman call that bright boy a moron! "She doesn't appear to have any understanding of what he's been through."

"Withdrawn? Silent? That's funny," he said, chuckling. "I can't seem to shut him up."

She smiled, thinking of his ongoing chatter with her father.

"Then, you should see what I mean. It's the teacher, not Eric."

"So he has to adjust, as he'll have to with lots of teachers, bosses or whoever he encounters in life. I had this algebra teacher, Mrs. Strasso, who was giving me hell. It wasn't my fault, either, and it would have been simple to transfer, but my father said—"

"I don't want to hear what your father said!" She was suddenly angry. And curious. "Didn't your mother have anything to say about anything?"

She looked at the man before her, seeing a boy. A grubby boy with reddish-brown hair and endearing dark eyes. A mother would put loving arms around him, would comfort and console.

"Not much. At least I don't remember her saying much beyond 'Your father wouldn't like that.'" There was a reminiscent twinkle in those dark eyes. "Guess she was too involved with Dad to pay attention to us. She absolutely adored him. He traveled a lot on business, and she never let him make a trip without her. Guess that's why they kept us in boarding school."

"Oh." The image of Dave as a boy switched to an image of his father. As handsome and virile as Dave. As irresistible. No wonder his wife was scared to let him out of her sight! "Did he adore her?" she couldn't help asking.

"Absolutely. I've never seen two people so much

in love." Dave chuckled again. "They still don't need us, though we pop in every now and then."

"Where do they live?" Somehow she hadn't thought of him as still connected with parents.

"Italy. He's retired now and they seem happy, just the two of them at their villa. Oh, maybe a discreet servant or two."

Italy. Servants. That said it. Distant. Rich.

But the image had shifted. What would it be like? Alone with Dave in some beautiful remote villa, her arms around him, free to give in to these new feelings, to the exciting erotic urges that teased her.

She shook her head. Blinked. What had gotten into her? She'd never had such fantasies, even about Robert. So why was she having them about Dave Archer, who, according to gossip, must have had dozens of affairs? And something, she didn't know exactly what, was surely going on between him and Val Langstrom right now!

She wasn't jealous. She hardly knew him, for goodness' sake! Anyway, who wanted the kind of love that made you neglect your own children?

"We survived," he said, as if in answer. "We knew they were always there and we always had everything we needed."

Maybe that was how the rich did it, she thought. Things, instead of love.

"Dad taught us to rely on ourselves. And that's what I want Eric to learn."

He got off the stool, walked over and put his hands on her shoulders. Gently. Not pulling her to him. But her skin burned from the touch, her pulse accelerated, and she could hardly breathe. "I like you, Monica. I like that...sparkle you show when you're not hiding behind your prim facade. You're a warm caring desirable woman. I think you're pretty special."

The words were music, his voice hypnotic, his touch magnetic. She felt weak, willing, wanting....

"You're pretty smart, too, about kids, psychology and all that stuff. But I want you to know this," he said, smiling, his eyes holding hers. "No matter how desirable, how smart, you can't maneuver me."

"Wh-what?" she managed.

"I'm not going to let you talk me into spoiling the boy," he said, settling back on the bar stool.

The boy? Lord, she'd forgotten all about Eric. She reached for mugs and poured coffee with trembling fingers. She handed one to him, then sipped hers cautiously, hoping the coffee would calm her, and finally managed to say, "I'm not...trying to maneuver you."

"Well, good, because you're not going to change my mind," he said, stretching out his long legs. "So let's forget that agenda and discuss the other one. What have you got against me, Monica?"

She stared at him. Was he kidding? Or was that a technique? A tease. Getting her all worked up and then backing off—

For heaven's sake! All he'd done was touch her lightly on the shoulder. And thank God he did back off before she made a fool of herself. Again.

"Come on. Tell me. What do you have against me?" he coaxed.

"Nothing. I...I don't have anything against you."

"So why are you avoiding me? I've phoned several times to ask you out, and all I get is the office-hour routine. I don't want to use Eric and I don't want to push. If you'd rather not be bothered, just say so."

"It's...it's just that I don't want to get involved."

"With anyone? Or with me in particular?"

Yes! With you in particular! she wanted to shout. No other man had ever made her feel so...so weird! But she couldn't say that. She didn't want to lie, either; she really *didn't* want to get involved with him.

"I don't like the business you're in," she said, giving him what she hoped was a teasing smile. Keep it light!

"What?"

"I told you I had a thing against professional sports."

"And I own a baseball team." He looked more puzzled than exasperated. "That's crazy!"

"I know. But there it is." A poor excuse, but better than the real one. She couldn't tell him that she didn't play games with relationships. That would sound stupid. Like asking his intentions or accusing *him* of playing games, which from all accounts, he probably did.

"In the first place," he said, "I'm me, not a baseball team. And in the second place— Wait a minute.

What's wrong with baseball, anyway? It's a game, a perfectly healthy sport.''

"A professional sport.''

"So?''

"I'm thinking of the mercenary aspects.''

"Mercenary? Right. An industry, a big boost to the economy. Lots of money going round and round for sportswear, equipment and such. Lots of paychecks. Players, trainers, sportscasters, popcorn vendors, you name it. What's wrong with that?''

"Nothing. Only...the players. Most are so young,'' she said, thinking of Zero. "Not used to the kind of paychecks they get.''

"They earn it. Couldn't have the games without them, could we? Do you know how many people are vicariously involved, just watching, in the stands or on television?''

"Yes, I know that.'' Half, no, practically all, the kids at Central, worshiped, emulated sports figures. "The players are instant heroes. And sometimes that's not good, neither for them nor for those who watch.''

"More good than bad. Better than those tear-jerking soap operas or the violence in some of those police shows.'' He paused to give her a keen look. "What's the matter? Did one of your pets get boosted into fame and big bucks and couldn't handle it?''

The flush that burned her cheeks gave him his answer.

"Well, well.'' He took a deep breath. "Come on,

Monica. Remember what I said about umbrellas? You can't shelter kids from life.''

''I'm a teacher, aren't I? I can at least direct them. There was this very bright boy I was grooming for college, Zero Perkins, and—''

''Zero Perkins! I remember him. Running back for the Chicago Rebels about two years ago?''

''Right. He dropped out of school when they drafted him.''

''And you thought he should have stayed in and gone to college.'' He shook his head. ''A million right now versus a four-year college stint and *maybe* a job afterward? What kind of choice is that for a kid who's been poor all his life?''

''I know. It's the money.''

''Not just money. Zero was great. I still remember that game with the Cowboys. He—'' Abruptly Dave broke off. ''I know. I guess the big bucks and the drug-pushers got to him. But it's not your fault, nor the fault of professional sport. Like my Dad always said—'' He broke off again, giving her a sheepish grin. ''Okay, forget Dad. But you must know the old saying, 'You can lead a horse to water, but you can't make him drink.' People make their own choices.''

''I know.'' She knew he was right. But a little feeling of guilt persisted. She'd been preparing Zero for college when she knew he was aiming for the NFL.

''I'll tell you something else,'' Dave went on. ''A guy like Zero's in the minority.'' He ran a hand through his hair. "Okay, there are some screwups, sure. But you don't throw out the barrel on account of one rotten apple. Many of our players come from deprived circumstances. Leroy Jones did."

"Who's Leroy Jones?"

"Catcher for the Yankees for about ten years." Retired last year at age thirty-two and has already started a multimillion-dollar restaurant franchise."

"I see what you mean." She sighed. "I was teaching Zero about Shakespeare, when I should have been telling him how to handle fame and money."

He shook his head. "There you go again. Taking everything on yourself. People are people, Monica, whether they play ball, build skyscrapers or dig ditches. They're responsible for themselves."

"I know, but—"

"All I'm saying," he interrupted passionately, "is that we give young players an opportunity that many would never have if they couldn't play ball. And that's good, isn't it? They've got a talent that gets them out of rat-infested tenements and into the good life. Most make the best of it too—for themselves *and* their families. I could tell you stories—"

Eric ran into the room, beaming. "We got it fixed real good!" he exclaimed. "It's a pretty pot, too, Miss Powell. We picked up all the broken pieces, and Grandpa says—" He stopped and threw a look at Dave. "He said Mr. Powell was too formal and I could call him Grandpa. That's all right, isn't it?"

When Dave nodded, he turned to Monica. "Come and see if you like it."

She followed him out, glad of the interruption. She wasn't sure that Dave would have gotten off his soapbox anytime soon. But he *had* given her a new slant on professional sports. How had they gotten on the subject of her pet peeve, anyway?

CHAPTER NINE

"YOU DID WELL today," Lisa told Duke as he was leaving the paddock. "You're really improving."

"Yeah." Eric grinned. "Pretty soon, I might let you out of the corral."

"Watch it, big mouth! Unless you don't plan to do any more trading."

Lisa's eyes widened. Those autographed baseball cards that the kids would die for. Eric had been trading them and winning friends. He got them from Duke. She smiled.

"Kidding! Just kidding!" Eric was saying, and his whole face creased into an impish smile. "You looked like Sol Aiken on that horse."

"Who's he?"

"Best jockey in the country. Maybe in the world. He rode Folly in the derby and he rode Sir Patton in the steeplechase."

"Now you're talking," Duke said, winking at Lisa. "Okay. I'm outta here. See you later."

"Later," Eric echoed as Duke strode out.

Lisa looked at the boy. She'd grown quite fond of him. "You sure know about horse racing, don't you?"

"Yeah. At least I used to when I lived at the

stables. Gramps was a trainer, and that's what I'm gonna be when I grow up. I'm gonna have a spread with lots of horse stalls and a bunkhouse and a race-track and everything, just like at Greenlea.''

"You really miss it, huh?" Here he was, still hanging around this little stable, even though he was off work duty.

"Yeah."

"I know how you feel." And she really did, she thought, with a surge of bitterness. If her father hadn't lost their ranch in Wyoming, that was where she'd be right now!

She rumpled Eric's hair. "I like having you here. You're a big help. And you're going to star in the spring horse show. That is, if I ever catch up with your father."

"You wanna talk to him?"

"Sure do."

"I'll tell him. He phones me at the dorm every Wednesday night from wherever he is."

"He does?" she asked, surprised. So Eric wasn't totally neglected.

"And he'll be here next week. For Parents' Day."

"Great!" What an idiot she was. She'd asked ev-erybody but Eric how to contact his father. "I'm glad he'll be here. He can check out the Mosley Ranch where we're having the show. Hopefully he'll give his okay for you to participate and we can start your training. Would you like that?"

"Yeah."

She noted the lack of enthusiasm in his voice. *No*

big deal for him, I guess, she thought. Just like this eight-horse stable wasn't enough for her. "It'll be fun," she told him. "You can help me with the others." She looked at her watch. "Dinnertime. Hadn't you better scoot?"

"Yeah. See you."

Poor kid, she thought, as she stood by the fence and watched him walk away. His loss was greater than hers. Greenlea Stables. She'd seen pictures. Acres of lush Kentucky bluegrass country, surrounded by the typical white rustic fencing. Home of so many famous Thoroughbreds. Idly she wondered what would happen to it. Would the family dispose of it? Boy, would *she* like to have it!

No. Not really. She wasn't aiming *that* high, nor was she into racing. She just loved ranch life. All that space and all those horses. She wouldn't be closed in, the way she felt in this small but too-posh paddock. And she wouldn't have to teach gym. She could just work with horses. And...okay, people.

Truth to tell, she'd liked handling the people, as well as the horses, at her family's Rolling Hills Ranch, a dude ranch in summer, easily transformed into a ski lodge during Wyoming's snowy winters. She liked planning and arranging the excursions. She liked to joke and laugh with the visitors, liked to maneuver them into having fun. She was good at it.

Like her father, dammit!

Her father. She leaned on the fence and sighed. Tup Hamilton was a devil. A handsome, manipulative, lying, thoroughly likable, utterly charming devil. He could charm a timid old lady into the fantasy that she was a daring young horsewoman and get her to cheerfully mount any horse he suggested. And he could charm any young woman—though he only went for the pretty ones of course—into believing she was *the one*, the enticing beauty who had, at last, captured his heart. He charmed Carol, her mother, who forgave him time after time.

Well, give the devil his due. It was largely Tup's lovable dynamic personality that made their dude ranch such a roaring success. Even she, since she'd first mounted a pony, had been his shadow, admiring, emulating his ways, while Mother, bless her, had directed and seen to the dull amenities like cooking and laundry. A pity she hadn't handled the accounts, as well.

Tup might have been the cause of their success, she thought as she made her way back inside, but he was certainly the cause of their downfall. He was as extravagant with money as he was with charm. Expensive gifts for the current lady of choice, and yes, for Mother and her, too. Too generous and easygoing with the hands. Hardworking with ranch chores, but careless with accounts. No wonder he'd finally gone bankrupt and lost the ranch.

His heart was failing now, too weak for the hard ranch work and harsh Wyoming winters, as well as the endless affairs. But he still retained the infectious smile and easy charm.

"Good night, Frank," she called to the stable manager as she picked up her purse.

She sighed as she walked to her car. Yes, she still loved her father, in spite of his faults. She did not begrudge the money she sent every month to supplement what Mother earned as a hostess in that small Laramie restaurant. Carol Hamilton was as staunch, pretty, stable and reliable as ever. And as much in love with Tup Hamilton as she'd ever been.

Lisa got into her car, shoved the key into the ignition and wondered how that could be. She'd witnessed her mother's humiliation many times and she knew how it hurt. Never, she promised herself, would she fall under the spell of such a man. She could thank Tup for one thing. She'd observed the way he operated long enough to immediately recognize the type.

Maybe that was why she had never fallen for a man. Maybe she never would.

I DON'T UNDERSTAND her, Dave thought, as the screen door banged shut behind him. He walked across the back lawn followed by the two dogs, the beautiful long-haired collie and the grubby little mutt; the mutt was filling out, though, starting to look quite presentable.

Of all the family houses, this place had been Dad's smartest buy, he thought as he stepped over the retaining wall and headed for the beach. No way could anyone get this much beach frontage now.

He strode leisurely, the sedate collie at his heels,

the mutt darting in and out of the quietly lapping waves looking for God knew what. Crabs, maybe? Dave smiled at the dog's antics.

Lord, how he loved the peace and quiet of a private beach. Much as he liked the thrill and excitement of a baseball game, the crowds got to him every now and then. At which point he could leave the noisy games and come to the quiet beach. The best of both worlds.

So what's bugging me?

Monica Powell. He got the cold shoulder, even over the phone. *What's* with *her?*

What's with *you? Why can't you just walk away?*

He was damned if he knew! Why, of all the women he'd ever encountered, did he feel that at last he'd found the only woman for him?

And the only woman who'd summarily rejected him. Surprise, surprise.

This really *was* a surprise. Usually he had to fend them off. Val made a good buffer.

Buffer, huh? Savvy businesswoman, sex partner and buffer, too? Not bad.

Dammit, Val had been the one to make the rules. Spelled everything out, right from the beginning. Safe, comfortable, nobody taking advantage of anybody.

Looks like she's changing the rules, chum.

Yeah. And he'd better back out before somebody got hurt.

Nothing to do with Monica Powell of course.

He called sharply to Jumbo. The dog was pretty

good in the water, but he was getting too far out. One big wave and he'd disappear forever.

Jumbo raced over to him, and Dave fastened the leash to his collar, thinking of that night on the beach with Monica. She'd kissed him with a take-me-I'm-yours fervor that had him spinning.

Had it simply been the moonlight, a mood of the moment?

Maybe. But it sure didn't seem that way. It seemed that nothing and no one existed but the two of them. It was that way for her, too, he was sure of it. And it hadn't been banished by the rain. It was still just the two of them, laughing together, as they raced home.

Then...*wham!* Back to the daily routine and the cold shoulder.

Maybe what she needed was more moods of the moment. But he couldn't seem to get her out again. She hovered over her father as if he were a delicate piece of crystal. Not good for her or for him. If she didn't coddle him so, he'd "walk as easily as anything," Eric had said.

Dave also remembered what Monica had said about the doctor's recommendation for physical therapy, and that her father would not leave home.

Well, like his dad always said, If the mountain won't come to Mohammed...

HERB HEARD the knocking, but he didn't budge. Whoever it was would go away and come back later.

"Mr. Powell, are you there?"

It sounded like the boy's uncle. "Yes, I'm here. Who is it?"

"Dave Archer. I'd like very much to speak with you."

"Just a minute." Herb grasped the walker and laboriously made his way to the door. "Good morn—no, afternoon," he said, opening it. "Sorry, but Monica's not here. She's—"

"At school. I know. I came to see you."

Herb moved back. "Oh, well. Please, come in."

"Happened to be in the vicinity." Dave stepped in, closed the door with his back. He nodded toward the two paper bags in his arms. "Lunchtime. Thought maybe you'd like to share. Just a change from the usual routine."

He set the two bags on the table beside Herb's chair. One contained a large platter of shrimp with two cups of sauce. The other, raw vegetables, crisp rye crackers and fruit juice.

"Just what the doctor ordered," Herb said, smiling. "Why don't you get plates and glasses from the kitchen," he added, thinking that this young man seemed to be awfully familiar with the household, considering this was only his second visit.

But, then, maybe it was a good thing. After all, Edna, his wife, had become ill before they'd been here long enough to make friends, Monica was also new to the area, and the Powell household was usually devoid of company. So now, for once, he was enjoying male companionship, as well as the delicious lunch, and ate with a heartier appetite than usual. That would please Monica.

It occurred to him that this was why the young man had come—to please Monica. *Perhaps I should ask his intentions,* he thought, suppressing a smile.

"Really good of you to do this, Dave," he said when the food was gone. "I enjoyed it."

"Me, too," Dave said. He seemed in no hurry to leave. He cleared away the lunch debris, then settled back just to talk. Interesting talk, mostly about baseball, but other topics, too. As they talked, Herb silently studied the young man. Notorious, Monica had said. Racehorses and women.

No. That was the boy's father. This was the uncle, who seemed thoroughly likable. Herb decided he didn't care what his intentions were or if he, too, was notorious for something. Monica needed a break in her routine, and she needed interesting male companionship more than he did.

"I really came here to talk about you, Mr. Powell," Dave said.

"After that lunch, please call me Herb, son." He gave a dismissive gesture. "What about me?"

"Eric keeps bugging me. He was very close to his grandfather, and in June..." He paused. "Do you know his story?"

Herb nodded. "Quite a blow for the boy."

"Yes. And he seems to think of you as...well, not a replacement exactly, but maybe a temporary substitute. Do you mind if I bring him over sometime?"

"Not at all. I like him, too."

"Thanks. I'd appreciate that. And there's another thing. Eric thinks you should have the kind of therapy his grandfather had when he suffered a stroke some years ago." Not exactly a lie, Dave told himself, suddenly nervous now that he'd reached the point of his visit.

Herb smiled. "Yes, he made that quite clear."

So he did, Dave remembered, and felt relieved. "What does your doctor think?" he asked, though he also remembered what Monica had said.

"Strongly recommended it. But I'd have to move into Ocean Villa, and I'd hate to leave Monica alone at this time. She puts up a good front, but she's taking her mother's death pretty hard. Maybe, after a few months..."

Each concerned for the other, Dave thought, to the detriment of both. "You shouldn't wait," he said. "And I have a solution."

"You do?" Herb looked at Dave in surprise.

"Yup. One of the best physical therapists in the country is at the Demons' clubhouse in San Diego."

"Yes, I suppose so. But working with athletes is different from—"

"Not so different. And Joseph has medical expertise. Five years at John Hopkins before he came to me."

"And he would—" Herb broke off. "What am I talking about? San Diego is much farther than Ocean Villa."

"I've thought of that, too. My pitcher, Duke Lucas, drives to San Diego five days a week for therapy for himself. He'd be glad to take you, and you'd be home before Monica returns from school. How about it?''

"I can't...I mean, I can't conceive of a better plan. For me, that is. But these people, this Joseph and Duke Lucas. Do you think they'd want to...?''

"They'd do anything for me. And I'd do anything for a guy who'd play Grandpa to my nephew. Deal?''

CHAPTER TEN

MOST PARENTS made a point of coming for Parents' Day at the Joel E. Smith Academy. From wherever they were, even as far away as Europe or Fiji. They could afford it, Lisa thought, and they looked the part. They wore their priceless gems and Armani suits with the same careless ease with which she wore her old frayed jeans.

No jeans this evening, however. She, like the rest of the faculty, was decked out in her best clothes to receive the bill-paying visitors at the formal reception. Dean Simmons, in his tuxedo, was the epitome of obsequious solicitude and Professor Atwood the epitome of academia; even Ada Johnson was in a sequined dress and fairly simpered with graciousness.

Only Monica seemed herself. She'd simply added pearls to her black sheath and was greeting everyone with her usual warm sincerity. Dave Archer hovered near her, but so far had failed to capture her attention. What was he doing here, anyway? There was no need. Eric's father was here now.

Lyndon Archer, whom I need to see, Lisa thought, as her gaze circled the room. Found him. Stayed on him.

She took several deep breaths to counteract the sharp jolt of attraction she felt. Good Lord. What was with her? She'd grown accustomed to rich and influential men during her dude-ranch days and had never been fazed by any of them. So what was it about *this* one? Maybe it was the ease, assurance and expectancy with which he received the respect of every man in the place, the admiring glances of every female. The cordial and relaxed acceptance. The infectious smile and easy charm....

She couldn't take her eyes off him. What held her was...recognition! Tup Hamilton all over again. The captivating smile. The easy charm. Everything Tup had. Only more.

Especially more money. Tup had always been on the brink.

What was it like to have all that money? Lyndon Archer could have anything he wanted. He already had Greenlea Stables, that beautiful Kentucky farm.

No. That wasn't his. It would probably go to Eric's mother, his second, no, first wife, she guessed. Anyway, too far away for inheritance. The boy's beloved Gramps and Grandma were *maternal* grandparents.

But he could certainly afford to buy it if he wanted to. He could buy anything.

He wasn't currently married. His last divorce was six months ago. Or was it a year? Well, whatever. According to Eric, he wasn't married now. Nor seeing anybody steadily, either.

He was available.

How did one go about marrying a rich man who could buy you anything you wanted?

How could she even think such a thing!

She was so busy watching him that she wasn't aware he was watching her. He did it very surreptitiously. Out of the corner of his eye, even while making conversation with someone else. A trick he had of sizing up every available woman and making his choice.

"Same old, same old." Elaine McAfee, who, like him, saw little of her son, was at his side. She stifled a yawn. "If you've seen one Parents' Day, you've seen them all. Right?"

"Well, since this is my first, I'm not the best judge," Lyndon answered, his eye on the blonde across the room.

Women always watched him. He was quite accustomed to it. So what was different about this one?

Nothing covert about that stare. It was blatant. And it had been going on for nearly ten minutes. What was with her?

Rather nice-looking, too. And something about that slim coltish figure, the way she stands. Like she's loaded with energy, about to toss off those heels and shirtwaist dress and run. Barefoot, free.

"Boring, isn't it?" Elaine said.

"Not really." He would have agreed wholeheartedly before the eye-to-eye showdown between himself and the blonde across the room. "I'm learning. I'm learning a lot," he continued, his eyes still on the shirtwaisted woman. Who *was* she?

Elaine noted his preoccupation, but chattered on. "We need to talk. You know your Eric and my Bertram have had a bit of a run-in, big enough to be noted by the dean."

"No, I didn't. Is it cleared up, I hope?"

"Yes. I'm told there's an uneasy peace."

"Good."

"Yes, and I want them to be friends, now that Eric is here and we live so close."

Yeah, he thought. The McAfees lived on the property just to the north of his. He'd like his son to have a friend.

Just then the dean approached and latched on to Elaine, which gave Lyn a chance to get away. He maneuvered through the crowd to stand directly in front of the woman who'd been watching him. He noted her big blue eyes. The red-gold hair, cut in what would have been pixie-style except the curls were untamable. A few freckles, which only enhanced her fresh vibrant look. A very attractive package altogether.

"Are you planning to seduce me?" he asked.

"What?" She looked startled, considering how long she'd watched him.

"I seem to sense an interest," he said. "I wondered if you were planning to seduce me."

Only *the* Lyndon Archer would ask such a question in such a setting, she thought. Or maybe a Tup Hamilton. Her eyes twinkled with laughter as she slipped easily into her flirtatious dude-ranch role. "I was thinking about it."

"Oh? You're intrigued by my good looks? My obvious virility? My—"

"Your money."

That threw him. She could tell. But he rallied in an instant. "You don't beat about the bush, do you? You get directly to the point."

"Saves time."

"I see. And you're in need of money?"

"Not really. I was just thinking it must be nice to have lots of it."

"You have a heart's desire that lots of money could fulfill?"

"Yes. No." A gurgle of laughter erupted. "This is a crazy conversation, Mr. Archer. What I wanted to ask you—"

"Lyndon. So you won't confuse me with the other Mr. Archer, Dave, my brother."

"Yes. All right." She was beginning to feel embarrassed. "I wanted to ask—"

"Answer my question first. Is it yes or no?"

"What?"

"Your heart's desire? Money?"

"Will you please forget all that nonsense? Because nonsense is all it was, and I need to get on the right track before you have me fired."

"Could I do that?"

"Probably. For harassment or unprofessional behavior or something. I'm Lisa Hamilton, Mr. Archer, phys ed and equestrian instructor."

"I'm delighted to meet you, Ms. Hamilton." *Delighted to know you're not a parent,* he thought, *and maybe not married.* No wedding ring, but that didn't mean anything.

"I did want to talk to you. Your son, Eric, is a fantastic horseman and I'm anxious for him to participate in the spring horse show. I need your consent."

"Not mine. Eric's. He makes that kind of decision for himself."

"Oh?" She wondered what other decisions Eric was allowed to make. Did this man know what his son really wanted? "Oh, Eric's quite willing," she said. "But...rules and regulations, Mr. Archer. I have to have your written consent. After I've explained the procedure and you've inspected the facility where we're having the show. You know the Mosley Ranch?"

He knew it very well. But on the other hand... "Quite some time since I've been there," he said. "Perhaps you could give me a tour."

"Yes. Then you can sign the disclaimer."

PARENTS' DAY was officially over, but many had remained for a private outing with their children. Lyndon Archer had remained to inspect the Mosley Ranch. Or rather, he thought with characteristic honesty, so that Eric could inspect the facilities and he could become further acquainted with the fetching Ms. Hamilton.

He and Eric spent the night with Dave. The three of them did a little surfing in the morning, then he and Eric took the Jeep to pick up Lisa. She'd suggested they meet at the ranch, but Lyn had said he wasn't sure about the direction. Truth was, he could have driven there blindfolded, but he wanted his inspection to begin at the beginning—where the lady lived.

The tenant list at the modest apartment complex indicated that "L. Hamilton" resided in 2-B. He pressed the bell and she said she'd be right down.

Not the kind to keep a guy waiting, he thought when she descended the steps a moment later. He liked that. And he liked the look of her slim figure in black jodhpurs. Definitely appealing.

"Hi," she said. "Perfect day, huh?"

"Perfect," he said, appreciating the freshly scrubbed look of her face, the sprinkle of freckles. Maybe she'd run a comb through those untamable curls, but she sure hadn't wasted time on makeup.

She sat in the passenger seat beside him, but all her attention was on Eric in the back. "Your dad says we'll have to get *your* approval to be in the horse show, Eric, so I hope you like the Mosley Ranch. It's smaller than Greenlea, but it's also a training stable. We're lucky Ted lets us use the track for our shows."

"Lyn!" Ted Mosley headed straight for Lyndon as soon as they climbed out of the Jeep. "Long time no see! Welcome back!" He gave Lyndon a hearty slap on the shoulder before turning to Lisa. "Couldn't get rid of him when he was a teenager. He was one of my best workers."

"Really?" she asked in surprise, then cast Lyn an arch look. "Hard worker, short memory, huh?"

He smiled, knowing she referred to his "not quite sure of the direction." "*Convenient* memory. I hope you enjoyed the drive out as much as I did."

"Yes," she said, and turned quickly to Ted, explaining why they'd come. But all the while she talked, she thought how much she *had* enjoyed the drive. How nice not to have to drag out the old station wagon and pick them up as she did other parents.

She gave herself a shake. Why was she making such a big deal of it, like she was being coddled or something? And why was she so conscious of his eyes on her as she showed Eric the facilities, like he was inspecting her.

What *was* it about this man that made her feel so awkward?

Nothing awkward about her, Lyn thought. He liked the way she moved. Graceful and precise, her hands demonstrating each phase of the proposed performance. It was clear she thoroughly enjoyed it. Her face was flushed and her tone vivacious as she proudly described triumphs of previous shows; laughter would bubble forth as she recalled disasters. Even Eric, he noticed, who heretofore had evidenced little interest, seemed to be caught up in her buoyant enthusiasm.

This was fun, Eric thought. He really didn't care about a show where you rode around and made a few jumps just so you could demonstrate that you could ride a horse. But Lisa made everything sound great, even a dumb horse show. He liked her. He could tell Dad liked her, too. He guessed Lisa was the *only* lady both of them liked.

He hadn't liked the last two wives, Jane or Dierdre. Not that he'd seen much of them, just the few times he'd had to visit Dad. They'd been really different in looks. Jane was tall with lots of long black hair, and Dierdre was short with red hair. But they acted exactly the same. All mushy over him, calling him a darling boy and telling him how glad they were to see him, then forgetting all about him while they went back to whatever they were doing before he'd arrived.

Nothing mushy about Lisa, though. Just a lot of teasing and laughing and saying things like "Better get on with that mucking if you want to take a ride like I know you're dying to."

He was dying to take a ride now. On that gray mare Mr. Mosley called Cindy. And not just a gallop around the track, but through the whole ranch. Nothing like in Kentucky, but it was the closest he'd come to a place remotely resembling Greenlea. Just the smell—of hay, horses, stables—was a pleasant reminder. He was beside himself with delight when Mr. Mosley did suggest that the three of them might enjoy a canter. Doubly delighted when he was allowed to mount Cindy.

It was so much fun! Come to think of it, it was the most fun he'd ever had with Dad, even counting the times they'd gone riding in Central Park in New

York when they'd stayed at his penthouse. Maybe it was Lisa, riding like the wind and looking like she was having the greatest time ever. And urging you on with her "Race you!"

He was sorry when they returned to the stable. He hated to see the day end. As they walked toward the car, he was glad to hear Dad ask Lisa to have dinner with him.

"I'll drop Eric off and pick you up about seven," Dad said. Eric knew that didn't include him, but that was okay. He could see that Dad liked Lisa, and he wanted him to keep on liking her. And if she liked Dad...

She didn't. He heard her say very politely, "Thank you. That would be nice. But I can't. I have another engagement."

"Oh?" Dad was surprised, Eric could tell. "An important unbreakable engagement?" he persisted.

"Yes," she said.

"Male?" By this time they were in the car, and Eric leaned closer to the front so he could hear her answer. He didn't want Lisa to have an engagement with a male friend. Not an important unbreakable one, anyway.

"Yes," she said, and Eric's heart fell. Then she turned to Dad, her eyes sparkling, and smiled in that teasing way she had. "A few men. But more women."

"You're putting me on." Lyn's mouth quirked.

"No, I'm not. I do have another engagement. It's a meeting."

"What kind of meeting?"

"Just a meeting. Listen, don't let me forget to have you sign the disclaimer. The papers are at my place."

"Okay. But let's not get off the subject. What kind of meeting?"

"A discussion group. We get together once a week and talk about…things."

"Can't you skip it this once?"

"I could, but I don't like to. They…well, they've kinda elected me the leader."

"I see. What time is this meeting?"

"Seven."

"You have to eat, don't you? We could go to dinner after your meeting."

Dad wasn't going to give up. *Good,* Eric thought. But she wasn't going to give in.

"Too late. We have a habit of going on and on. Usually I grab a sandwich before I go."

"So, why don't we do that?" Lyn said. "Or maybe a burger, instead." And he turned the car into the Hamburger Palace. Which was all right with Eric. It was his favorite place to eat.

At least one of us is pleased, Lyndon thought as he glanced at his son. *I prefer candlelight and soft music when I'm with a new interest.* But this new interest obviously preferred to dash home for a sandwich and off to pursue her own business. Which was…what, exactly? He couldn't help but wonder. What kind of "things" did such a group talk about?

Never mind the group. He wanted to know all

about her. This wasn't the place. Not with his son gaping and that rock music blasting from every direction.

Hard to believe that this had once been his thing. The days of his youth seemed long ago. Of all the family residences, he guessed he'd spent the most time here in Pueblo. The house at the beach was where he and Dave were usually dumped when there was no school or camp. Dave spent his time at the beach, while he practically lived at the Mosley Ranch. Then off with his latest crush to the hamburger joint. Not this relatively new place, but a place with the same booths, the same boisterous atmosphere—which was now driving him crazy.

No. Not exactly crazy. More like he was taking a strange backward-in-time flight. Back to when all that mattered was here and now. No pending deals or mergers, no pressures. Just comfortably absorbed in the pleasure of today and the knowledge that tomorrow would be like it.

Such a strange feeling. Like coming home. And that was stranger still. Since he'd never really had a *home*. Many residences. No home. But now—

Damn! He was getting downright sentimental. He shook his head in an effort to ward it off. But the peculiar feeling persisted.

What had prompted it? The exhilarating race through the ranch? The nostalgic reminders?

Or the woman with the untamable pixie curls and mustard on her chin, who grinned at him from across the booth. ''Thank you, sir. Much better than a peanut-butter sandwich. This place makes the best burgers, and their strawberry shake is to die for. It's my favorite place."

"Oh? Then we'll dine here often."

"Of course," she said, but it sounded more like *Ha ha! That'll be the day!*

"I mean it. I want to know you better. I want you to know *me*."

The blue eyes twinkled. "Oh, I already know all about you."

"Don't judge me by the press," he said, smarting. His reputation was not as bad as the media reported.

"No. I wouldn't. I have much better criteria. I've seen you on a horse."

"What are you talking about?"

"I was reminded of Tup. Something he always said."

"Who's Tup?" he asked, more interested in what this Tup meant to her than what Tup said. And irritated by the spark of jealousy he felt.

"My father."

Oh. That was a relief. "Why do you call him Tup?"

"Because he's that kind of man. Everybody calls him Tup, and that's not even his name."

Lyn sighed. "Okay. So what did he say?"

"He said that if you want to know about the inside of a man, just watch him on the backside of a horse."

"I see. So from our short ride, you now have a clear reading of my background and character?"

"Definitely."

"All right. Then tell me."

"Why?" There was that fun-filled teasing look again. "You already know you."

"Of course. I just want to know how much you've learned from the backside of a horse," he said, aware that Eric was listening intently, his gaze shifting from one to the other.

She laughed. "You look so scared. You shouldn't be. Actually it's a pretty good reading," she said, as if rather surprised.

"So tell me!"

"Well, let's see. First, a bit of background. Life has been good to you. You're quite accustomed to having anything you want. Even to this day. Everything goes your way."

"Oh?" He thought about that. He couldn't remember wanting much. Possibly because he had it all.

She nodded. "That's why you're always in control. You're so used to being in command that you don't expect things any other way."

"No, I—"

She held up a hand. "Hush. This is my reading. Horseback analysis. Okay. You get what you ask for—instant obedience. Easy. The person, or horse, doesn't even realize he's being controlled. The lightest tug on the reins or a gentle nudge with the knee. Or, in the case of a person, that charming smile. Do you know what a sweet smile you have?"

He swallowed. Something wrong here.

She could tell he was disconcerted. No doubt he was usually the one laying on the compliments. It was fun turning things around. Fun to slip back into her old dude-ranch role, joking, flirting, teasing.

"So much of what you are is transmitted to the horse, or person of course. Your serenity, calm confidence, your gentleness. No horse or person could be skittish or nervous around you. The gentle touch of your hand..." She hesitated.

"Yes. Go on. The touch of my hand?" His voice was a gentle nudge and she caught her breath, suddenly aware that she had stopped breathing. The touch of his hand, gentle, commanding, loving... Dear Lord, what had come over her?

"Hey, look!" she said, glancing at her watch. "Almost seven. I have to go. Please. Will you drop me by so I can pick up my car?"

"Must you really go?"

"Well..." She did want to stay. Laughing, teasing, having fun with this man. Being Tup Hamilton's happy carefree flirtatious daughter.

But she was Carol Hamilton's daughter, too. She knew that a woman could get hurt.

"I have to go," she said.

CHAPTER ELEVEN

ERIC DIDN'T KNOW what Lisa's meeting was about. But he knew that any meeting Dad went to was about business. So he was surprised to hear him say, "Don't bother about your car. We'll just tag along with you. That's okay, isn't it?"

Lisa said, "Sure. Okay." But she looked like she was surprised, too, and like she really didn't want them to come.

Lisa, in fact, *didn't* want Lyndon Archer to tag along. She knew this wasn't his thing. She did suggest that he might be bored, but there seemed no graceful way to tell him to forget it.

The meeting was always held in a small room of the local church, courtesy of one of the members who was on the council. Lisa led their little trio through the church, deserted now, except for a few people working in the bookstore.

"Sorry I'm late," she said to her friends, and introduced the Archers. "They wanted to join us tonight. Hope you don't mind."

Naturally no one objected, but Lisa was concerned. Eric and Lyndon were not part of this cohesive group, whose members used the meetings to air deeply personal problems in a supportive atmosphere. She could only hope Eric and Lyndon's presence would not inhibit the regulars, make them reluctant to speak up.

She was wrong. Nothing and no one was going to keep Alice Abercrombie from bewailing her broken marriage and pending divorce.

Lisa, with the support of other members, assured the woman once again that the failure was a learning experience. "The best is yet to be," she said. "When one door closes, another door opens. So let go and see what happens."

She was talking to Alice, but her mind was on Lyndon Archer, sitting quietly in the back listening. He'd been through *three* divorces. Were any as vicious, as painful as Alice's? Hardly—at least not for him. Probably he was already on the lookout for something better. Ha! More likely, had already found her.

Still. Three divorces. She couldn't help but wonder what he was thinking.

Lyn, in fact, was thinking about her. Was this the same woman who'd flirted so blatantly with him last night? The vibrant delightful woman, so full of fun and jokes, who'd galloped beside him today? Yes, it was. And now she was crackling with the same enthusiastic vitality, but spouting all that sanctimonious nonsense.

Let go and see what happens! Yeah, right. She ought to tell that woman to get a good lawyer. That was what all his ex-wives had done. He didn't know about the pain, but they left well padded.

Now Lisa was giving the same line to the man who'd just lost his job. *Another door opens....* The name of the game today was downsizing, and the guy had better start opening some doors for himself. Hit the pavement, study the want ads, find another field.

As the discussion went on, Lyn tried to reconcile the unearthly theories he was hearing with his own practicality. But it was Lisa who captured his interest. Which woman was she? She'd sounded pretty practical last night, hadn't she? *Your money!* It had fairly popped out. No joke.

No problem, lady. He had plenty of money, and he liked an honest approach. He liked *her.* That natural unchic look of her, the turned-up nose, the sprinkle of freckles. He liked the outrageous way she flirted and teased. He might argue the soul-searching crap, but he was certainly intrigued by her rendition. It would be his pleasure, he thought, to give her whatever her heart desired.

"It's God's pleasure to give you the kingdom." Eric's bored ears perked up at the statement, delivered by one of the members, a small white-haired lady whose hands were clasped like she was praying.

Oh, sure, he thought. All you had to do was pray, thank God, and believe, and you got whatever you wanted. That wasn't true. Because no matter how much he prayed and thanked God, it wouldn't bring Gramps and Grandma back. And he couldn't live at Greenlea.

The man who'd lost his job thought the same

thing. He said the company had gone bankrupt and closed down. No way could he get his job back.

"Then there's something better waiting for you," Lisa said. Jeez. Like she really believed it.

Eric sighed. There couldn't be anything better than being back at Greenlea with Gramps and Grandma. Just thinking about it made him feel sad. He felt even sadder when another woman started talking about Christmas.

"We just got through Halloween, and the stores already have the decorations up," she said. "Christmas is becoming too commercial. All this expensive giving!"

Gramps had been planning to give him a horse. A racehorse he could train himself.

"Hey, don't knock the giving!" one of the men said. "We store owners count on holiday givers to boost the economy." That made everybody laugh for some reason, but the man kept talking. He said that was *real* giving to lots of people—store owners, clerks, delivery folks and people who you didn't even know you were giving to.

Then Lisa said that giving was one of the messages of Christmas. "Love is the greatest gift, and without it, any gift is meaningless. It's good to give, a diamond bracelet or a chocolate bar, even a kind word. As long as it's given with love."

Funny, Eric thought. It sounded like what Duke had said. Only he'd said it different.

Anyway, he was tired of this meeting, and he was glad when they all filed out. Only, they stopped at the little bookstore they'd passed when they came in. Lisa was showing folks certain books to buy, ones she said would be good for them to read. Dad was watching Lisa. Eric watched the two teenage girls who were sitting at a table. They had a basketful of little candles, and they were folding pieces of paper and securing each to a candle with a rubber band.

"You want one?" the girl with red hair asked.

He really didn't, but he was about to say yes when the black-haired girl said he couldn't have one.

"Not unless you come on Christmas Eve," she said. "That's when we have the candlelight service."

"What's that?" he asked.

"That's how we celebrate Christmas here at church," she said. She told him how at the end of service, they passed out these little candles so everybody had one. Then they turned out all the electric lights and the candles were lit by passing one to another. "It's so beautiful," she said. "Then everybody holds up their candle high and makes a pledge for the coming year."

"How come you're putting that paper around it?" he asked.

"It's your fortune for the year, whichever candle you get," said the redhead.

The other girl giggled. "It's not really a fortune."

"It's almost like one," the redhead insisted. "At least it's a message from God. And sometimes it's a fortune. Last year I got one that said—" She stopped. "I forgot. You're never supposed to tell anybody what your message says. It's just between you and God."

"That's dumb," Eric said. "How can it be from God when you, or somebody wrote whatever's on there? And anyway, you don't know who's going to get which candle!"

"God knows."

Eric stared at the girl. She sounded so sure. He was going to ask more, but Dad motioned to him that they were ready to leave. He followed them out, wondering. He'd ask Lisa. Maybe, if he wasn't somewhere with Dad, he'd ask her to bring him Christmas Eve. He'd hold up his candle, get his own message, even if it did sound dumb.

"GOOD NIGHT, SON. I'll be back shortly," Lyn said when he dropped Eric at the house. "We'll get up early and do some more surfing before I take off. Would you like that?"

"Yeah."

"Better hit the sack, then. It's been a long day, but I enjoyed it," he said, rubbing a knuckle against Eric's cheek.

He shut the door and started back to the Jeep. It occurred to him that this was the first time he'd spent a whole day with his son. Divorced when Eric was only two, except for a few short visits, he'd left him to Marion's care. Actually to her parents' care, for Marion hadn't seen much more of Eric than he. He felt a deep sense of regret. He'd missed so much.

Now fate had given him another chance, and he meant to take advantage. His boy was growing up and becoming a real personality. A little bumpy on the surfboard, but with a bit of instruction...

And maybe, he thought, grinning at the glow of pride he felt, Eric could teach him more about handling a horse. He definitely meant to see more of him.

And of Lisa, he decided as he climbed back into the Jeep where she waited. The mystery woman beside him had certainly been a big part of the day's fun. He was just as anxious to see more of her.

What now? Would the prim serious lady of the discussion group bid him a cool good-night and race to her apartment alone? Or would last night's money-hungry temptress invite him up for a nightcap or coffee—and possibly more?

"Care to come up for a drink?" she asked when he stopped at the complex.

Are you kidding? he thought. "Sure," he said, and followed the trim figure in the snug jodhpurs up the stairs to the second floor.

Yes, he thought, as he surveyed the apartment. It was *her*. The same comfortable disorderly appeal as her tangle of curls. The same spark of vitality—tennis racket on the sofa, running shoes on the floor, open book on the coffee table. But also a bed, glimpsed through the open bedroom door, neatly made, fresh flowers on the table by the window.

"Not much of a choice," she said, moving about,

picking up the racket, the shoes, putting things in order. "Which?" she asked.

"Pardon?" he said. What had she offered?

"Wine or hot chocolate?"

"Hot chocolate?"

She shrugged. "Sorry. I don't drink coffee."

"Wine, thank you." Lord. When had he last tasted hot chocolate?

"Coming right up." And she disappeared into the bedroom with the shoes and racket. She was back in a moment on her way to the kitchen.

Curious, he sat on the sofa and picked up the open book—*The Art of Meditation*. Careful not to lose her place, he thumbed through the pages, trying to see Lisa still and quiet, in the meditative posture. Couldn't imagine it.

She returned with a tray. A bottle of chilled white wine, two long-stem glasses, crackers and a selection of cheeses. "You pour," she said.

He poured, handed her a glass, touched it with his. "To you and me."

She hesitated, sipped, but said nothing.

Not very encouraging. He changed the subject. "Isn't that an Eastern ritual?" he asked, gesturing toward the book. "Somewhat contrary to your Christian principles?"

"Oh, come on. Everybody does meditation now of one form or another, even nonbelievers."

"Really?"

"Really. Besides, I'm ecumenical."

"Are you, now?"

"Sure. My mother says people have different faiths or rituals, take different paths, so to speak. If someone else has found a shortcut or, in this case, a handy vehicle, it makes good sense to borrow, doesn't it? We're all seeking the same thing."

"And what's that?"

"Peace, joy..."

"Love?" He leaned toward her, not quite touching those very kissable lips.

She drew back. "Of course love," she said, making it sound universal. "Love is the answer to all problems, all controversy."

"You're finding meditation a handy vehicle to the...delights of love?"

Her face burned. He was mocking her. She wouldn't let him get away with it. She helped herself to a piece of cheese and spoke seriously. "Many of the great sages meditated. And many of today's leaders, in business, government or whatever, find meditation a stimulating and powerful tool in their much-too-busy world."

"And you?"

"All right. It hasn't worked for me," she said honestly. Not yet, but she intended to keep trying.

"I wouldn't think so," he said. "You're far too...physical to just sit and think about love."

She ignored the implication. "No problem," she said, determined to keep the discussion impersonal. "I can sit. I just can't listen."

"Oh?"

"Meditation is for listening. I'm so busy talking

to God I never hear what He says." That was quite true, she thought, and very frustrating.

His mouth twitched. She sounded like she'd been conversing with a neighbor. "And what do you talk to Him about?"

"Oh...things."

"Earthly things?"

"Well, yes, I suppose you could say that." She stopped, staring at him. Maybe that was the trouble. Dwelling on mundane earthly things when she ought to be listening for divine guidance. And why the dickens was she talking about this to him of all people! Why had she started it?

No. *He* had started it. Asking about that book. Then things had just popped out. Why did he affect her like that? One look, and out came whatever was on her mind.

Abruptly she got up and went to her desk. "I almost forgot the disclaimer," she said, taking it from the drawer. "This is what I want you to sign."

He took the papers, scrawled his signature where indicated, handed them back to her.

"You didn't read it," she said.

"The first rule of business is knowing whom to trust. I trust you."

"You shouldn't judge a book by its cover," she said lightly, slipping back into her old dude-ranch role. "For all you know, you could have just signed over a big hunk of...of something to me."

"Some earthly desire you've been bugging God about?"

"What?"

He stood, moved closer to her. "Perhaps you should talk to me about...earthly things."

She blushed. Last night the word "money" had just popped out. Did he think she was for sale? She picked up his jacket, handed it to him. "I'm afraid we'd better call it a night. Thanks for an enjoyable day, and for this," she said, holding up the disclaimer. "Eric's going to be the star of the show. And before you go, I want you to know that I'm not some sort of Jesus freak. I don't picket travelers at the airport—"

"Okay, but—"

She held up her hand. "Don't interrupt. I don't fast, and I don't solicit converts. You asked to come to the meeting, and you witnessed an activity I enjoy and believe necessary to keep one healthy in today's world. So there! And thanks again. Good night." She kissed her finger and pasted it on his cheek.

Lyndon went back down the stairs, feeling dismissed, disappointed, frustrated. What was with Lisa Hamilton? He didn't know. But she was certainly different.

CHAPTER TWELVE

"WHAT A CHARMING little place!" Val Langstrom said, her eyes sweeping over Monica's living room. She'd come in with Dave. Or rather, followed him in, Monica thought. Dave had seemed surprised to find her behind him when he brought Eric in.

But always the gentleman, he said, "You remember Val Langstrom? You met at the Beach House."

"Of course," Monica replied, acutely aware of Val's sleek perfection beside her own grubby jean-clad self. "Nice to see you again."

"Hi, Monica," Eric said. "Where's Grandpa? Is it all right if I stay?"

"I think so," she said, smiling at his eagerness. "But check with Dad. He's on the patio."

So Dave and Eric had gone out to check.

Val stayed behind, smiling her catlike smile, explaining, "We're off to another Demons' board meeting. Dave and I are the controlling owners, you know, so we can't afford to miss one." She shook her head. "It's a lot of work managing a baseball team."

"I imagine so," Monica said, though she thought, Didn't they employ managers for that? Her expression must have betrayed her, for Val answered her unspoken question.

"Of course we have a manager who takes care of the baseball *playing*. The board handles contracts, trade agreements and the like. Dave and I keep the business afloat, so the big decisions are up to us."

"I see," Monica said, wondering why all this information was being imparted. To let her know that Val and Dave were a team?

"To *me*, actually," Val went on. "Dave leaves all the major decisions to me."

Monica wasn't sure how she was supposed to respond to that. "That's nice," she said.

"More than nice. It's necessary. Dave's too generous, you see. If I weren't right beside him, he'd give away the store. It's so sweet of you to lend us a hand with Eric."

"We're always glad to have him." More than glad. Eric's visits had made Dad come alive again.

"Well, we certainly appreciate it. He's a darling boy, but every weekend can be a burden. Dave and I are always on the go, you know. Constantly between here and San Diego, and last week we were in Vegas, and goodness knows where from one week to the next. Well, you see how it is," Val said, with a vague wave of her hand.

"Yes." Monica's ears burned. She got the *we, us* and *Dave and I*. No need to cram it down her throat. Did Val think she was trying to break up the cozy little twosome? Dave meant nothing to her!

"This is lovely. Is it an orchid?" Val touched a finger to one of the delicate blossoms.

"Keep—" Monica caught herself, and stopped, shocked by the hot wave of fury. Had she really started to tell Val to keep her greedy hands off that plant? But it was *hers*. Dave had given it to her. Val had no right...

"Yes," she said, hardly able to restrain herself from snatching Val's hand away. What on earth was wrong with her? It was only a plant. She realized Val was staring at her and managed to speak in quiet conversational tones.

"A *kind* of orchid, a phalaenopsis. It does need special care."

She'd bought a book on the subject. The roots were still embedded in bark shingles, and the container rested on a tray above the pebbles immersed in water. The plant itself must never touch water and was to be kept in a semi-sunny area. Talked to. Loved!

Not poked at with long painted nails!

"Okay, let's go!"

Val, to Monica's relief, turned at the sound of Dave's voice. "You're ready?"

He nodded, looking at Monica. "Herb says it's all right. I should be back before eight. Is that okay with you?"

Before Monica could answer, Val's honeyed tones cut in. "Don't make any promises, sweetheart. We'll probably stop for dinner on the way back."

"You're coming back here?" he asked, sounding less than enchanted with the prospect.

But Val didn't seem to notice. "Of course. Don't worry. I won't desert you." She turned an arch glance on Monica. "Don't be surprised if you're stuck with Eric again tonight, huh, Dave?"

But Dave had spotted the orchid. "Hey, it's really flourishing. Looks like it's getting plenty of tender loving care." He smiled down at Monica, his eyes warm, enveloping, questioning—

"Dave!" Val's voice was sharp. "We'd better go. We're already late."

Thank goodness, Monica thought as they hurried out. What was it about Dave Archer that drew her to him? If Val hadn't been there, she would have—

No. Surely she wouldn't have!

But she'd wanted to. Oh, how she'd wanted to. She'd longed to go to him, wrap her arms around him and—

She had to get hold of herself. He'd kissed her once. That long-ago night on the beach. Why did it haunt her so? Why did the feeling linger? Unfinished. A teasing burning desire waiting to be fulfilled.

Idiot! Mooning over a kiss. Giving TLC to the orchids he'd sent her.

And the bracelet. Hidden in her jewelry box when she knew darn well she should return it.

But she couldn't let it go, that endearing lopsided shoe. No more than she could resist the way he looked at her, like...

Like he looked at *all* women! Lisa's words came back to taunt her. *Archer men...loaded with humor, charm and sex appeal...whatever it takes to make them irresistible to women.*

And I'm just as vulnerable as any other dumb female!

Deliberately she pushed Dave Archer from her mind and went into the little laundry room. As she transferred towels from the washer to the dryer, she could hear Eric's voice from the patio in rapid conversation with Herb. She recalled something else Lisa had said: *grandparent-isolation syndrome.* So Dad was a comfortable bridge from the past to the present, she thought. Eric certainly seemed happier.

Dad was happier, too. She hadn't realized how lonely he was, how starved for company.

Then, too, he'd felt so awkward about using a walker. She smiled. Eric, in his outspoken way, had banished all that. *My gramps had a walker. You gonna get rid of yours?*

Now Dad *had* rid himself of the walker. In just two weeks he was managing with a cane and just a little help. Duke said the therapist was amazed at Dad's agility. Relatively young muscles, he'd said, younger than Dad's fifty-five years. He said Dad would soon be walking normally.

Thanks to Eric, she thought, delighting in the sound of the child's voice and her father's resounding laughter.

But it wasn't only Eric. It was Dave. He was truly a friend. He'd brought Eric over, had arranged for the therapy at his club and wouldn't even allow them to pay for it. Even arranged for transportation with Duke whose jokes and conversation had proved a real tonic for Dad.

Vicky, Duke's wife, was also a delight. She turned out to be very different from how she'd appeared to Monica that memorable night at the Beach House. Monica remembered thinking that she looked very exotic and very remote, as if she would rather not be there.

She certainly wasn't remote with her and Dad, hadn't been right from the very first moment Duke brought her to the house. She'd greeted them warmly. "So nice of you to have us. Duke talks so much about Herb. I've been dying to meet him."

"I've been anxious to meet you," Herb had responded. "According to Duke, you're the most beautiful, most desirable, sweetest woman in creation."

"You forgot to mention nagging, demanding, fussiest—" Duke began.

"Watch it!" Vicky warned with mock anger. "And thank your lucky stars you have me. Isn't that right, Monica?" she'd added with a wink.

They were like a breath of fresh air, Monica thought, as the good-natured banter had continued and the usually quiet house rang with laughter. Since then, the young couple had become almost a part of the family.

I'd better get a move on, Monica thought now. The couple were due for dinner that night.

When they arrived, she was surprised to find they both knew Eric. In fact, there was quite a capping session going on between Duke and Eric.

"I see you two are good friends. Or enemies," Monica joked when they were seated at the table. "I suppose your being on Dave's team..." Her voice trailed off as she thought about it. Was Dave spending more time with Eric, taking him to the clubhouse, introducing him to the players? "I suppose you two met through Dave."

"You got it," Duke answered. "Dave arranged it with the academy stable for Eric to give me a few tips on, uh, perfecting my riding skills." Duke looked hard at Eric.

Eric giggled.

"I see," Monica said. "So you two hit it off right away?"

"No," Eric piped up. "He started bawling me out like everything. Just 'cause I said I didn't like it there."

"I did not," said Duke.

"Yes, you did. You kept saying things like 'You hungry? Got a bed to sleep in? Anybody beating you?' Kept at me. You know you did. And you were real mad!"

"Well, I guess I did rub it in. You were acting like a spoiled brat. Too dumb to know when he's well-off. Sitting on a gold cushion, a loaf of bread under both arms and cryin' the blues!"

"I wasn't crying!"

"And making fun of me to boot!"

Eric grinned. "Well, you couldn't ride. Still can't."

"Oh, yeah?"

They were at it again and eventually Herb played referee and broke it up. "Hold on, you two! After such a shaky beginning, I'd like to know how you became reconciled. At least to some extent," he added, grinning.

"Duke started telling me how bad he had it when *he* was a kid," Eric said.

"Wait a minute." Herb turned to Duke. "I thought you said it was a good life, even fun, this home you lived in."

"Oh, it was...is. I'm talkin' about before."

"Yeah," Eric said. "Before Dave found him and saw all those bruises on him where he'd been beaten."

"Dave?" Monica's heart gave a lurch. "Your uncle Dave?"

"Yeah." The whole story about hiding in the school john tumbled out in Eric's childish but dramatic words.

Monica's heart throbbed as she listened. Dave. Of course. That was the kind of thing he'd do. Just as he'd seen to Dad's needs and taken Eric under his wing. He cared. He cared about a poor hungry hurting black boy. Her heart swelled with a warmth that spread through her, gentle and tender, as strong as the sexual pull she felt. Dave. She was overwhelmed with longing.

"And Dave said Duke wasn't ever gonna go hun-

gry again and nobody was gonna beat him, either,''
Eric finished.

"He kept that promise, too,'' Duke added. "And
it sure wasn't easy for him.''

"What was the problem?'' Herb asked. Monica
wondered, too. Surely it wasn't money.

"All the legal complications,'' Duke said. "Single man. Dave must have been about twenty-four
or -five then. I was twelve. Lots of judicial crap.
Adoptions by singles frowned on. Interracial adoptions taboo.''

"I see,'' Herb said. "An impossible situation.''

"Not for Dave.'' Duke cut into his roast beef.
"He's got a way of cutting through the red tape to
get what he wants. He got a pack of lawyers, called
in the county politicos and used his family muscle.
In less than a month the San Diego Demons' Home
for Boys was started, with me the first and for some
time the *only* occupant.''

Duke chewed, paused, stuck a forkful of food in
his mouth and swallowed. "*Man,* this is good, Monica! Best home-cooked meal I've had in a long
time.''

"There you go again,'' Vicky said. "You're
about to talk yourself out of getting any more from
me.''

"Right.'' He grinned. "Best one since last night,
honey.'' His eyes shone with love as he looked at
his wife. "Herb, did I also mention the best cook?''

"Come to think of it, I believe you did. And I
agree,'' Herb said, nodding toward Vicky. "My

mouth's watering for those barbecued ribs of yours again!''

Vicky smiled at him. "Ribs and baked sweet potatoes next week."

"Promise?" Herb asked.

The talk went on about when and what she would cook, but Monica wasn't listening. Her food was growing cold on her plate. All she could think about was Dave. He came on so tough. All that about her holding umbrellas over people who ought to be looking out for themselves. Ha! Like he wasn't doing the same thing. Outwitting the bureaucrats to take care of one little boy. More than one, she realized as Herb started asking questions, and the talk again reverted to the home.

"This home, according to what you've told me, has become quite an institution," Herb said.

"Oh, sure. So big now, Dave is thinking about opening another one. Mandy and Jim Ross, the couple he first put in charge, are still the folks in charge. But they've added to the staff just as they've added to the building. Would you like to see it sometime?"

"I certainly would."

"Okay, I'll take you over. And say, we're having a fund-raiser next week. An exhibition baseball game at the Demons' stadium. You all should come."

"You bet," Herb said. "Any home that's produced a guy like you deserves support."

"Oh, Dave supports the home," Duke said. "But, well, he has a way of making the boys think they have to pay their own way. Chores around the home, community service and the like. And this game the boys have every year. It's to raise money for their Christmas giving to poor families and children who might not otherwise have a Christmas.''

A chain of love and giving. Monica was impressed. She got up. ''Better see about dessert,'' she said, retreating to the kitchen.

Vicky followed, bringing in the empty plates. ''Touching story, isn't it?''

''It is. I would never have known all that about Dave.''

''No. Dave's pretty quiet about his giving,'' Vicky said. ''Shall I serve the coffee while you do the pie?''

After dessert and coffee, Eric and the two men went out to the yard to play catch with a softball Duke had brought over. ''You can sit in a chair, Grandpa,'' Eric said. ''If you miss, I'll get it.''

Monica watched them through the kitchen window, delighted to hear her Dad laugh, not seeming embarrassed even when he missed. ''Eric's done wonders for Dad,'' she told Vicky, who was helping clear up. ''So has Duke. Your husband's a pretty special guy, Vicky.''

''I know. I love him to pieces. But he does bug me sometimes.''

''Really? Why?''

''He's such a showoff. Like he's always got to prove himself.''

Monica hesitated. "He doesn't seem like a show-off to me."

"Well, he is!" Vicky stopped rinsing dishes and leaned against the counter. "All these rich people with their fancy houses and stupid horses. They put on such airs. You're the first person I've felt comfortable with since we moved to Pueblo. You and Herb and Lisa."

Monica laughed. "That's because we don't have anything to put on airs about."

"No," Vicky said seriously. "I think it's because you have the kind of ordinary but stable life-style I've always had." She sighed. "That's something Duke never had."

"But the group home sounds pretty stable and secure."

"He was twelve when he got there, remember?"

Monica nodded.

"That was just half his life," Vicky said. "He's only twenty-three now, and before that his life was a mess. Even with his mother before he was put into those horrible foster homes. Now don't get me wrong. She was quite a lady, a good woman with sound values that have remained with Duke to this day. Made him the guy he is."

"So what's the problem?"

"It's like he has to do everything, have everything that anybody else has. Maybe because he was spurned as a child, even when he was with his mother—poorer than anybody else, left out of things. Now he has to make sure he's not left out of *anything*. He not only has to keep up with the Joneses, he has to keep up with the Rockefellers!''

Again Monica laughed. ''Oh, Vicky—''

''It's true!'' she insisted. ''Like our moving here. I'd much rather live in San Diego in a simple condo, where most of the players, at least those not in the big bucks, stay. But no. Duke has to move out here—big house, stable, those darn horses. I'd rather fill the place with children.''

''Would you, Vicky? Children are a big responsibility, and you're both so young.''

''That's what Duke says. He thinks we should wait. But I don't want to wait.'' Monica was struck by the pathos in her voice. ''I want my children while I'm young enough to enjoy them. Anyway, we sure don't need horses. Eric was right. Duke can't ride.''

Vicky shook her head in disgust. ''And he doesn't have to. We don't have to give big parties, suck up to these folks who've been rich all their lives. But Duke thrives on it, especially the adulation. And these *women.* You wouldn't believe how they go after him! They—''

''Wait a minute. Does he go after *them?*''

''No,'' Vicky admitted. ''But he *loves* that kind of attention. He—''

''We better hit the road, honey,'' Duke said, coming into the kitchen. ''We'll be late, but we ought to make the Daltons' reception, don't you think?''

Vicky gave Monica a ''See what I mean?'' look. Monica had no idea who the Daltons were, but gathered they were people Duke felt he needed to keep up with.

She shook her head as she closed the door behind them. They were such a great young couple. Kind, good-humored, down-to-earth. And both so vulnerable. Duke, like Zero, was too much enthralled with the sudden fame and fortune fate had bestowed. Vicky, so much in love, so possessive, so eager for a real family life. Scared. Jealous.

Monica knew how it felt to be jealous. Or perhaps *envious* was the better word, if the man didn't belong to you.

CHAPTER THIRTEEN

As THEY LEFT the boardroom, Val glanced at Dave's expressionless face. He'd opposed her tonight on almost every issue.

"You were sure on a share-the-profits kick tonight," she said crossly.

"It's only fair."

"Fair to whom? Additional personnel, big contracts. Sure cuts dividends."

He shrugged as if he hadn't just given away a big hunk of what was rightfully theirs, she thought, her anger mounting. Well, she wasn't a broker for nothing! And things would be different when she got control.

"Well, if that's the way you want it, sweetheart, so be it." She hooked an arm through his. "I'm with you."

"Didn't sound like it back there." He'd increased his stride and she had to run to keep up.

"Oh, honey, you know me. Sometimes I get blown away by dollars and cents." And she'd better watch it, she thought. The Demons were small potatoes compared to his community property. "Truly, what I want is what you want. So what's on for tonight? Steak or fish?"

"Neither for me," he said, touching the remote that unlocked the car. "I need to get back. I'll just drop you and—"

"Drop me!" She stood by the door he opened. "I'm going back with you. Remember?"

"Not a good idea tonight, Val."

She couldn't just stand there. She got in the car. But she was furious.

"What's the matter?" she asked when he slid into the seat beside her and drove off. "Mad because I tried to stop your little giveaway game tonight?"

"Of course not. You're a good businesswoman and I respect your opinion. I might disagree with you at times, but that's no reason to be mad."

"Then what's with this 'Not a good idea tonight' stuff?"

"I've got things to do. For one thing I have to pick up Eric and—"

"Eric?" *Jeez, that kid!* she thought. Dave hadn't spent one night with her since the brat had gotten here. "You know something, Dave, that kid is Lyndon's. Not yours. Anyway, why is he such a problem? Why can't you just call and ask that he stay overnight with what's her name?"

"I didn't say he was a problem. I said I had to pick him up." He'd stopped in front of Val's condo and started to open his door. "Come on. Let me see you in. I promised Monica I'd be back early."

"Oh! I see. Monica. Is she the reason you're so anxious to get rid of me?"

Dave had started to climb out of the car. But he

got back in, closed the door and turned to face her.
"Val, we need to talk."

"Talk?" Uh-oh. Had she gone too far? "We *are*
talking."

"Well, I'd like to remind you of a discussion we
had a long time ago. Soon after we first met, in
fact."

"Oh?"

"Right here. Upstairs in your condo. You laid
down certain rules. No promises, no ties, no com-
mitments. Remember?"

"Yes." Of course she remembered. He'd eaten it
up, just as she'd known he would.

"You meant it, didn't you?"

"Of course." Meant it as a starter, a gimmick to
make him feel comfortable, give her time to get under his skin, bring him closer. Damn! She hadn't yet
worked up to a live-in relationship, much less a marriage. Well, she wasn't giving up yet!

She touched his hand. "Oh, honey, you know me.
I talk hardball. But inside I'm soft, as vulnerable as
any other woman. And we *have* been close, haven't
we?"

"Yes. Good friends, good business partners."

"It's been more than that and you know it!" she
snapped.

"Come on, Val. You called the shots. No
chains."

She *had* gone too far. "Oh, Dave, let's not quar-
rel. We're both tired. You shouldn't rush back to
Pueblo tonight. Come on up and—"

"No. Look, Val, we've always been honest with each other. Maybe it's time to—"

"Don't say it!" She put her hand over his mouth. "We are good together, aren't we, Dave?"

"Yes, but I'll say it again—you're a great business partner and a good friend. I'd like to keep it that way."

"Me, too." She paused. "You must forgive me. I get a little cranky sometimes because I worry about you. All women aren't like me, you know. And when I see one after you tooth and nail it burns me up. Like—"

She stopped. Best not mention that teacher, counselor, whatever she was. "Oh, you know what I mean. I do worry about you. You're such a sweet guy, Dave." She reached up to tenderly caress his cheek. "So trusting, so...vulnerable. You need someone to protect you."

"Not really. I'm a big boy, Val."

"Of course you are. And I'm not going to keep you out here bickering over nothing, because we're both tired. No, don't get out. I'll see myself in and I'll call you tomorrow. We still need to decide whom we're trading."

She got out quickly and rushed into her condo. She slammed the door and leaned against it, breathing hard. Damn! She'd had to get away before he said what he was trying to say. She didn't intend to make it easy for him.

HE *WAS* A BIG BOY, Dave thought as he drove away. Big enough to know when he was being conned, in bed or out. From now on, it would be business only between him and Val. And he'd watch her business tactics, too. He wasn't going to let his baseball team become just some stock-market commodity.

As he drove toward Pueblo, his thoughts took another turn....

ERIC STOOD WITH MONICA and Herb, watching as Duke and Vicky drove away, his face split in a huge grin. "Duke's funny!"

"Talks funny, but makes sense," Herb said.

"Yeah. He told me love was catching, like measles." Eric giggled. "He said what you give out, you get back."

Monica smiled. "Did he really say that?"

"Yeah, and it works, too. Even on people you hate. Like my teacher. Only it was more *her* not liking *me*."

So he'd been aware of Ada Johnson's feelings, too, Monica thought. Pretty perceptive for a ten-year-old.

"Duke said you're s'posed to say something nice to people like that, only I couldn't think of anything nice to say to Mrs. Johnson. But then one day she wore a blue dress that sorta made her eyes look pretty, and...well, I told her so. She just smiled like everything, and after that, I think she did like me more better."

"Just better," Monica corrected.

"Yeah, better. And you know something? I found out you can be nice by *not* saying something, too."

"How's that?"

"Well, you know Bert McAfee? I really hated him. Me and him had that big fight in the dorm that night, you know?"

"He and I."

"Right. I hit him in the nose and he didn't even cry. But he sure was crying the day after Parents' Day. I saw him. My dad brought me back to the dorm to get my boots, and I remembered I'd left them at the stable and I was gonna borrow Tommy's, only I couldn't find him. He and Bert are big buddies, so I went there looking and that's when I saw him. Bert, I mean. Lying on his bed bawling like anything. And when he saw me, he started yelling like he wanted to fight again. But I just shut the door and went out. I didn't find Tommy, but I took his boots, anyway. He didn't care. We're friends now."

"What about you and Bert?" Herb asked.

"Oh, yeah. That was what I was gonna tell you. About not saying something. I felt sorry for Bert. Wasn't hardly anybody else in the dorm, on account everybody was out with their folks like I was with Dad, you see. Except for Bert."

"Oh, poor kid," Monica said. "His mother was here. She didn't stay to spend time with him?"

"Guess not. Maybe she was busy like Marion."

"Marion?"

"My mother. She likes me to call her Marion.

And she's always busy. Fittings, hairdresser, stuff like that.''

"I see.''

"So I know how he felt, and that's why I felt sorry for him and I didn't tell anybody I saw him crying like he thought I was gonna. Specially when he gets to bragging like he always does.''

"That was good of you,'' Monica said.

"Yeah, and now me and Bert are pretty good friends, too.'' Suddenly he turned to her beseechingly. "Monica, can I have another piece of pie?''

"You may,'' Monica said, giving him a hug. "Because you're a pretty special boy.'' A boy who was finding his own way, she thought. Just as Dave said he would. Had it been left to her, she would have snatched him out of Ada Johnson's class right away, and he would have missed a good learning experience.

Dave was right. People had to help themselves; other people could get in the way. Like she'd done with Zero. He'd been big enough to find his own way; it wasn't her fault if he hadn't. She wondered what had happened to him. She'd completely lost touch.

She was in the kitchen cutting the pie when the doorbell rang. She hurried to the door.

"Told you I'd be back by eight,'' Dave said. "It's only ten after.''

She glanced over his shoulder. No Val. Not in the car, either. Empty, as far as she could tell. The rush of elation made her body tingle and her face grow warm. He was here! Alone!

"It's just me. Dave. Were you expecting someone else?"

"No, I thought... Never mind," she said, irked that his perceptive eyes had caught her looking for Val.

"Aren't you going to ask me in?"

"Oh! Of course. Come in." She managed to get control of herself and spoke quite normally. "Dad and Eric are having pie. Come and join them."

"Back already?" Herb asked as Dave followed her into the kitchen. "Good. Sit down. Have some pie. It's delicious."

"Yeah," Eric said. "Monica cooks as good as Rosella. Duke ate three pieces."

"Duke was here?"

"For dinner. He and Vicky." Herb looked at Dave. "Were your ears burning?"

"Pardon?"

"Duke talked a lot about you."

"Yeah," Eric said. "About how you got mad when you saw somebody had beat him up and how you—"

"Duke talks too much and so do you," Dave said.

"Maybe," Monica said as she set pie and coffee before him. "But I did learn a lot about umbrellas."

"We didn't talk about umbrellas, did we?" Eric asked Herb. Herb, looking puzzled, shook his head.

Dave, who'd caught Monica's teasing smile, looked embarrassed. "Well, I hope Duke told you

about the game the boys are sponsoring next week,"
he said, changing the subject. "It's called the Lucky
Bowl, and it's the Demons' pony league against the
L.A. pony league championship team. Some of
those guys are really good. The scouts are already
watching them." He said it was a big event and they
shouldn't miss it, and the conversation changed to
baseball.

Monica stopped listening. She slowly sipped her
coffee and thought about what she'd learned tonight.
Dave Archer wasn't just some rich playboy. He was
a deeply caring giving man who—

*Oh, for goodness' sake, you didn't fall in love
with a man just because he was a do-gooder.*

In love? She couldn't be in love with a man she'd
known only...what was it? A couple of months?

No. She wasn't. She couldn't be.

But the feeling, deep inside her, had nothing to
do with his being a do-gooder or a rich playboy. He
was Dave. Dave, whose penetrating dark eyes could
read her every thought. Dave, whose kiss still
burned in her memory. Dave, who haunted her
dreams. Who had only to open his arms and she'd
run into them.

Good Lord! That wasn't love. That was sex.

She tore her gaze from him. "More pie? Coffee,
anyone?"

"I'M GLAD you let us ride with you," Monica said
as Vicky maneuvered her Mercedes into her re-
served parking space at the San Diego stadium.

"I'm glad to have the company. Duke's busy doing his thing, you know," Vicky said. "Lisa was coming with us, but she's been drafted."

"Drafted?" Herb asked from the back seat.

Monica turned to her father. "Apparently. Dave always buys blocks of tickets and has kids bussed from various schools. This year, on account of Eric, Joel E. Smith Academy was included, and Lisa's one of the chaperons."

"I see. Wow. This *is* a big event."

As they climbed to their seats, she saw that the stadium was almost half-full, and the crowd was still pouring in.

"Oh, yes. The boys work hard to make it a big success. Others, too. Like Duke. He heads the committee for corporations, who donate a lump sum or a block of seats. That's why we have to leave a bit before the game ends. We have to get back for the big bash Duke and I are hosting for corporate donors."

"My goodness, you do have your hands full!"

"No problem. It's being catered. Look, there's Eric with some of his buddies. They've got great seats."

Eric and some of his buddies. How good that sounded, Monica thought, as pleased to see Eric on good terms with other kids as she was to see Herb managing without his cane. And on these stairs, too. There really *were* miracles.

And Lisa. Wasn't that Lyndon Archer beside her? Volunteering as a chaperoning parent, she presumed.

Though he seemed more interested in Lisa than in his charges. But he had been turning up more often lately, which was certainly good for Eric. She wasn't sure about Lisa, who'd confided that she didn't intend to give *the* Lyndon Archer the time of day. Monica wondered...

"I'd like you to meet my friends," Vicky said, referring to the two women who were joining them. "Their husbands are on the Demons' team. And Link, Doris's husband, was at the group home," she added. "Our men are either in the dugout or coaching from the sidelines, so we have to hang together," she explained.

"I'm beginning to feel like a fox in the henhouse," Herb complained.

"More like a fox about to be caught by the hounds, I'd say, as handsome as you are. Watch out," Doris warned as the others laughed.

Monica was amused to see her father blush. These young people were good for him. She was glad they'd come.

"Is this the section for baseball widows?" a familiar voice sang out.

Monica's heart sank. Val Langstrom. Monica and Vicky slid over to make room, but Val squeezed in between them, much to Monica's annoyance. She was not in the mood for the "Dave and me" bit.

She needn't have worried. There was no chance for small talk during such an exciting game. Even the opening ceremony held everyone spellbound.

It started out simply enough. The national anthem

sung by a young girl, still in her teens, with a fabulous voice. Then Jim Ross, manager of the San Diego Demons' Home for Boys, thanked them for coming and said, "I want to introduce someone who's going to tell you more about today's project. Our first resident and one of whom we are extremely proud—Duke Lucas!"

There was a great roar from the crowd, then everyone stood, with cheers and whistles, as Duke stepped to the podium.

"Thank you, thank you," he said as the ovation quieted. "I see you know me."

Laughter from the crowd.

Duke continued, taking a cocky stance as he pointed to himself. "I'm Duke Lucas. I pitch for the Demons. I'm great, they say. Okay, okay, I slipped a little last season, but I'll be back. Just watch my smoke."

Cheers and cries of "You're the greatest, Duke!"

"Yeah. I'm still the greatest. You know about my contract, don't you? It's all over the media." This brought more laughter, which continued as Duke bragged about his house in Pueblo Beach, his cars, his horses, his beautiful wife. "But I want to tell you," he said so quietly that the crowd hushed, "I wouldn't have all this if I hadn't got lucky. *Lucky,* I tell you! Eleven years ago, I was roaming the streets of this city all alone, hungry, bruised and beaten. But somebody found me, somebody fed me, somebody cared. Somebody gave me a home and a chance to be what I am. I call that lucky."

The crowd was very quiet now, and Duke continued, "Now I know you're not here for a sermon,
but I got to do a little preaching. The man who fed
me fed others, too, by founding the Demons' Home
for Boys." Duke raised a hand to stop the cheers.
"But he gave us more than food. He gave us a way
of life and a philosophy. You earn your own way
and you give back what you get. We worked at the
home and in the community, and we got a sense of
pride in ourselves."

He paused. "Three years ago one of the boys volunteering at a food shelter was touched by the sight
of a woman who'd brought her six grandchildren by
bus to be fed at the shelter. It was around Christ-
mastime, and he got his friends at the home to round
up some toys for the kids and food for a Christmas
at the shack they called home. 'But that's just one
family,' one of the boys said. 'Yeah,' said another.
'We oughtta do more. If we had a big event, raised
a lot of money, we could give presents and food to
lots of people.' And with a name like Demons, what
other event could they dream up? You got it! A
baseball game!

"So two years ago, this project was started, right
there in the Demons' Home for Boys. They wanted
it named like the Rose Bowl or the Cotton Bowl,"
he said, gaining more laughter from the crowd.
"'We could call it the Empty Bowl,' said one boy.
'You know—like we wanted to fill it up.' Another
kid said, 'Hey. How 'bout the Lucky Bowl? 'Cause

we been lucky and we gonna make others lucky, too.'

"So that was it," Duke said. "Two years ago, this project, Lucky Bowl, was started. This one event has not only provided toys and a Christmas party for over five hundred kids, but has provided food and clothing for many families during the past two years. It's the boys' project. But they couldn't have done it without all of you here today. You're the real contributors. You've brought luck to many, and we thank you."

There was another standing ovation, and it was some time before Duke could say, "On with the game between the San Diego and L.A. pony leaguers. We'll be cheering for both teams. Everybody wins at the Lucky Bowl!"

Then Dave came out to make the first pitch and the game began.

Monica, though, couldn't keep her mind on the game. Her heart was so full of all that had come from what one man started. A man whose name had not even been mentioned today. She turned to the woman beside her.

"Wasn't that a wonderful thing Dave did?" she asked. "I mean, taking Duke on and starting the group home?"

"Yes," Val answered. "It's a great tax deduction."

CHAPTER FOURTEEN

THEY LEFT after the eighth inning, and Vicky broke the speed limit on the drive back, anxious to get there before guests arrived.

"I never know who's going to show up," she said. "Duke's invitations are the Come-on-everybody kind."

Herb laughed. "Duke's quite a guy. That was some speech."

"I guess," Vicky said. "But don't you think he laid it on kinda thick? All that bragging about what he has."

"He wasn't bragging," Herb said. "He was making a point. A good one. There's a striking difference between what he was and what he's become."

"And he really wasn't talking about himself at all," Monica said, still a little irked by Val Langstrom's comment. The group home just a tax deduction? Amazing how people could see things in such different lights!

"I think," she went on, "that Duke just used himself as an example. What it can mean if someone cares. I think it was a touching story."

"Okay, okay!" Vicky lifted her shoulders defensively. "You're right of course. It's just that I've heard it many many times. Duke so full of what was done for him. At least,'' she added, laughing, ''he didn't go into all that about hiding in the john.''

"No, he didn't, did he?'' Monica said, remembering that was the way she'd first heard it. ''And if I hadn't heard it before, I wouldn't have known it was Dave he was talking about.''

She stopped, drew a sharp breath. ''Hey, you're driving too fast, Vicky.''

Vicky lifted her foot from the gas pedal and the Mercedes slowed a little. ''I guess he can't help telling it. He's so grateful. Always trying to give back. Can't do enough for Mandy and Jim or those boys at the home. And Dave!'' She shook her head. ''As far as Duke's concerned, Dave is the Lord God Almighty.''

"But he never even mentioned his name,'' Monica murmured.

"He knew better than to do that. Dave hates the limelight.'' Vicky turned into a long driveway. ''Well, here we are. Good. We beat the crowd.''

"You're right. No cars,'' Monica said, her eyes scanning the spacious parking area. Duke had something to brag about, all right. She and Herb had become regular visitors, and she was quite familiar with the five-bedroom house, guest house, stable and swimming pool. She never ceased to be amazed at what two people, still in their early twenties, had achieved. Really, what Duke had achieved. Because of baseball.

Baseball. Again she thought of Dave. *Sure,* she

remembered him saying. *It's a business. A big business.*

Yes, she was beginning to get a better opinion of professional sports. A golden opportunity for a good ballplayer.

Too bad opportunities weren't as golden for a scientist or a schoolteacher, she thought, smiling, as she followed Vicky into the house.

They hadn't been there but a few minutes before guests started flowing in. They gathered inside the house, around the swimming pool and the stable or strolled about the grounds, partaking of the bountiful supply of food and drinks. Their numbers were astonishing.

"Vicky was right about Duke's everybody-come propensity," Monica said to Lisa, who'd arrived rather early, accompanied by Lyndon Archer.

"That explains the presence of Frank, the academy's stable manager," Lisa said. "He looks rather lost. I'd better go over and talk to him."

Monica watched Lisa and Lyndon move off. Together.

IT WAS LIKE walking beside a block of ice, Lyn thought. Okay, a scintillating enthralling block that sparkled with life and held him captive. But ice just the same.

What the devil did she have against him?

He joined her conversation with the rather shy Frank, but his attention was really focused on *her*, the woman with the spray of freckles and no makeup at all.

How was it he'd become besotted with someone he'd never even kissed?

This whole situation was new to him. He usually only had to select from those that pursued. This one he'd pursued relentlessly. Up to and including chaperoning a busload of noisy kids, not to mention going to that discussion group.

The thing was, he couldn't figure her out. One minute she was an alluring anything-goes siren, and the next she was distant, as remote as a nun. She was an enigma. A challenge.

"Hi!" Duke greeted, joining them. "Glad you all came. And thanks for the generous donation, Lyn. The boys appreciate it."

"I hope they appreciate your strong-arm persuasion," Lyn said.

"They do, they do!" Duke said, laughing. Then he turned to Frank. "Glad you could make it. Would you like to see the mare I bought from Mosley?"

"Sure thing," Frank replied.

"Me, too," Lisa said, starting to follow, but Lyn's hand closed on her wrist.

"No," he said. "I've had enough of horses and horse analysis."

"Okay, sir. What's your preference?"

"You."

"I'll drink to that! That is, I would—" her eyes sparkled "—if I had a drink."

"No problem," he said, taking a bottle of champagne and two glasses from a passing waiter.

"Wait," she called as he started toward an empty table. "Woman cannot live by drink alone." By the time she'd filled a plate from a nearby buffet, he'd found a more secluded table, to which they retreated.

He poured the champagne and seated himself across from her. "Now. Tell me about you."

She dipped a fat shrimp into the sauce and looked at it, as if considering. "What would you like to know?"

"Everything. Where you came from and where *we* go from here."

She bit into the shrimp, choked. "Spicy!" she said, fanning her mouth.

"Quit stalling."

She took a hasty swallow of champagne. "All right. I came from a dude ranch in Wyoming, and we're not going anywhere from here."

"A ranch?" Of course. That shouldn't surprise him. "A dude ranch in… Oh, the hell with that! Why aren't we going anywhere?"

"I'm not sure," she said slowly. "I think it's because you remind me too much of…someone."

"Someone you loved?"

She nodded. "Still love." She chewed on an olive, picked up a sandwich. "Aren't you hungry?"

He felt like he might never be hungry again. "You're in love with someone else? Someone who—"

"I'm not *in* love. I love him. My father, Tup. I think I've mentioned him."

"Oh, yes. I remember. He said you could judge the inside of a man by how he was on the backside of a horse, or something."

She nodded.

"So I take it," Lyndon went on, "that, even though Tup's wise, he's not a very nice person."

"Oh, yes, he's very nice. Like you," she said, her eyes twinkling.

"But something about him bugs the hell out of you, and since I remind you of him... You might be mistaken, you know."

"Oh?"

"I might not be as much like him as you think. Why don't you give yourself a chance to know me better and find out?"

Lisa smiled. "That would take time. More time than a busy man like you can spare."

"More than *you* can spare, you mean. What with school, riding lessons and all those meetings!" He bent toward her eagerly as an idea presented itself. "Look, your Thanksgiving break is coming up. Why don't we take a little trip? There's a great spot in Acapulco I think you'd like. We could—"

"No." She shook her head. "I don't do that."

"You don't do what? Travel?"

"I don't bed hop."

"You don't..." He felt stung as if she'd slapped his face. "I didn't ask you to. I merely suggested—"

"But that's what you meant, didn't you? A cozy little suite overlooking the ocean. For just the two of us."

She was right. That was *exactly* what he'd meant. But that didn't keep him from being shocked. Never had he been so bluntly rejected. He wasn't even sure he'd ever been rejected, bluntly or otherwise. "This bed hopping, as you put it...I suppose it's against your religion?"

"Health hazard," she said, grinning.

"Don't be naive." But he was the naive one. Her shocking tell-it-like-it-is made a farce of an invitation to...become better acquainted. Hell, that was the usual procedure, wasn't it?

"Forgive me," she said quickly, as if sensing his irritation. "I shouldn't have put it that way. And to be perfectly honest, it's not physical but emotional hazards that concern me."

"Emotional? You've been hurt?"

"Someone close to me has. And...well, I could be." She paused. "I... Look, it's a long story and I'd rather not talk about it," she said earnestly. She touched his hand. "I'm sorry. I don't think I'm the right type of woman for...for you."

Further insult. What type was his type? He said nothing, feeling utterly at a loss.

"Anyway, I'm planning to visit my folks during Thanksgiving, but I do thank you for the invitation," she said as if to end on a polite and pleasant note.

So why hadn't she just said that in the first place? Infinitely less embarrassing. "The dude ranch?"

"No. Laramie. The dude ranch is no more."

There was such a sad note in her voice that he could have forgiven her anything.

MONICA DIDN'T QUITE KNOW what to do with herself.

Herb had retreated to the TV room where several fans were watching football. Maybe they'd just come from an exhibition baseball game, but this was football season, and she gathered this was a major game. Vicky, the perfect hostess, was busy introducing her dozens of guests to each other. "At least, the ones I know," she'd confided to Monica.

Monica would have liked to help, but she hardly knew anyone at all. Might as well join the football fans, she thought. She accepted a glass of wine from a passing waiter and walked to the TV room. She went in and took a seat near Herb, then looked at the screen, prepared to be interested, though she didn't even know who was playing.

Nobody was playing.

"Game's over," Herb said. "Rebels won."

"Oh." No wonder people were deserting, everybody talking excitedly as they filed out to the bar or buffet. Monica sipped her drink, relaxed.

Suddenly she sat bolt upright. There, on the screen, in a football uniform, was…"Zero! That's Zero!" She thumped her father's knee in excitement.

"Yes," Herb said. "Zero Perkins. Running back for the Rebels. Ran forty-five yards for the winning touchdown."

Monica felt a warm glow, as much relief as pleasure. Zero was back! Healthy. Confident. She couldn't take her eyes from the screen.

After a replay and an analysis of the spectacular run, the reporter said, "Congratulations! You've made a great comeback, Zero."

"Thank you."

"Not only have you regained your football skills, but you overcame a harmful addiction," the interviewer continued. "And I understand you're advising others who are victims of drug abuse. What advice do you give them?"

"I tell them what a teacher told me when I was at Central High in Philadelphia. I was pretty cocky, I guess. Big football hero, you know. But this teacher said I couldn't be a hero to anyone else until I was a hero to myself. I kept remembering that, even during the worst times. You sure ain't no hero to yourself if you're all messed up with drugs."

Monica gasped. She remembered. She'd been trying to make him understand Shakespeare. "This above all: to thine own self be true."

One little sentence. One he'd taken as a lesson for life. He'd grasped it, held on. Now he was passing it on to others!

She brought a hand to her mouth in awe. She'd never felt so proud. Imagine. Just one little sentence.

But as Dave had said, *Whatever works.*

Dave. Where was he?

DAVE WAS MAKING his way through Duke's mob of guests when Val Langstrom finally spotted him.

"Dave, you're here at last! I've been waiting for you!" she exclaimed, latching on to him. He might reject her in private, but she knew he was too much of a gentleman to do so in public. "What took you so long?"

"I stopped by the home on the way here. The boys are having a little celebration of their own."

"That's nice. But it's been a long day for you. Tired? Hungry?"

"I guess."

She saw his eyes scanning the groups of people, obviously searching, but she had no intention of letting him get away from her. "Then come on and let me take care of you."

She grabbed his hand firmly and pulled him into a room where several tables were set and a lavish buffet was available. "Stay here," she said, seating him in one of the chairs at a small table for two. "I'll serve us. I know what you like."

She signaled a waiter and ordered two margaritas, then proceeded to the buffet. She made a great show of selecting various delicacies, then bringing them to him and begging him to "taste this. See if you like it."

This is what Monica saw. Val, bending over Dave, holding a tidbit to his parted lips. The image flashed in sharp focus before her. Blurred. It was lost in the fire of red-hot fury that blazed all around and deep inside her. This was Dave. Dave, who haunted her dreams, whose eyes teased, tantalized and held her spellbound, whose lips had touched hers and turned her world upside down. He was the only man who could set it right again. She wanted, needed...*loved* him.

The words rang in her ears. *This above all: to thine own self be true.*

Val? She wasn't married to him, despite all the *we* and *us* innuendoes.

Anyway, Monica thought in a burst of defiance and confidence, *I'm better for him. I can make him happy. I love him.*

Her thoughts spun and flickered like sparks from the love/anger fire for only a moment. A moment in which Val hurried back to the table for more tidbits.

A moment in which Monica walked over to Dave, bent and kissed him full on the mouth. An intimate kiss but so swift that no one in the room took notice. No one except Val Langstrom.

"Hello," Monica said, sliding into the chair beside him.

Dave, the kiss still tingling on his lips, was too stunned to speak. This was the prim schoolteacher?

Monica smiled at the waiter who brought the drinks. "Thank you," she said, and sipped the margarita.

"Hey! That's *my* drink!" Val, carrying two loaded plates, pushed a couple of other guests out of the way in her haste to reach them.

"Oh, I'm sorry," Monica said. "I'll order another for you."

"And *my* chair!"

Dave, ever the gentleman, stood. "Take mine. I'll get—"

"Not you," Val snapped. "Don't you move. She…" Her green eyes shot daggers at Monica. She moved rapidly, eager to reclaim her territory, and bumped right into Dave. The loaded plates crashed to the floor, their contents splattering Val's chic Armani suit and Bally loafers.

Utter confusion. People cleared the area as a pair of waiters hurried to clean up the mess.

Monica spotted an earring among the debris and retrieved it. *Must be Val's,* she thought, and handed it to her. She also held out her cocktail napkin. "I'm so sorry."

Val glared at her, then down at herself. It was obvious that no quick wipe with a damp cloth would do. A complete change was necessary.

But where? How? Borrow something from Vicky? No, anything of hers was too small, dammit!

She'd have to leave. Leave Dave with that damn schoolteacher!

Hell! She glared at Monica again, then stormed from the room.

Monica made her apology to Dave. "I'm sorry. I didn't mean to cause so much trouble."

"It wasn't your fault," he said. But his mouth twitched. Why did it seem she'd almost choreographed the whole thing? "Sit down. Let's finish our drinks."

She sat. "But all your treats, spoiled. Shall we select more?"

"I'm not hungry."

"Neither am I." Not for food, she thought, as her gaze fastened on him. That crease in his cheek, the way one corner of his mouth lifted. She felt weak, consumed with longing.

The message in the clear hazel eyes confused him. An invitation? Seduction from the elusive Ms. Powell?

It couldn't be.

Or *could* it? That kiss she'd planted on him minutes ago...

Monica's courage began to return. All in all, she was quite pleased with herself. Smart move, that kiss. Unhooked Val, hadn't it? And hooked Dave—at least for the moment. But this was a new game for Monica, and she wasn't sure of the next play. She lifted her glass and tasted, as if to find the answer in the frosty drink.

He watched her lips touch the rim of the glass, watched her sip, then retreat, watched the tip of her tongue lick the salt from her top lip.

Felt a stirring in his groin.

His restless movement startled her. She'd better say something. What?

"I..." She hesitated, then spoke quickly. "I came over because I wanted to tell you something. Something important."

"So tell me." *Tell me in that sexy voice,* he thought, remembering the first time he'd heard it. He'd been right. A woman with a voice like that was no ordinary woman.

'I've changed my mind about professional sports,'' she said.

"Oh?'' That wasn't important, but he wanted her to keep talking. "What changed your mind?''

"*You* did. Remember what you said about it being a business, and money going round and round?''

He nodded.

"You were right.'' As she talked on, her words floated like music to his ears, though the meaning barely registered. He was caught off guard when she asked, "It does something for you, too, doesn't it?''

"What?'' He'd heard the song, but only the melody lingered.

"What your business does for these boys, I mean. Giving them an opportunity to use their talents. It makes you feel you're a part of what they've become. Like I did today when I saw one of my students on TV.''

She went on to tell him about seeing Zero being interviewed. "I know football did more for him than I ever did, but I still felt proud, like I'd made a contribution. Not like you, of course.'' There was that look again, that intense dark gaze. "What you do for all those boys. You're pretty special, Dave.''

"Thank you.'' He was more interested in what she *wasn't* saying. "That was all you wanted to tell me?''

"Not quite." She paused, looked down at her wrist, wishing she'd worn the bracelet with the lop-sided shoe. She swallowed, and her next words came in a pleading whisper. "I guess what I really want to say is, can't we take another walk?"

"Why walk when we can dance!" He could stand it no longer—the sexy voice, the little tongue tasting the salt, the yearning in her eyes. He wanted her where she belonged. He stood and held out his arms.

Day had faded into night. The patio dance floor was cushioned in a warm subdued glow from the moon and stars. The music from the combo Duke had hired was soft and haunting.

Monica was in heaven. The other dancers didn't exist. She was only aware that she was in Dave's arms, her head against his chest, his chin rustling her hair. Now and again his lips nuzzled her ear.

Like the song said. Heaven.

It was during a break in the music that she remembered Herb. "I'd better find Dad," she told Dave. "He must be tired."

"Then I'll take you home," Dave said. "I'm not ready for this evening to end."

Monica was not ready for it to end, either. And she wanted to look her best. So, before searching for Herb, she searched for a powder room. The two downstairs were crowded, so she ran upstairs to Vicky's room.

No crowd. But quite a disturbance. A distraught Vicky was pacing the floor in a rage.

Lisa, who was trying in vain to calm her, ex-

plained, "She's upset because Duke has been dancing a long time with—"

"All evening!" Vicky cut in. "With that little
vixen who's always at the Beach House."

"All evening?" Monica asked. She hadn't noticed. But then, she really hadn't noticed anyone but
Dave.

"Well, at least three dances," Vicky admitted.
"But the way she had her arms around him! And
she's always making eyes at him. Oh, you know
what I mean. She's after him. She—"

"I should think you'd be used to it by now,"
Monica said musingly.

Both women looked at her in shock.

"Well," she said, "Duke's quite a guy. Wouldn't
you be after him?"

"What are you talking about? I'm *married* to
him."

"I know. But don't you want to keep him?"

Vicky stared at her. "I love him. Of course I want
to keep him."

"Then you'd better go down and lay on the
'Come here, sweetheart, I need you' stuff. Make him
know you need and love—"

"Sweetheart, my foot! I'd like to bash him on the
head with the nearest champagne bottle!"

"No." Monica's full smile grew into a chuckle
as she recalled the departure of a furious Val Langstrom, her chic outfit drenched with shrimp sauce,
her play for Dave's attention aborted. Sure, it had

been an accident, but accidents could be created....
She laughed out loud.

"This is nothing to laugh about!" Vicky gritted
her teeth. "She's dishing out all that 'You're so
wonderful' stuff and he's eating it up!"

"Men!" Lisa said in disgust.

"Yes, they like it," Monica said. "But so do we.
Vicky, my advice, as I put on my professional hat,
is to outdish her. Or any other woman, for that matter," she added, as her knowledge of psychology
combined with the enlightening experience of the
past hour.

A quiet descended as her words bounced about
the room.

Then Lisa spoke. "Monica, this is the twentieth
century. Men are no longer lords and masters to be
bowed and catered to. At last women have come
into their own. Our needs are recognized, our
rights—"

"Can't go to bed with rights, so let's talk statis-
tics." Monica sat on a divan, pulling Vicky down
beside her. "Do you know that women outnumber
men? At least, the good ones do. Duke's pretty special, you know."

Like Dave, she thought as a warmth stole through
her.

"What exactly are you saying?" Lisa asked.

"I'm saying good men are scarce and women are
hungry. If you want a good man, or want to keep a
good man—" she looked at Vicky "—you better
learn to compete."

"That sounds like the old bowing and catering," Lisa said. "You're saying we should—"

"I'm saying, pass out the sugar, not the salt. Love is catching." Monica again looked at Vicky. "I'm quoting Duke. He said what you give out, you get back. He's right." What she'd given Zero two years ago had come back to her this very day, hadn't it? "If you're true to yourself, Vicky, you'll go downstairs and take over as only you can."

Vicky stared at Monica for a moment. Then she stood. Smiled. "Ladies, stay as long as you like. I have work to do." She spun around and left the room.

Monica got to her feet and turned to Lisa. "If I were you, I wouldn't let old hurts haunt me out of being true to myself. Love, life—anything in life—can be risky. But it's worth fighting for, isn't it?"

She found a mirror, freshened her makeup, then headed back to Dave.

Dave. She wanted more than tonight. She wanted to love him. Make love with him. Be alone with him.

How did one go about inviting a man to come away with you for a weekend?

Maybe longer. Thanksgiving break…

CHAPTER FIFTEEN

VAL LANGSTROM pounded her fist on the steering wheel and stepped hard on the gas pedal as she drove to San Diego. She'd never been so angry.

That little bitch did that deliberately! I'll get even. Somehow. Some way.

She glanced down at the mess that had been spewed all over her designer outfit and cursed some more. She'd swear that schoolteacher bitch tripped her. Just walked in and took over like she owned Dave—and tripped her!

Val just knew it. The bitch couldn't keep the smirk off her face. So proper and polite! Picking up her earring and holding out that tiny napkin—as if it would have done any good!—and coming on with all that sweet "I'm so sorry" crap.

Sorry, hell! I ought to go back and...

Val couldn't go back. She could have if she'd planned to stay at the hotel and brought a change of clothes. But the truth was she'd been hoping to entice Dave to drive to San Diego with her and spend the night at her place, as he often did.

It'd been a while, though, she realized. A long while.

Since he'd met that schoolteacher?

She thought about that.

Slow down! her good sense told her as she whizzed past several cars like they were standing still.

She did. She also slowed her breathing and tried to think rationally. Carefully she recounted each time she'd heard Monica Powell's name, each time she'd seen her in person. Yes, Val admitted with a grimace, there was certainly a connection between Monica's arrival on the scene and Dave's lack of interest in being with her, Val. Okay, so Dave was attracted to the woman.

Why?

Well, she was pretty enough. A little younger than Val. Not much. Two, three years maybe, and half a size smaller. And not much on the ball, as far as *she* could see.

Val firmed her jaw. She'd tackled tougher competition. And won. She'd held on to Dave Archer for two years, and she was not about to let him get away now! Yes, dammit! She'd be Mrs. Dave Archer before that harlot could blink those big hungry schoolteacher eyes or her name wasn't Val Langstrom!

She parked, shut her car door with a bang and entered her condo. She stripped and showered, then began to map out her plan of conquest.

IT WAS A BEAUTIFUL Sunday morning, and Monica felt on top of the world as she sat with her father in their sunny breakfast room. She sipped her coffee, toyed with her fruit and relived the past evening. It had been so wonderful, just being with Dave, laughing, talking, dancing.

"More coffee?"

She looked up to see that her father was pouring himself a second cup. She nodded. "Thank you."

She watched the steaming liquid fill her cup, but what she saw was Dave. The way his mouth curved when he smiled, the way he looked at her when—

The phone rang. She jumped up to get it, eager. Maybe it was Dave.

"Is this Monica Powell?"

"Yes. Who's this?"

"Val Langstrom. The woman you dumped those trays of food on last evening."

Monica's jaw dropped. She gulped and managed to say, "Oh, no. Indeed. Miss Langstrom, you're wrong. I didn't, well, yes, I was there. But so were others. All trying to use the same space at the same time. Remember?"

"You're damn right I remember. You, smiling, as you pretended innocence. Smiling while you helped clean up the mess. Saying nothing to me except a very fake 'I'm so sorry.'"

"It wasn't fake. I meant it. Your beautiful suit—"

"Cut the crap! I know what you're up to. I know you're after Dave Archer. Right?"

"I will not dignify that with an answer."

"Of course not, because it's true," Val said, and added a few choice epithets that made Monica's ears turn red. She was unaccustomed to this kind of talk. Her mouth refused to move.

Val, noting the silence, said more forcefully, "Hello? Do you hear me?"

"No...yes," Monica said, her senses returning.

"You did hand me my earring that fell during the fiasco. But the other one is still missing. Did you see it?"

"No, I didn't."

"I'd hate to lose it. It's more than an expensive gem. Those earrings have great meaning. Dave gave them to me."

Monica swallowed. *Okay, Val. I hear you.*

"Maybe he picked it up," Val said. "I'll check with him when he gets here. Sorry I bothered you. Have a good day."

Monica returned to the table, her spirits considerably dampened. She knew why. Not just Val's vicious stream of invective but that "Dave and me" stuff again. *Dave gave them to me.* And *I'll check with him when he gets here.*

And the insinuation that no matter *who* was after him, Val had the inside track.

Well, okay. She shouldn't be so shocked by Val's accusation. After all, hadn't she decided to do just that last night?

Yes, she had. Monica shook her head. But she really didn't care for this game. Maybe Mom was right. Let the man do the pursuing.

She thought about the earrings. *Great meaning. Dave gave them to me.* But hey, no big surprise. Of course he'd have given Val some jewelry. They've been...friends for a long time. *He gave me that bracelet the day after he met me.* Obviously things like that didn't mean a lot to him.

Did they?

Herb looked up from his crossword puzzle. "Not drinking your coffee, honey?"

"It's cold."

VAL LANGSTROM smiled. That ought to start the little schoolmarm thinking.

She picked up the phone again and dialed.

"Yes, Val, what's up?" Dave asked.

"Truthfully, Dave, I'm upset."

"About what, babe?"

She liked it when he called her babe. She softened her voice and purred, "Your schoolteacher friend was just on the phone with me."

"Oh?" He sounded surprised.

"I asked her if she found my other earring."

"I have it right here. I saw it in the hallway. You'd already gone."

Val was relieved. "I'm still upset, though," she said.

"Now what?"

"That little lady is after you, Dave. Can't you see that?"

"You're wrong. Her interest is in my nephew. You know—Eric."

"I suppose that's why she tripped me last night!"

"Come on, Val. She didn't trip you. It was…an accident."

She caught the hint of laughter beneath his words, and her voice grew sharp. "Oh, she managed it all right. She's a little—"

Val broke off. Just in time, she thought, as again her voice softened. "Dave, I know these women better than you. Monica Powell might pretend an interest in your nephew, but at the end of the hook is bait for Dave Archer. Not Eric."

"Look, Val, I'd rather not talk about Monica."

"I sure don't want to talk about her. What we need to talk about is this threatened strike."

"Yes. It looks serious." Dave's stomach churned. If the players walked out, there'd be no games next year, no season, no series. Nothing.

"You know we have this owners' meeting in New York on Tuesday. Don't you think you'd better get over here so we can work out our strategy?"

"Guess I'd better." Val was good at the money game. And strategy so often came down to money.

"See you about noon, then?"

"Yes," Dave said, and rang off. He'd thought about spending the day with Monica, if she was available. Last night it had seemed as if some invisible barrier was suddenly down. He'd thought they were beginning to get…somewhere.

But now, the strike. Duty called. He hated to think of his beloved baseball game turning into a free-for-all grab bag! He intended to do his best to prevent it.

IT WAS AN UGLY FIGHT. And a long one. The New York meeting was the first of several sparring sessions. The owners were not about to give in to the players' demands for free agency and a greater share of the profits.

"They're so greedy," Dave said to Val.

"So are the players," Val answered. "Most of those guys are making more money in one month than they'd ever make in a lifetime if they weren't playing ball. They ought to be satisfied."

"Guess you're right. Everybody's greedy."

"Everybody but you, Dave Archer. Money doesn't interest you, because you've never had to scratch for it like the rest of us."

"Maybe." He wondered if he should feel guilty.

"Anyway, the players are absolutely dependent on us. We supply the arena—stadiums, organization, training grounds. The whole setup. There'd be no games without us."

"Or without players," he answered. "We're dependent on each other."

He just wanted the controversy to end so that it wouldn't drag on into the new year, the new season. He kept thinking about the rookies like Stu Harmon, who'd grown up in the boys' home. He'd just been picked up by the Giants for a measly forty thousand, which probably looked like a million to him, and he was eager to show what he could do.

Dave knew Val was not as much in sympathy with the players as he was, but he had to give her credit. She fought on his side and was a valuable ally. She knew the game and she played hardball. It was a pleasure to watch her tackle their opponents in meeting after meeting.

MONICA WAS a little perplexed.

From the first day they met, Dave Archer had acted as if he wanted to be...well, more than just a friend. But when she capitulated, if that was what she could call her brazen actions at the Lucases that evening, he'd withdrawn. At least, she'd hardly seen him since. Twice to be exact. Once, a short visit when he'd dropped Eric off. And once he'd taken her out to dinner, but both times he'd seemed preoccupied.

"Is the threat of a strike getting to you?" she'd asked.

"Yes," he'd replied. "But I don't want to talk about it. I just want to enjoy you."

So she hadn't pressed. It was a pleasure just being together. But if that was the case, why weren't they together more often?

True, he'd been traveling a lot. He'd phoned once, checking on Eric, he'd said, and to say he missed her. But the business held sway. He and Val were mentioned in some of the newspaper reports on the progress of the negotiations.

But he wasn't *always* away. From a few tidbits Eric had let drop, he was often closeted with Val Langstrom. And Val's telephone call still pricked at her.

Monica tried to restrain her jealousy and doubt.

Tried to hold on to the confident expectancy she'd felt that night at the Lucases, tried to hold on to the reassuring warmth of *his* telephone calls.

But it wasn't much to hold on to.

So, she found herself sometimes up and sometimes down, a real roller-coaster ride. As she undressed for bed one night shortly before Thanksgiving, she thought, *It's worth it,* remembering Dave's kiss, the way he'd looked at her.

Her phone rang. Lord, it was late. Who could it be?

"Monica." Val Langstrom's voice was as sweet as honey. "I'm sorry to disturb you at this time of night. But I'm trying to arrange something and I need your help."

"Oh?" Monica's radar went on alert. *Val* needed her help?

"All right. I know you and I aren't the best of friends, but we both care about Dave. And this is a favor, really, for him."

"Oh?" That seemed to be all Monica could manage.

"He's really bushed, Monica. The poor guy's been working like a house on fire trying to avert a baseball strike. I suppose you heard about it?"

"Yes."

"Well, it's over. We won. And we're having a big celebration in Vegas."

"That's nice."

"The celebration's for Dave. He worked so hard and was the main force in reaching an agreement."

Yes, Monica thought. Dave would do all he could to save the game, to keep the thriving business that meant so much to so many. Her heart warmed. "I'm glad you reached an agreement," she said.

"I knew you would be," Val said. "And that's why I'm calling you. Dave doesn't know about this party. It's to be a surprise. I've been delegated to see that he gets there, and I'm trying to remove any hindrance that would prevent his leaving here. And that's why I'm calling on you."

"What can *I* do?"

"Eric, you see. It's during Thanksgiving, and Eric will be out of school. I haven't been able to reach Lyn, but I thought if you invite Eric to stay with you... He's so fond of you and your father— Uh-oh! I'll have to go. There's Dave now."

Monica heard a sound like a hand being clapped over the receiver and a muffled "Come on in, Dave. I'm on the phone. Be with you in a moment." Then Val's voice again, unmuffled. "We'll talk later. Think about it, okay?" Val finished, then the line disengaged.

Monica hung up and the roller coaster plunged again.

"OKAY, VAL," DAVE SAID. "What's so urgent that I had to rush over right away? You said it was about the strike. Has something come up?"

"No, no. Everything's settled. All papers signed, sealed and delivered."

"Then what's going on? Why'd you have me race over?"

"Surprise!" Her eyes twinkled as she held up...

He stared. Plane tickets?

"What's going on?" he asked, his suspicions aroused. "Haven't we done enough traveling during the past two weeks?"

"But that was busy time. This is fun time."

"What is?"

"I've arranged everything, Dave. You...we've both been working so hard and this is a time to celebrate. I have the plane tickets and I've arranged for us to stay at the MGM Grand the whole Thanksgiving week. We deserve it, don't we?"

Dave took a deep breath. He didn't want to hurt Val. Had it not been for her, the battle between players and owners would still be on. "Sorry, Val. I...I have other plans for that week."

"Dave Archer, you're avoiding me!"

"No, indeed I'm not. I—"

"Indeed you are. You haven't been near me for weeks!"

"For God's sake, Val. I've been with you almost every minute since—"

"You know what I mean." Her voice lowered, became huskier. "And don't pretend you don't."

He knew. "Look, Val, we're good business partners, but—"

"It wasn't always just business!" Now her voice went up an octave.

"Okay." He might as well face it. Val played

hardball at more than business. "I think we've had this conversation before, Val."

"Well, we're having it again. You've been using me in business, and by God you're not going to embarrass me. We've arranged this celebration in Vegas and I told all the guys I'd have you there."

"Wait. About this 'using.' This is your business, as well as mine. For your benefit, as well as mine."

"I know," she said in resignation. "But I really thought you'd enjoy a change in pace, because *I* really would. And, stupid me, but I arranged this R and R with all the doves. A couple of the hawks have even agreed to come. So don't embarrass me...please."

Dave thought, juggled his schedule in his head and answered. "Okay, I'll go. I'll make an appearance and leave. Look, babe, you gotta understand. I *have* made other plans and they aren't with the guys and...you. And don't give me that hangdog look—you're the best associate any businessman could have. A relationship, though, is just not in the cards, babe. Okay?"

Val felt whipped. The term "babe" didn't have the meaning she thought it did. She'd lost.

She quickly revived, reviewed her portfolio and sought to cut her losses. "I hear you. And since I started the charade, I'll end it. You don't need to go. I'll scrub it all. And graciously. Okay?"

"Thanks," he said, relieved. "You're tops, Val."

"And you're dismissed," she said with a brave smile. "I'll see you when I see you."

CHAPTER SIXTEEN

"YOUR EGGS are getting cold," Dave said. The two brothers were having breakfast on the veranda, awaiting the arrival of the company chopper that would whisk Lyn to the San Diego airport.

Lyn ignored the eggs, took a swallow of coffee. "I can't figure her out."

Dave glanced up from his newspaper. "Who?"

"Lisa," Lyn grunted.

"Woman trouble? I thought you were the expert in that department."

"Not when I'm dealing with a nun."

"Lisa?"

"Pretty close. She took me to church on our first date, and twice since then. Some discussion group of hers meets there."

"Boring?"

"Not really. She makes it all palatable. Even fun sometimes," he said with a wry smile.

"Good for the soul, I suppose?"

"I can take it. What upsets me is her up-front nononsense response to my proposal."

"Proposal?" Dave asked in awe. "Marriage?"

"No, no. My invite to take a holiday trip with me."

"Which was?"

"Doesn't bear repeating."

"That bad!" Dave's lips twitched. "Sounds like she's not your type."

Lyn stared at him. "Funny. That's exactly what *she* said."

"So what's next? Another proposal?" Dave grinned. "Or another woman." At that he waved his hand, dismissing the subject. "Which reminds me. What are your plans for Thanksgiving?"

"I don't know. Why?"

"I was thinking of Eric," Dave replied. "He'll be out of school. I'd hate for him to be here with just the housekeeper. I may be away."

He *would* be away. If Monica didn't stop hinting and ask him outright, he'd take charge himself.

"Don't worry about Eric. I'm taking him skiing."

"Really? Aspen?"

"No. Thought I'd try the slopes in Wyoming," Lyn said, his eye on the descending chopper. "There are some good spots near Laramie."

MONICA'S SPIRITS soared as the roller coaster took an upward swing. Dave had spent almost every evening with her since the baseball trouble had been settled. Usually they walked on the beach. She loved it. It was a wonderful, exhilarating, satisfying time.

Well, not quite satisfying. Somehow the stars above, the sand on her feet and the touch of his hand made her long for more.

Much more.

She hadn't yet gathered the courage to suggest

they go away together. She stooped to pick up a
seashell. Looked at it, tossed it away. "Dad is driving with Duke and Vicky to Atlanta for Thanksgiving," she said.

"They're *driving?*"

"Yes. They don't have any time limit, and Duke
has some places he'd like to stop off at for Dad to
see."

"Herb and Duke. Funny how close those two
have become," Dave mused.

She smiled. "You'd think they were the same
age. But then, when Dad's with Eric, it's like he's
his age."

Dave laughed. "A man of all ages, your dad!"

"Like he was before Mom and the stroke," she
said, feeling a warm glow. She looked up at Dave.
"Much of the credit is due to you. Did I ever thank
you?"

"About a million times. I need to thank Herb.
Eric's a changed boy."

"Isn't he! Some good changes for a change, huh?
This Thanksgiving trip'll be great for Dad." She
gave a rueful smile. "I'm glad. I've been dreading
the holidays," she said, thinking of last Christmas,
her mother...

"I know." Dave's hand tightened on hers reas-
suringly. Comforting to be with someone who
sensed your every mood.

"Vicky thought she enticed Dad with her promise
of real Southern cooking," she said. "But Dad
grabbed at the chance to get away."

"And what about you?"

"Me?"

"Don't you need a change, too?"

"I suppose. I do have a few days." Her pulse quickened. Was this a good time to ask him? "Actually I thought I might go away."

"Where?"

"I hadn't gotten that far."

"Would you like a change in the weather?"

That made her laugh. "A change from one beautiful day after another?"

He nodded. "Yes. Someplace where it's frigid outside, but—" even in the dim light, she saw the teasing glint in his eyes "—inside is warm and cozy."

She tried for a casual note. "I presume you know of such a place."

"Sure do. There's a family cabin at Lake Tahoe that I might arrange for you to borrow."

"Yeah?"

"The thing is, I'd have to be part of the loan."

Monica smacked him on the shoulder. "Dave Archer, you knew I wanted...that I was going to ask..."

"It was taking you too long. I couldn't wait," he said, laughing. "So what about it? Shall we go up and...well...get warm and cozy?"

WHEN HE SAID they'd fly to Reno, she'd assumed they'd take a commercial flight. Certainly not a private two-decker two-bedroom jet with all the other just-like-at-home amenities!

She saw Dave in a different light. Not just a rich

guy who owned a baseball team and a house on the beach.

He was an Archer, of Archer Enterprises, with a private jet fleet, Italian villas and God knew what else. This was going to take some getting used to.

If indeed she had that chance! How many other women had sat on these very cushions and been whisked off to some exotic place?

Been replaced by another when their polish wore off.

"I thought we should have a snack before we land," he said. "Tea and sandwiches okay?" Now he was just Dave, smiling down at her with that sweet smile.

"Very okay." She reached up to touch his cheek. One moment with this man was worth a thousand with any other. Whether on a private jet or a crowded Greyhound bus.

The view of the snow-covered slopes from the plane was spectacular, but driving through them was breathtaking. And just a bit awesome. Crystal peaks stretching heavenward and rugged depths of white stretching endlessly downward.

"It's like a picture postcard," she breathed.

Dave only nodded, his eyes on the treacherous mountain road.

Like a Christmas card, she thought next, and with it came the little pang of grief for her mother. But suddenly she felt content and at peace.

"Everything so still and white and peaceful—and yet so grand!" she marveled. "It's telling us something." She smiled. "Can't you hear it?"

He grinned. "Not very well. What's it saying?"

"That we are here and this is *now*. A happy wonderful now, and we ought to enjoy every moment."

"That, my love, is what we intend to do."

It was dark by the time they arrived at the cabin. It was set back from the road in a grove, and Dave drove through snow-tipped fir trees to reach the front of the house.

"I'll take you in and come back for the bags," he said. His arm was around her as they made their way through drifting snow to the door.

He drew her inside and a welcoming warmth enveloped her. It stemmed from the rich splashes of burnt orange in the low-slung sofas, the soft glow of lamplight and the crackle of logs in the big stone fireplace. Instantly, without hesitation, she turned to him. "Oh, Dave. I love it!"

"You haven't seen it yet," he teased as his hands slipped beneath her jacket to pull her close. "Glad you came?" he whispered, his lips tantalizing against her ear.

"Uh-huh." Glad to be here in his arms. Alone with him.

"Plan to stay awhile?"

She nodded against his sweater. Forever if she could.

"Then you'd better let me go so I can grab your things from the car."

She pushed him away, suddenly conscious and thoroughly embarrassed that she'd been clinging as if she never wanted to let go. "Oh, you!"

He laughed. "Don't go away. I'll be right back." The door banged shut behind him.

She walked to the fireplace, ran her fingers over the large stones that framed it, turned to survey the room with its walnut paneling on one side, floor-to-ceiling windows on the other. Some cabin!

"How long have you had this place?" she asked when he returned with their bags.

"Forever. One of Mom and Dad's getaway places."

But his parents were in Italy. And the place sure didn't look neglected. She brushed the thought away.

"Want a tour?"

She nodded.

"Okay," he said with a gesture. "You see the living room. And here." He led her through an arch to a dining area, containing only a small buffet, a round glass-topped table and four chairs. It opened onto a compact well-stocked kitchen.

"Now—" he winked at her "—shall we visit the main room, the focal point, so to speak?"

He took her hand and she followed him down a hall to the master bedroom.

Again she sensed a feeling of warmth and welcome. This room was even more cozy and inviting. Plush carpeting, exquisite furnishings. Her eyes skirted the colorful pillows on the king-size bed and focused on the merrily crackling fire in another massive stone fireplace.

"That's it," Dave said.

"That's it? All? Not even more bedrooms?"
There ought to be, for guests, shouldn't there?

He shook his head. "Only one."

She thought about that. Not a cabin. A luxurious
hideaway. Designed for two. "It's a love nest," she
said.

He nodded. "Does that bother you?"

"I...I don't know." A hideaway for two. How
many twosomes had been here?

"Come here, sweetheart."

She could no more have resisted the magnetic pull
of his eyes than she could have stopped breathing.
She went to him as if in a trance.

He sat in the big chair before the fire and pulled
her onto his lap. "Let's talk about it." He brushed
back a lock of hair, pressed a kiss to her temple.
"Got a thing against love nests?"

She shook her head against his chest.

"Perfect place for lovers." His lips traced a path
along her cheek, and his hand slipped beneath her
pullover to lightly caress bare skin, sending tremors
of delight rippling through her. "Private. Wonderful
place to make love."

She stirred, her body ignited by his touch. She
clutched his sweater, put her mouth to the hollow of
his throat, tasted his skin.

His hand was gently stroking, urging. "Do you
want to make love?"

"Yes, oh, yes! But..." She couldn't think. She
could only feel. The gentle caress of his hands, the
irrepressible yearning that possessed her. "Yes.
Only..."

"What is it, sweetheart?" he whispered, his lips hovering over hers.

She desperately wanted his kiss, but she had to know. "You...do you come here often?"

"No. It's been ages, my love."

She trembled slightly at his endearment. Did it mean...? She wasn't sure. And it didn't matter. She was hearing something else—*to thine own self be true.* True to the rush of feeling, the whirlwind of passion sweeping through her. "Dave...Dave," she whispered. "I need... I want..."

"I know, sweetheart, I know." He lifted her in his arms and carried her to the bed.

SHE AWOKE to complete quiet. The fire had died to mere smoldering embers and she sensed, rather than heard, the fall of snow. Occasionally there was the sound of an icicle snapping off a tree outside; only the soft glow of a bedside lamp illuminated the face of the sleeping man whose body lay entwined with hers.

She studied that face. The strong nose, the upward tilt of the right eyebrow, the generous mouth, which, even in sleep, retained the hint of a smile.

She thought how she wouldn't have missed this night for the world. No matter what.

His eyes suddenly flew open, stared into hers. The hint became a full smile. "Hello."

"Hello."

"Happy?"

"Yes. I really am." She wrapped her arms around

him and said with perfect honesty, "Last night was the most wonderful night of my life."

"Well, then—" his smile widened "—you're almost as happy as you've made me. Happy Thanksgiving, love."

"Already? Oh, yes, it is, isn't it?"

"A bit early, but Thanksgiving just the same," he said, and started to get out of bed.

"Don't!" She clung to him. "Don't leave me."

He drew her close and kissed her. "I'll never leave you, sweetheart. But...just to the kitchen? I thought you might be hungry."

"Hungry?" She glanced at the bedside clock. "It's only three in the morning! Much too early for Thanksgiving dinner."

"But not too early for the dinner we didn't eat last night. Aren't you hungry?"

"No. And I don't want you to go. I want—" She stopped, feeling her face grow hot. "All right! Quit grinning. I know what you're thinking."

He chuckled and sat up. "I think you're the sweetest, most desirable, lovable, sexiest woman in creation. And if I'm to keep up my strength, I'd better eat."

The pillow she threw cut off his next words and he fell back, laughing. "Tell you what," he said as he got up and walked, unabashedly naked, to the closet. "You come with me to make sure I don't get away." He took two heavy matching terry-cloth robes from the closet, handed one to her.

She eyed the robe dubiously. Who else had worn

it? Who else had climbed out of this bed and put it on against the November chill?

"It's Mom's," he said. "I swear it. Been here forever. Came with the place."

She gave him a suspicious look, but pulled on the robe. It had a faint sweet smell she couldn't define. "How long since your mother's been here?" she asked.

"Let's see. Two or three years, I guess."

Well, she thought, everything else had been kept in readiness. Why not a robe?

She found she was hungry, after all. The casserole, piping hot from the microwave, was delicious, the French bread crunchy, the salad crisp. It was fun to sit at the little dinette at three-thirty in the morning with the man you loved, wearing matching robes and eating dinner.

"Where are they?" she asked, taking a sip of the zesty wine.

He gave her a puzzled look. "They?"

"Those invisible somebodies." She frowned. "Maybe just one somebody."

"What are you talking about?"

"Somebody laid the fires, stocked the fridge, made the casserole. Kept everything in readiness."

"Oh. That."

"Yes, that." She flashed a teasing smile. "Do you keep an invisible staff or maybe a couple of extremely efficient robots?"

"Just a plain very efficient Mr. and Mrs."

"Who know when to appear and when to disappear?"

"Right. Never fear, my love. They won't be appearing while we're here."

"What? Oh, my!" She glanced at the plates and glasses on the table, looked at her hands. "Hands that have flown in a private jet—how could they possibly be plunged in dirty dishwater?" she said in mock horror.

"Right." He walked around the table, pulled her to him. "Let's go back to bed," he said, holding her close and nuzzling her neck.

A flood of desire surfaced from deep inside her, and she lifted her mouth to his. But then old habits surfaced, too. "Wait," she said breathlessly. "This mess. We can't leave these dishes. Come on, it'll only take a minute."

"Hang the dishes!"

Startled—and pleased—by his fervor, she made a weak protest. But his arm only tightened around her, almost lifting her from the floor. "Grab the glasses," he said. "I have the wine."

Heaven.

It was long past noon on Thanksgiving day when they awoke. Made love. Showered together in the bathroom.

Late in the afternoon when they'd finally cleaned the kitchen and breakfasted on toast and coffee, they sat on the living-room floor before the fire Dave had revived, drank wine and played Scrabble. Argued over a word. Laughed. Pushed the Scrabble board aside.

Made love again.

It was after seven when Dave remembered dinner reservations he'd made at the Tahoe Inn.

"I don't want to move," Monica murmured. "I like it here in your arms."

Much later they feasted on cheese, cold cuts and crackers. "The best Thanksgiving dinner I've ever had," she said, lifting her glass to his.

The days passed in a blur of happiness. Once or twice in an uncertain moment, the old doubts and fears emerged. *The Archer men...irresistible to women. How many others have been here?*

Then, she'd brush the doubts aside and remind herself that a good man was worth fighting for. Furthermore he seemed as happy, as fulfilled as she.

Yes, these were perhaps the most precious moments of her existence. These moments, here and now, with Dave. She would treasure them forever. She would enjoy them now. No matter when they might end.

"I hope Dad's enjoying his holiday as much as I'm enjoying mine," she said. They'd put on their boots and were walking through the white drifts. The air was crisp and cold, and tiny flakes of snow were slowly descending.

"Somehow," Dave said wryly, "I think his holiday is a little different from yours."

She laughed delightedly. "Yes, I expect it is. But I hope he's enjoying the change and having fun." She stuck out her tongue to taste a frosty flake of snow. "Did you ever make snow ice cream?"

"No. Is there such a thing?"

"Of course. We did. When we lived in Ohio

where it snowed all the time. My friends and I used to put some clean snow in a bowl, then add vanilla and sugar. It was delicious.''

"And germ-ridden, I bet."

"Nonsense," she scoffed. "Didn't bother us at all. I'm surprised you never tried it. Especially around here where the snow looks so clean and pure."

"Never came here as a kid. To the slopes, yes. But never to the cabin. Off-limits. Just for Mom and Dad."

"Oh." Her eyes flew to his. So, when he'd said it'd been ages since he was here, it must have been with his parents?

He took her by the shoulders and shook her gently. "Stop thinking what you're thinking. When I did come here, I came alone. Once with Lyn when he wanted to get away and talk. After one of his breakups. He always took them hard. He comes on as callous. But deep down he's quite sensitive, vulnerable."

Like you, she thought.

"So, except for that one time with Lyn, I always came here alone. Never with anyone else."

"But..." She looked at him doubtfully.

"All right! I'm thirty-six years old. There've been women in my life. You didn't expect me to be celibate, did you?"

"No." She bit her lip, felt her face grow hot. When a person could read your every thought...

"I didn't want to bring anyone here," he said. "It wouldn't have been right."

She stared at him. "Why not?"

"It would've been a sacrilege. This place was special for Mom and Dad. It had to be special for me." He paused. "With only a special someone. Do you understand?"

"Oh, Dave..." That was all she could say. She clung to him, drowning in wonder and delight as she absorbed the word. *Special.* She was special. What they had was special.

After a moment they walked on through the grove of trees. Fir trees, perfectly shaped, gloriously decked in pure white snow. Again she was struck by the likeness to an image on a Christmas card.

"I can't believe I was dreading the holidays," she said. "Now I'm even looking forward to Christmas."

"We'll make it a wonderful Christmas. I understand Eric's going to be in the Christmas pageant being put on at school."

"Yes," she said. "Helen Montrose, the music teacher, has asked me to help her. We'll start rehearsals as soon as we get back."

"Eric's all excited about some Christmas Eve service at Lisa's church, too. Lyn plans to spend Christmas at our house in Pueblo." He reached for her hand. "Shall we have breakfast at your house and dinner at mine?"

She laughed, and they walked on, hand in hand, making plans.

All too soon, it was the last day. The last night.

"We've sampled everything but the hot tub," Dave said.

"I was going to ask about that. Don't tell me your folks installed it twenty years ago."

"No. Lyn had it installed during his last marriage. He was always hoping…" Dave shrugged. "But that one didn't work, either."

Poor Lyn, she thought. A strange way to think about the confident handsome rich Lyndon Archer. But…always hoping? Hard to believe.

"So get ready," Dave said.

"For what?"

"The tub. It's hot and waiting."

She stared at him. "It's outside!"

"But hot!" He smiled. "And, forgive the cliché, but we'll have our love to keep us warm."

Monica had never had an experience like it. Bathed in hot swirling water, her body warm, even on a cold winter night. Dark except for the reflection from the outside light over the deck. Snow falling, flakes splluttering as they disappeared in the steaming water. Champagne tickling her nose.

Her body was tingling with desire and anticipation. At last, enveloping themselves in the soft terry robes, they went indoors and made love, spasms of fulfillment exploding deep inside her.

"My love, my love," he murmured as she nestled against him. Content.

CHAPTER SEVENTEEN

"'IT CAME UPON a midnight clear/that glorious song of old./From angels bending near the earth/to touch their harps of gold!'"

Monica heard the resounding childish voices before she reached the auditorium. She hummed along with them, feeling the tug of Christmas, with all the old carols, stars and angels. Mom wasn't with her in body, but she was in spirit. Monica could almost see her, hear her telling her to be happy.

She smiled. Her mother *had* her wish. She *was* happy. That time in the mountains had healed her. Being in his arms had erased all thoughts of sad yesterdays, all past pain and grief. The blissful feeling stayed with her as together they made plans for Christmas. Breakfast at her house, dinner at his. It was time to buy a tree, pull out the old decorations.

Dad. She was hesitating because of him. It was true that the Thanksgiving holiday had been good for him. He'd been positively glowing when he returned from Atlanta. But now he was restless, and that haunted look had returned.

She knew he was thinking of Mom and last Christmas. He did not, as she did, have a happy now to sustain him. He did not even have the daily treks with Duke, for there was no more need for therapy. His physical health had returned, but the emotional trauma remained.

I'm all he has, she thought. Maybe she should talk with him, try to impart something of what she'd been feeling about Mom and how Mom would have wanted them to go on with the old traditions.

"'Peace on earth, good will to men,/from Heaven's all gracious King./The earth in solemn stillness lay,/to hear the angels sing!'" The voices rang out louder as she swung the door open and went into the auditorium. Where, it seemed, there was more pandemonium than peace.

"Thank goodness you're here," said a harried Helen Montrose. "Would you please… Wait a minute." She turned to speak to the pianist, signaled the chorus to quiet. "Hold it for a minute. Then we'll try again."

She turned back to Monica. "Will you see what you can do with the gang over there? They're really distracting everybody."

Monica nodded, smiled as she saw that Eric was one of the kids being distracting. It pleased her to see that he was "one of the gang." In fact, he, Tommy Atkins and Bert McAfee were the decided ringleaders, and she spoke sternly to all three.

"Sit right here and be quiet. Tommy, take your hat off, and not another sound from any of you until Miss Montrose is ready for you."

When they were called, Monica was surprised to see the disruptive trio transformed into the dignified "We three kings of Orient are." She was amazed to hear Eric's clear treble rising above the other two. She hadn't known he had such a beautiful voice.

Dad will love this, she thought. *He'll be so proud. As I am.* Eric had become very dear to them. Like one of their own.

Her own. How she'd love to have a mischievous boy, indulging in disruptive pranks one instant and behaving like an angel the next. Would she have such a boy? Would she and Dave...?

SHE STOPPED by the nursery and selected a tree that afternoon. "Only two weeks until Christmas," she said to her father after the man who'd delivered it departed.

"I try not to think about it," he said, his eye on the five-foot pine. It was as if the tree stared back in sturdy defiance, its pungent scent filling the room, its bare branches proudly outstretched, waiting to be adorned.

The tree was doing its part. She had to do hers, Monica knew. "I'll get the things from the garage," she said, keeping her voice bright. "That's where we packed them last year, right? The tree has a nice shape, don't you think? Is this a good spot, here by the window? Or maybe we should put it—"

"Monica, stop!" he said, then his voice broke. "Honey, I...I know what you're trying to do, but...it's too soon. I thought we might go away like we did for Thanksgiving." He made an attempt at a smile. "Skip Christmas this year."

"Oh, Dad, we can't do that!" She went to him, wrapped her arms around him. "Mom wouldn't like it. She wants us here, celebrating with her. I know it."

He stared at her. "She isn't—"

She put her hand over his mouth. "Don't say it. Part of Mom will always be with us, and we have to hold on to it. She always loved Christmas. She'll want the tree and she'll want the little white birds you bought when you were first married. She'll want the angel on top—remember you bought it at Stoke's? And how she fussed because you paid so much for it? And how tenderly and carefully she wrapped it every year? Of course, she was just as careful with those stupid bells I made when I was a Brownie." A lump rose in her throat, choking off her voice.

"All right, kitten. All right." Now he was comforting her. How long since he had called her "kitten"?

She cupped his face in her hands. "You do see, don't you, Dad? We have to keep Christmas to keep Mom. The old traditions to remind us that she was here and that she loved us."

He sighed heavily and nodded. "You're right, honey. I'll get the things from the garage. You stay here."

"Wait, Dad. I want you to know it will be a happy Christmas. *It will.* We won't be alone. Dave and Eric and his brother, Lyn, maybe Lisa and Duke and Vicky."

He smiled. "Quite a crowd."

"You'll like that, won't you? They'll be here for breakfast on Christmas Day, and then we'll have dinner at Dave's. I told you we're having a pageant at school the night before vacation begins. Oh, you should hear Eric sing! He's really good. He's one of the three kings.''

"I can't imagine that." Dad was laughing as he started toward the garage.

Lisa dropped by just as he was bringing in the last box. "Good," she said. "I don't have a tree, so I'll help decorate yours. I love doing that."

Dave came by just in time to help Herb untangle and test the lights.

It was an impromptu tree-decorating party, complete with snacks, wine and laughter. The old ornaments prompted all sorts of "remember when" anecdotes, and bittersweet memories of the past blended with the happy now. For Monica and Herb, especially, a beautiful healing transition.

The days flew by in a flurry of pleasant preparations. Monica had the whole house dressed for Christmas and had almost finished her Christmas shopping. Herb joined in the shopping, purchasing both a basketball and a baseball mitt for Eric.

"I don't know which he'll choose," he said. "Maybe he'll do both. He's a pretty active kid, right?"

Monica laughed and squeezed his arm in agreement.

Meanwhile, Eric was in trouble again. The three kings, filled, as only young boys could be, with the Christmas spirit, celebrated by throwing spitballs at one another during a pageant rehearsal. The behavior netted them three days' work duty each.

"At least Eric wasn't sitting alone, staring," Monica told Herb. The conversation with Ada back in October seemed as if it'd been about some other child, not the rambunctious talkative Eric.

Herb smiled. "What's his work assignment?"

"What else? The stable."

ERIC SANG the carol softly as he walked toward the stable. "'Star of wonder, star of light./Star of radiant beauty bright...'"

Theirs was the best part. Except for those silly turbans they had to wear. Tommy sure looked funny in his. And Bert couldn't sing. Eric giggled at the memory of their first rehearsal. At first Miss Montrose had looked like she was going to take Bert out, replace him with someone else, but she hadn't. He was glad. He and Bert and Tommy would—

"Hi, Eric."

"Hi, Mr. Chello." He'd entered the tack room where Frank Chello was munching a sandwich and watching a TV talk show.

"Aren't you a little early?"

"No. Well, yes," Eric replied. "I didn't want lunch. So I came here to finish my work. I'm off detention after today."

"Mmm. Too bad. I'd begun to think of you as a steady hand. So you skipped lunch. Want this apple?"

"Huh? Oh. No, thank you." But Eric wasn't looking at Frank now. His eyes were riveted to the television screen.

To Marion Holiday, his mother. She was wearing

a blue dress like she always did on account of her blue eyes, and she was looking up at the show host, smiling at him.

"So your new film, *My Son, My Heart,* opens the day after Christmas," the show host was saying. "Isn't this a rather different role for you, Marion? Single mom?"

"Different *film* role. But very real for me in life. I *am* a single mom, you know."

"Yes. That's right. I'd forgotten."

Eric knew she was referring to him. He didn't think she liked being a mom. But now she was talking about how much she loved it, about how her heart was torn when she was forced to be away from him.

"But you're not. I mean, your son's with you, isn't he?"

"Not...not just now. Circumstances—" She stopped, like she was choking or something. She looked like she was going to cry, and Eric wondered why. Then she sat up. Said something about relating to the mother in the role who had to fight for custody.

"But I'm luckier than she is," she went on. "I do have custody." She said her son was in boarding school right now because of her busy schedule, but she was to pick him up in a few days. He'd be with her for Christmas, he'd appear at the premiere "for all the world to see." She was so proud of him! "He'll remain with me always. We'll never be apart again."

Eric's heart stopped. He didn't *want* to be with

her! He certainly hadn't liked it that time he *had* stayed with her. Mostly she wasn't there. Just Mrs. Lennon, her housekeeper, in that big house, and all he did mostly was swim in the pool. By himself.

He'd been glad when Marion sent him to Dad. He hadn't liked that much, either, but at least Dad took him with him. Dad was fun, even though it got to be pretty boring just riding around in the company jet from one city to another and to some hotel, waiting while Dad went to meetings. No kids to play with. Then Dad said he had to get back in school, and he thought he would really like it at Joel E. Smith.

He didn't like that, either. At first.

But now he did. He liked living in the dorm. He and Bert and Tommy and the other guys had fun. And Jumbo and Silver were at Dave's and he could go to Dave's anytime he wanted.

Dad was always around now, too. And there was Monica and his new grandpa. And Grandpa said maybe he should sign up for Little League, and Duke said he'd show him how to pitch. And, well...he just liked it here now and he wanted to stay.

She was going to take him away! In a few days, she'd said. Before Christmas. No! He wanted to be *here* for Christmas. It wouldn't be Greenlea and he wouldn't get his horse, but it was going to be a real fun Christmas. Bert was going to stay with him at Dave's. Dave had said it was okay, because Bert's mom was going to be in Europe. But maybe Dave wouldn't let Bert stay if he wasn't here. Anyway, it

was going to be fun having another guy, especially
Bert. Dad was going to be there, too. And there was
the Christmas Eve candlelight thing at Lisa's church
where he would get his fortune. Then they were going to Monica's and...oh, lots of things!

It wasn't fair! Just when everything was beginning to get right again, Marion was going to snatch
him away.

Custody. He hated that word.

That was what they kept saying over and over
again after the plane crash. It was sad with Gramps
and Grandma gone, but he kept telling everybody
he could still stay at Greenlea, couldn't he? With
Rosella and Runt and all the farmhands? And Rosella put her arms around him and started crying as
hard as he was, and Runt said he would keep Silver
for him, but they couldn't keep *him.* His mom had
custody and so that was where he should be. With
his mother.

Suddenly Eric was all choked up and could hardly
breathe. Like the room was closing in on him. He
had to get out. He turned and ran outside. He heard
Frank calling to him, but he didn't stop. He just ran
and ran, not sure where he was going. He didn't stop
until he was behind the gym where he used to go to
train Jumbo, when the dog was a stray. He leaned
against the back of the gym and tried to think.

I won't go with Marion. I won't!
I'll tell Dave. Call Dad.

But Dad had been at the services for his grandparents. When Eric had told him he wanted to stay
at Greenlea, Dad had said, ''That's impossible, son.

There's no one here to take care of you. You'll be
happy with your mother. She has custody.''

Custody. It was some kind of law. It didn't matter
what a kid wanted to do.

Well, he wouldn't go. He wouldn't! Dave said a
guy had to learn to look out for himself, didn't he?
So if Marion couldn't find him...

Yes. That was it. He could hide somewhere until
she went away.

But where?

He sat for a long time, thinking. He had to hide
from everyone else, too. On account of they knew
Marion had custody. He wouldn't hide in a john like
Duke had when he was a kid. That was dumb.

He couldn't even stay here in Pueblo. They'd find
him.

They wouldn't find him in San Diego, though. It
was a big city. Plenty of places to hide. He wouldn't
have to hide long. Just till Marion went away. He
was sure he had enough money for the bus.

Lunch was just over. The bell had sounded and
everybody was going back to class. He had library
at this time. Instead of going there, he went to the
dorm. Nobody noticed.

In his room he counted out his money—twenty-
five dollars and seventeen cents. He put it in the
back pocket of his jeans and buttoned down the
pocket. Somehow just doing that made him
feel...well, almost grown-up. Anyway, like he could
take care of himself.

He packed some things, not much. Just a backpack full. Didn't want it to look like he was going

away. He went to his next class, the last for the day. Then he walked out through the front gate, along with the day students.

CHAPTER EIGHTEEN

"'HARK, THE HERALD ANGELS sing,/Glory to the newborn King...'" The lines didn't ring with the usual fervor.

Stupid to schedule a rehearsal on Friday afternoon, Monica thought. Many students, even the boarders, had weekend plans, and they took off as soon as their last class was over. But Helen insisted they go through the whole repertoire, and they pressed on.

"Where's Eric?" Monica asked as she prepared to line up the three kings.

"He's supposed to go to his uncle's today," Tommy offered. "Maybe he's gone."

"He shouldn't have," Monica said, a bit irritated. "He knows we have rehearsal."

"Maybe he's still at the dorm. Want me to go get him?" Bert asked.

"Don't *you* leave. I'll phone."

"No, he's not here," Matron said when Monica called. "I see he's signed out. He did have permission to visit his uncle."

The little scamp! He knew he was supposed to be here. Well, Dave's house was only a few blocks away and he could just get himself back here, pronto!

"No, Miss Powell," Dave's housekeeper said when Monica phoned. "He's not here. Mr. Lyn was here earlier. He must have picked him up and taken him somewhere."

Well, at least father and son were getting close, she thought. But darn! Eric's voice was sorely missed.

Oh, well. This was just one rehearsal. If Eric was with his father, that was good, wasn't it?

IT WAS ALMOST ELEVEN when Dave reached home. He called Monica immediately. "Sorry I missed our walk, sweetie. Things got pretty hot and I couldn't get away."

"What happened?"

"I got involved with that salary-cap fiasco at the league office, and then this business came up about how I'm using the boys' home."

"What do you mean, using the home?"

"As a training camp for the team."

"That's ridiculous!" Monica's temper flared. "It makes me furious! How people can twist something good into—"

"Cool it, honey. It could look that way. Duke's always around the home and so's Ramirez, the infielder who's batting 400. Naturally most of the boys want to follow suit. Lots of baseball, not to mention that Little League fund-raiser they've started. But not to worry. We'll straighten it out."

They talked of other things and were about to

break off when she remembered. "Is Eric still up? I'd like to speak with him."

"Still up? He's not even here. Mrs. Turner said—"

"I know. I called earlier and she told me his dad must have picked him up. They're not back yet?"

"Not yet."

"Well, when they do get in, you tell Eric I want to have a word with him. He knew he was due at rehearsal. He could at least have informed us if he had other plans."

"Okay. Will do. He's all yours."

But something nagged at Dave after he hung up. Eric was pretty reliable. Almost always where he was supposed to be. He glanced at his watch. Eleven-thirty. Where could Lyn have the kid at this hour? A movie? Or maybe they stayed at the corporate suite in town?

He phoned both the San Diego corporate office and the suite they maintained. The only response was the mechanical voice of the answering machine. He left a message at both places.

He tried Lisa. Maybe she'd seen them.

No, her sleepy voice answered, she hadn't seen either of them. She'd seen Eric at school earlier, though. He'd had work duty at the stable, but she hadn't been at the stable today. "Has something happened? Would you like me to call Frank?" she asked, sounding alert now and concerned.

"No. Nothing's happened. I just wondered where they were. Go back to sleep, Lisa."

Okay, maybe they'd gone to a movie.

Still the nagging worry persisted. When at last he heard Lyn's car pull into the driveway, he felt a great surge of relief. He met him at the door.

"Lyn! Why can't you let somebody know when—" He stopped and glanced around. "Where's Eric?"

"Eric? I haven't seen him." Lyn's voice grew loud with alarm. "What do you mean? He's not here?"

Dave, thoroughly disturbed, told what he knew. "Everyone assumed he was with you."

"No. I was here about two, had to pick up some material. I was at meetings all afternoon, a dinner tonight at about... Oh, hell! Never mind what *I* did. Where is Eric?"

Dave looked at his brother, not seeing him. "He was supposed to come here, had permission from the school, was signed out. Probably walked over as he often does. Or started to," he added slowly.

"What are you saying? It's only three blocks, for God's sake! And in broad daylight...what could have happened to him?"

"Nothing," Dave said quickly. *A lot of things*, he thought as a series of horrors raced through his mind—an accident, some sicko, a gang of hoodlums. He saw the same thoughts reflected in his brother's face before Lyn swung around and started out.

"Wait! Where're you going?" Dave demanded.

"To find my son," Lyn called as he charged out the door.

"Wait. I'm coming with you!"

They combed the street between house and school, the side streets near and around. But the streets were deserted and there was no sign of any disturbance.

"Sometimes he takes the beach route," Dave said. They walked along the beach all the way back to the house. Nothing but the quiet lapping of the waves, a reminder of what a vast ocean could hide.

"This is crazy," Lyn said. "He can't have disappeared into thin air. I'm calling the police."

"Wait, Lyn. Police. There'll be publicity and kooks from every direction. Maybe that's not good."

"I don't give a damn about publicity. I want my boy. I—" He pressed his lips together, took deep breaths, stared into space. "Okay. You're right. A private dick. I'll call Humphrey."

The detective was there at six Saturday morning. They reviewed the facts.

"Could he have just taken off?" was the first question the detective asked. "Sometimes a kid gets angry about something and then..."

Dave and Lyn looked at each other. No, they both agreed. Maybe when he'd first come here. But not now. He seemed so happy.

Humphrey cleared his throat. "Mr. Archer, have you thought of another possibility? You're a man of considerable means. This could be a kidnapping."

Lyn stared at him. "How's it possible? How would anybody know one kid from another?"

"They'd know. Kidnappers don't work on impulse. They gather the facts, plan. Watch. You say the kid often walks from the school to—''

"Lots of kids do. Anyway, there's no note, no call."

"Not until the culprits are out of reach, have the kid stashed away. Now look, don't be alarmed. I may be jumping the gun. But we can't ignore any possibility. Meanwhile, I'll make a few inquiries. You sit tight and wait."

It was hard to sit tight and wait. *He's ten years old*, Lyn thought, *but it's like I've just found him.* A sturdy little boy who could ride like the wind, who could joke and tease, who could be teased in return.

Plans. Lyn had made plans. He'd even talked to Mosley about buying a horse for Christmas. Eric had been so hyped up about what his grandpa at Greenlea had planned... Greenlea! That, too, he was planning as a surprise. A special Christmas gift. Now he might never know.

Then Lyn wondered why he was thinking about all these things that didn't matter a damn. Nothing mattered except that his boy was gone and no one knew where, and all he wanted to do was wrap his arms around him and hold him tight. By God, when he found him, he'd never let him out of his sight again! Lyn sat and waited and worried.

As the detective made inquiries, others worried.

Herb and Duke walked the streets of Pueblo together, making a wider sweep than Dave and Lyn had made. They looked for clues, a scrap of torn shirt, a sign of a scuffle.

They found nothing.

"Well," Herb said, "that kind of distraction would've been noticed."

"Yeah," Duke agreed. "He would've had to be lured."

"He's too smart for that."

"Unless," Duke said, "somebody needed help. Eric's a sucker if somebody needs something."

Yeah. Even if they don't ask, Herb thought, remembering that forthright *You gonna get rid of that walker?* He gave a rueful smile. "That kid has a way of making you realize something you should have realized for yourself."

"I know what you mean," Duke said. "He made me realize I couldn't ride a horse. Something everybody else tried to tell me and I should've realized myself. Anyway, I've given it up."

"Yeah?"

"Yeah, and it's all due to Eric. He was always putting me down. But in a way that...well, like it was okay I couldn't ride a horse, I was still a good guy and he liked me just the same. You know?"

Herb nodded. Like he was okay with Eric, walker or not.

"Made me think," Duke said. "You are what you are. Don't have to do everything, don't have to prove yourself to people. Know what I mean?"

Herb knew exactly what he meant. They went on searching, waiting, worrying.

The detective made discreet inquiries. Eric had attended his last class. One of the day students, a girl, had seen him walk through the gate toward his uncle's house, saw him stop, turn at the corner and walk toward town. Yes, the bus driver said, a boy of Eric's description—blond, freckled, sturdy—had boarded the four-fifteen bus Friday afternoon, got off in San Diego. There the trail ended.

"So it does appear he took off on his own," Humphrey said.

"BUT WHY?" Monica wondered aloud when Dave told her.

"I don't know," Dave said. "I thought he was feeling pretty settled. Had gotten used to being here. He certainly seemed satisfied."

"More than satisfied. He was happy," Monica said. She knew it.

She'd always had a good rapport with every student she counseled, and usually developed a kind of kinship with them. She had a way of thinking *with* as well as *for* them, which was a great help in solving their problems. And as for Eric, she had a special feeling for him; the boy was much more than a student to her. She'd grown really close to him, heard him talk, curiously and eagerly, about her house, watched her father come alive with his laughter. Moreover, she'd seen him change from a sullen withdrawn child into an active participating boy, full of fun and devilment. Oh, yes, he was happy. She knew that.

So why would he run away?

The detective retraced his steps, made more inquiries. Frank Chello was off for the weekend, but he located him through Lisa. Dave accompanied him to the interview.

"Yeah," Frank said. "He was here for his work duty. Came in singing a carol. But then—" Frank's brow wrinkled in puzzlement "—something happened. I don't know what. His mood sort of changed and then he left. Didn't even stay to finish his work. All of a sudden just took off like a bat out of hell."

"You don't know why?" Dave asked. "Did you say something to him he might've taken the wrong way? Or..."

"No, I didn't." The stable manager scratched his head. "Only...there was a talk show on and he seemed mighty interested. Yeah. I remember. Had his eyes glued to the set."

"Which talk show? Who was on?" Humphrey asked.

"Some actress. I wasn't paying much mind. Hard to remember.... Oh, yes, Marion Holiday."

"His mother!" Dave turned to the detective. "Marion Holiday. She's his mother."

"Okay. We'll get that tape," Humphrey said. "Might give us a clue."

After a hurried call, they received the tape late Saturday night. Monica huddled in the study with Dave, Lyn and the detective, to watch it.

She watched as Eric must have watched, thinking his thoughts, feeling what he felt. Her heart ached for him. He was going to be evicted again! Just as he was getting into a happy routine!

"Gad!" Humphrey exclaimed. "Why didn't we

think of that? Call her. Maybe he's run to his mother.''

"Like hell he has. He's running *away* from her!" Lyn declared. "But why didn't he come to me? He knew I would have stopped that.''

"How would he know that?'' Monica said. "He's been bounced from one place to another ever since his grandparents died. Without any say in the matter. Just for everybody's convenience but his own! And now he thinks he's going to be bounced again.''

She turned to the TV screen as if it somehow contained the boy. "Oh, Eric, no wonder. No wonder you ran.''

"Don't say that!'' Lyn snapped.

"I'm sorry. I'm sorry.'' Monica stared at Lyn's stricken face, appalled at herself. She was so wrapped up in the boy she'd forgotten about the father.

"I know it couldn't be helped,'' she said hastily. "You did make the best possible arrangement. He's been happy here, and I shouldn't have said what I said.''

"But you're right.'' Lyn's voice was flat. "Don't apologize, Monica. It's true. He didn't know he wouldn't be bounced again. Oh, God!'' He walked to the window, stared out into the night. "I should have told him, made him know he could come to me with whatever bothered him.''

"Or me,'' Dave said. "I'm the one here all the time.''

"I'm his father. I—''

"No.'' Monica waved her hand dismissively.

"Stop blaming yourselves." She touched Dave's hand, walked to Lyn and put her arms around him. "This hasn't been entirely your fault, Lyn. Circumstances are such that you didn't have much chance to be a father until the past five months. But so far you've done a wonderful job! Of course you had a little help from Dave. The main thing is you've made him happy. He's not running away from you. He's running away from *her!*" Her words seemed to comfort the brothers, but it was the detective who spoke.

"Do you think so, ma'am?" he asked, then went on as if he'd been trying to solve the disappearance problem while they indulged in emotional trauma. "I was thinking she might have spirited him away. You know, like asked him to meet her secretly at the bus station and—"

"Ha!" Lyn turned on him. "You believe all that publicity hogwash? In the first place she wouldn't have to spirit him away, and if she did, she'd make sure the press was there to see her do it! *God!* How did I marry such a woman! And how did I leave her custody of my boy!"

He stopped, shook his head. "No. I can't blame her. She was young and busy with her own career, just as I was. She got legal custody, but it was a joint decision that he should stay with his grandparents."

"Evidently a good decision," Monica said. "Those eight years made him the fine boy he is today."

"Thank God for that." Lyn's face brightened

with determination. "But I'm taking custody from now on. That is..."

He turned misery-filled eyes to the detective. "What now?"

"I'm starting at the San Diego bus station," Humphrey answered. "I'm heading there now."

After the detective left, Mrs. Turner, the housekeeper, came in with sandwiches and hot chocolate. "I'm taking this coffee away," she said. "Cocoa is more conducive to sleep, which you both need. Do you realize you've been on your feet for the past forty-eight hours?" She spoke in a low voice to Monica. "Try to get them to eat something if you can, Miss Powell. They'll have to keep up their strength if they're to find our boy."

Monica nodded, seeing the tears in the older woman's eyes. *Oh, Eric, we all love you,* she thought. *Why didn't you come to one of us, you foolish boy?*

At her prompting, the men did eat and drink a little. Then she asked Dave to take her home.

Lyn, alone, stared at his empty cup. Sleep? He might never sleep again.

The phone rang. He grabbed it. Maybe Eric...

It was Lisa. "I'm sorry, Lyn. I know it's a bad time to disturb you. But have you heard anything?"

"No, except that he probably left on his own. No guarantee he's safe," Lyn said, thinking of his boy alone on the streets of San Diego.

"Lyn, he's going to be all right," she said. "I know it. That's why I called."

He stared at the receiver. How could she *know it?* How could she be so confident? So positive?

"Lyn, are you there?"

"Yes."

"I called because I wanted to tell you something. You know how I told you I'd been trying to meditate and couldn't?"

"Yes, but not now, Lisa. I can't think about—"

"I know. You can only think about Eric. That's all I've been thinking about, too—you and Eric. I was almost crazy with worry, and... well, they say meditation can bring peace and I thought—"

"Lisa, I can't meditate. I can't think straight. I'm so—"

"Not you. *Me.* Lyn, listen. This is important. I tried to find peace by meditating, and... I know this sounds strange, but I had a vision! It was so clear. I saw you and Eric. He was on a horse and you were standing beside the horse, and you were both laughing. You were in front of a stable. On top of the stable was this statue of a running horse. Under the horse were some letters, but I couldn't quite read them. But everything else was so clear! Maybe it was just because I had you on my mind, but it did seem like a message. Like it was telling me Eric was safe and everything was going to be all right. And, well, I just wanted you to know." She paused. "Lyn?"

He couldn't speak. He'd seen the statue of the running horse many times. The printed words...

"Lyn? Are you there?"

"Yes."

"I know it was just a vision. But it did give me a kind of peace. I thought it might make you feel a little, well, better."

"It does. Lisa, this means a lot to me. I'll tell you about it later."

"All right. Let me know when you hear something."

Only Lisa could have had a vision, he thought. He shook his head. But it was Greenlea, clear as day. Would she have known that? He didn't think so.

A *clear* vision. If not peace, it did give him hope.

CHAPTER NINETEEN

NOBODY LOOKED at Eric in the big crowded San Diego bus station late Friday afternoon. Everybody seemed in a rush to get somewhere or do something. Except that girl in the shorts and that pack on her back. She was just sauntering along, eating popcorn. That fat woman, struggling with two suitcases and three children. Maybe he ought to help—

"Oh, sorry!" he said when he bumped into a man carrying a big suitcase. The man hardly noticed him.

Eric felt very much alone. And scared. Maybe he ought to call Dave or Dad.

No. Not till Marion went away.

When he'd left the school earlier that day, he'd hesitated at the first corner. Maybe, he'd thought, he ought to leave a note in Dave's mailbox. Let him know he was all right and would be back. He knew Dave wasn't at home.

But the housekeeper was always there, so better not. She might stop him. He'd trudged on to the bus station.

The bus driver had looked at him kind of strangely. So had some of the passengers. But Eric had handed over his ticket and shifted the backpack

on his shoulder like he was just going home from
school, and nobody had said anything.

So here, in the San Diego bus station, was as good
a place as anywhere to hide. Just sit on a bench like
he was waiting for a bus.

He sat there a long time watching people come
and go. Nobody paid him any mind. Except one lady
who had the look of a schoolteacher.

"All alone, little fellow?" she asked kindly.

"Just waiting," he said. When her eyebrow lifted,
he said, "My mother. I'm waiting for her to come."
And go, he added to himself, crossing his fingers.

That seemed to satisfy the lady, but she kept
watching him, and he was glad when she finally
boarded her bus.

He got hungry and bought a hamburger and a
milk shake. He'd have to be careful with his money.
He didn't know how long he'd have to hide. If he
ran out of money, he'd get hungry.

"Ever been hungry?" Duke had said.

Duke! Like a flash it came to him. The boys'
home. Duke said they took anybody in. If you were
hungry or somebody had been beating you or something. And they'd have a bed for him to sleep in.
He was getting awfully tired.

The home was in San Diego. He just didn't know
where.

That's easy, dummy! Look in the phone book.

There it was, in big black letters. San Diego Demons' Home for Boys, 1820 East Lennox.

Eric left the phone booth and walked through the
crowded bus station out to the equally crowded

streets. Everybody there seemed in a rush, too. Except the lady in the Salvation Army uniform. She just stood there, smiling, ringing that little bell. Nobody paid any attention to her, either. Eric felt sorry for her. He went over and dropped a dollar into her basket.

"Thank you," she said. "God bless you."

Eric hoped God would. It had just dawned on him that knowing where to go didn't make it easy to get there. Dad always stepped from the airport into a cab or a limousine and told the driver where to take him.

Eric glanced at the taxi stand. Felt his back pocket. But he knew. Six dollars and fifty-nine cents, after the bus and a hamburger and stuff. He didn't think it was enough for a cab. Anyway, the people at the group home wouldn't think he needed to stay there if he arrived in a cab.

He'd have to take a bus. Which one? Who to ask? Not a policeman or even the smiling Salvation Army lady. People like that would ask questions and try to help you—help you do what they *thought* you should. He was feeling pretty desperate when the bus station door swung open and the girl with the popcorn walked out. Maybe...

"Can you tell me which bus goes to East Lennox Street?" he asked her.

"Sure. Number 18." She pointed. "Go down to that corner and wait at the bus stop."

"Thanks," he said, and started off.

"Wait," she called to him. "You better ask the driver to call the street when he gets there."

He thanked her again. By the time he caught the bus it was getting too dark to read the street signs, so it was good the driver called, "Lennox!"

He got off, and watched the bus continue down the street it was on. Then he started up Lennox. The number on the first house was 1101. That meant several blocks to go. Almost no people and few cars on the street. It was totally dark now, but his way was lit by the Christmas lights that shone from many of the houses he passed.

At one house a boy about his age ran up the steps. The door was opened and the boy called, "Hey, Mom! Guess what!" before he disappeared into the warmth.

Eric felt cold and lonely. Tired. His feet dragged. Suppose they wouldn't let him stay?

He saw 1820 before he reached it. It was a big house with a lit-up Santa Claus on the roof. The house took up the whole block, or at least the fence that surrounded it did. Colored lights along the fence and around the door and windows. Lots of ground. Toward the back he saw a basketball court, also lit up, where some big boys were playing. The bounce of the ball, shouts and laughter echoed through the night. A happy sound.

He sure hoped they'd let him stay.

He mounted the steps and pushed the bell.

The door was opened by a man who seemed to be on his way out. But when he saw Eric, he greeted him with a cheerful "Hello!"

"Hello." Eric stepped into a wide entry hall, which seemed to open into several areas. From some of those areas came the murmur of voices, laughter, the slap of a Ping Pong ball, back and forth, back and forth.

The man looked down at him like he was inspecting him. "Haven't seen you before. New around here?"

"No. Uh, yes."

"Come on. Yes, no. What kind of answer is that?" The man's grin made him think of Duke. He didn't look like Duke. He was blond and blue-eyed, not as tall and not as skinny as Duke.

"I...I mean, I want to be around. Stay here, I mean. Please."

"Oh. I see." The man's grin faded. "Got a problem?"

Eric nodded.

"Well, you've come to the right place."

"I can stay?"

"Well, now, that's not for me to say. You'll have to talk to Mrs. Ross." Eric stepped back a pace. "Don't be scared." The man put a hand on Eric's shoulder. "You can talk to her. Just tell her your problem. She's real good with problems."

He took Eric to a big room on the right of the hall. There was no carpet on the polished wood floor, and the chairs and sofas were upholstered in sturdy dark brown leather. Gratefully Eric let his tired body sink into the soft leather of one sofa. Somehow he knew that, in this room, it didn't matter that his jeans were kind of dusty. A Christmas tree almost as big as the one at school stood in one cor-

ner. Two boys about Eric's age sat on the floor by
the tree, playing some kind of game.

"Wait here," the man said. "I'll get her."

Eric hated to see him go. He seemed like somebody he could talk to. He wasn't sure about this
Mrs.... What was her name? He looked at the two
boys. But they were too intent on their game and
minor disagreements with each other to notice him.
He still felt very much alone.

IN HER OFFICE at the back of the house, Mandy Ross
was making notes. Managing a home for sixteen
boys wasn't easy, and she was beat. But she was
determined to be ready for the committee from the
baseball commissioner's office when they came on
Monday. Dammit, they didn't have the right to in-
vestigate her home! Didn't she have enough trouble
with the state and county welfare agencies?

Okay, be fair, she told herself. Mostly those agencies just wanted to show her place to other group-
home supervisors as a good example. But it took
money for the facilities, staff and the kind of atmosphere she was able to create. Most group homes
didn't have Dave Archer's financial backing. It really got her dander up when the baseball commissioner accused him of running a Demons' base-
ball-training camp under the guise of charity.
Naturally some of these kids were into baseball, and
some, like Duke Lucas—

She looked up as the door opened. "Scot. I
thought you were gone."

"I was on my way out when—"

"Hang on a minute," she said as the noise from the basketball court floated through the window. "Since you're here, would you go out there and tell those boys to get in here? It's lights-out time."

"Sure. I will. But first, Mandy, there's this kid..." He told her about Eric. "Looks pretty washed-out. Like he's come a long way to get here."

A boy in trouble. First things first, Mandy thought as she hurried out.

Eric looked up when she came in. He saw a tall black woman in a neat pink dress, sort of like the kind his grandmother wore. And there was a wide streak of gray in the hair piled on top of her head.

He stood up, just as he had been taught to do when someone entered a room.

Good manners, Mandy thought. She noted, also, that he seemed to brace himself. His shoulders squared and his chest rose and fell with sharply drawn breaths. Her heart went out to him. He was scared.

"Good evening, young man," she said.

"Good evening, Mrs.... Mrs...."

"Mrs. Ross. But you can call me Mandy. All my boys do. Sit down and we'll talk."

She turned to send the two boys playing by the Christmas tree to the games room, but her mind was on the boy on the sofa. Many boys came to her door—hungry, brutalized, troubled.

This one... Even his tennis shoes and the cut of his jeans spelled money. And as far as she could tell, not a scratch on him. Still, trouble didn't discriminate.

She sat beside him and took his hand in hers. "What's your name?"

"Eric."

"No last name?"

"Please. Couldn't you just call me Eric?" Better not to tell his real name, but he didn't want to lie to this woman with eyes like Grandma's. They were a dark velvety brown, not blue like Grandma's, but warm and kind and trusting like hers.

"All right, Eric. What can we do for you?"

"I want to stay here. Please."

"Why? Don't you have a home?"

"No, ma'am." That was true. No home of his own. Not since Greenlea.

"Are you sure? You must live somewhere."

"Yes, ma'am. Lots of places." Eric hesitated, wondering how to explain. "Well, I've been... I move about a lot and... Please, can't I stay here? It wouldn't be for long. Maybe just a little while, and then I'll go back and not bother you anymore. I'd be good and do anything you told me to. Please..."

Mandy could tell he was at a breaking point. She put an arm around his shoulders and held him for a moment as she had many a troubled boy. "How did you get here?"

"On the bus."

"Oh. But why...how did you know about this place?"

"Du—" He stopped himself. "At that game. They talked about it."

"Oh." The dark eyes studied him. "All right,

Eric. You can stay—for now. We'll talk in the morning. Are you hungry?''

"No, ma'am. Just tired."

"I expect you are." She touched a bell and pretty soon another woman came into the room. "Lucy, take Eric up to the spare and see that he has what he needs. He's staying with us tonight."

"Thank you," Eric said, his relief and gratitude unmistakable.

Mandy sighed as she watched him leave. She would try to find his parents tomorrow. It was not her policy to report a runaway until she was fairly certain of the situation. Often the facts could be satisfactorily ferreted out and the child returned home without the blemish of a police record. Surely this boy, Eric, would open up in the morning, and she would know whom to contact.

VAL LANGSTROM was really miffed at Dave Archer. This was *his* headache, not hers! But when she called last night to remind him of this morning's meeting with the baseball commissioner, he'd practically slammed the phone down before she got a word in.

Family crisis indeed! What could be more important than this meeting? Of course it was all a stupid mix-up. They never should have called it the San Diego Demons' Home for Boys in the first place. That alone connected the team with the home, at least in the public's eye.

Well, it was the commissioner's eye that counted. He was probably being pushed by complaints from some soreheads who noted the number of boys from the home who'd moved in and up in baseball, usually on the Demons' team. It really wasn't fair to Dave, whose policy was to take in "any poor kid who needs."

Well, she wasn't a bleeding heart like Dave, but she was a darn good businesswoman. No venture she was involved in was going to be charged with irregularities, and by God, she'd have these charges dropped. Today. She had records in her briefcase to prove they were invalid.

Promptly at nine-thirty Monday morning she climbed in her car and headed for the group home. She had a meeting there at ten and didn't want to be late. When she arrived, the hotshots from the league were already waiting. So was Scot Palmer, a medical student, and Elmer Reid, currently an engineer with Headback Aircraft Corporation. Both men were former residents of the home and prime examples of the many boys who'd been housed there but were never involved in baseball.

Neither Mr. nor Mrs. Ross were there. So they waited.

It was almost ten-fifteen when a harried Mrs. Ross appeared. "Sorry to be late," she said. "We had a bit of a crisis here this weekend."

Another crisis, Val thought, remembering Dave's excuse. "What's the problem?" she asked idly.

"Oh, a little boy turned up here Friday night, obviously a runaway. I hated to involve the authorities, but perhaps I'd better. All we can get out of him is that his name is Eric. No last name."

Eric? Family crisis? A lightbulb went on in Val's head.

"LOOK, VAL," Dave said into the phone. "I don't give a damn about any meeting. Later!"

"Dave Archer, don't you dare hang up! You said you had a family crisis? Would it involve a boy named Eric? If so, you'd better listen to me."

"Val, what are you saying?"

"I'm saying I have Eric right here with me. Would you like me to bring him home?"

CHAPTER TWENTY

ERIC FELT HIS HEART beat faster the closer Val's car got to his dad and uncle's house. She'd said everything was going to be all right, but he wasn't so sure.

Had Marion come? Gone?

Were his dad and Dave both mad at him?

His trepidation mounted as they pulled into the driveway. Then his father ran down the steps and to the car. He opened the door and gathered Eric into his arms like he wasn't mad at all.

Eric couldn't believe it. "Are you mad?" he asked.

"Mad as hell. I don't know why I'm hugging you," Lyn said. Still holding him tight, he carried Eric up the steps and into the house. "I ought to tan your hide."

"I'll do it for you," Dave said. "You're in big trouble, boy!" But even as he scolded, Dave reached out to tousle Eric's hair. "Didn't I tell you to call me when you had a problem?"

Eric looked at him over his dad's shoulder. "I know. And I was going to, only...you would've stopped me and then..."

They were in the hall now, and his father loosened

his hold and let him slip to the floor. "I don't want to live with Marion, Dad. Is...is she here?" Eric asked in a whisper.

"No, she's not," Lyn said, tight-lipped. "And you should know better than to take off because of something you heard on television. You should have come to me."

"I know. But you said...you said she had custody." He couldn't get the word out of his mind.

Lyn bent toward him. "Listen, son, let's get one thing straight. You'll *always* be in my care. And from now on, we, you and I together, will decide the best place for you to be. Okay?"

"Okay." Eric felt a great surge of relief.

Lyn looked a little troubled. "Things being what they are, I want you to understand that it might not always be the perfect place, but—"

"Oh, it is! Perfect I mean. Here." The words tumbled out. "Tommy and Bert and me, we always have fun. I can be here with Dave anytime I want. I like being at this school, even like it when I have to work at the stable. And there's Monica and Grandpa Herb and Duke and everybody. I like it here, Dad."

"Then maybe you'd better come in here and apologize to these people you've kept on pins and needles for the past two days."

Lyn led him into the sitting room, where all the people he'd named, except the boys, were waiting to welcome him back.

"I'm sorry," he said, after the round of greetings.

"I didn't mean to worry anybody. I...I was just scared that somebody would take me away."

"So you took yourself away," Duke said. "That was dumb. I told you it was tough out in the streets."

"But you told me where to go, too, didn't you?"

"What?"

"The home. You know you told me all about it. How they would be good to you and wouldn't beat you or anything, and I remembered when I was in the bus station. I found it all by myself, but then I was scared they wouldn't let me stay. But they did and it was okay. I kinda had fun."

MONICA WAS TOUCHED by Eric's glowing report of his time at the home. It really did sound like a haven. And wasn't it astonishing that a place Dave had founded had provided a haven for his own nephew!

Duke made the point. "Didn't I tell you? What goes around comes around. If Dave hadn't started it, it wouldn't have been there for you."

"Yeah," Eric said. "Mandy told me I could come back anytime I want to, on account of it really belongs to Dave."

"Well, you won't be going there or anywhere else for a while, young man," Lyn said. "You're grounded, and you better come with me. You and I need to talk. First, though, don't you want to thank somebody for bringing you back where you belong?"

Lyn reached for Val's hand. "I can't thank you enough. You don't know what this means to me."

"I just happened to be there," Val said, returning the pressure of his hand. "But I'm glad I was. And I must say I was pretty proud of your boy. Mrs. Ross said he was really well behaved and never lied to her. When she asked for his last name, he said, 'Couldn't you just call me Eric?' And he was having such a good time! Were you sorry to be found, Eric?"

"Yes, that is, no, ma'am." Eric looked up at Val, seeming confused. "Thank you," he said before his dad bore him away.

"I thank you, too," Dave said. "I owe you one, Val."

Monica's breath caught as Dave not only took Val's hand but gave her a hug. She was instantly ashamed of herself. Wasn't she glad to have Eric safely back, no matter who'd found him? She joined the others. "We're all grateful to you, Val," she said. "We were so worried."

"Well, it was just chance," Val said. "I was in the dark, you know. I was pretty sore at Dave for missing that meeting on account of some crisis, but when Mrs. Ross also talked about a crisis with some boy named Eric, I just put two and two together. And you, Mr. Archer, owe me more than one. I bested the league committee in that battle about your precious home, too." Val's finger tapped Dave's chest as she delivered this last.

It was to emphasize her point, not an intimate gesture, Monica told herself. All the same she did feel left out when Dave and Val went into a huddle about the league and team business.

Maybe it wasn't enough just to be special.

MARION HOLIDAY did come to Pueblo Beach. She came in a flurry of press people with lightbulbs flashing. She was photographed with her son in his classroom, talking with his teacher, at the stable, in his dorm room and holding his hand as they walked about the campus together.

A lot of pictures were taken at one of the rehearsals of the Christmas pageant. "Following in his mother's footsteps," was the caption under one picture, as the paper noted the remarkable resemblance—her eyes, the narrow face, the blond hair.

She even spent one whole evening with Eric at Lyn and Dave's house for a private mother-and-son chat, the ever-present reporters kept at a distance.

Then, as suddenly as she'd come, she was gone.

Later, in one of their patio conversations, Eric confided to Herb and Monica that he was glad Marion had been to see him. Then he turned to Tommy, who'd accompanied him on this visit with Monica and her father. "Fun, wasn't it?" he asked.

"Yeah," Tommy said, his mouth full of Monica's cookies. "Taking all those pictures and stuff. Neat."

"And all the guys kept saying, 'wow, your mom's sure pretty,'" Eric added, with a touch of pride.

Tommy giggled. "Did you see Bert? The man with the camera kept telling him to throw that ball, like we were playing, and he just kept staring at your mom like he'd gone dumb or something."

Herb smiled. "So you enjoyed the visit."

"Yeah," Eric said. "She's nice and she says it's

okay if I stay with Dad. Dad says I should visit her sometimes, but I'm glad he fixed it so I live with him all the time.''

"We're glad you're glad," Monica said, grinning.

"Yeah. I like it here, because I get to do lots of stuff, but I don't *have* to do it unless I really want to. When I'm with Marion it's do this, do that, just so's I can get my picture taken doing it.''

"Well, grab that volleyball and let's go down to the beach and not do much of anything," Herb suggested.

As she watched her father and the boys depart, Monica felt sorry for Marion Holiday. She wouldn't see her boy very often. Did she not know what she was missing?

Still, Monica *was* glad Eric had reached a kind of happy reconciliation with his mother and a truly compatible and loving relationship with his father. She was also glad the Hollywood star had made her brilliant appearance *before* the Christmas pageant. That was the children's time to shine. They didn't need someone else stealing the limelight.

The pageant was held two weeks before Christmas before an auditorium filled with teachers, parents and other close relatives of the children. There were only two mishaps—an angel lost her halo, and a shepherd stumbled over his staff—but no one in the enthralled audience appeared to notice. The simulated star cast its light over the manger and sleeping baby. The angels sang beautifully.

When the three kings made their way down the aisle, their eyes fixed on the star, singing "'We three kings of Orient are..."'" Bert remembered to keep his voice low and Tommy forgot some lines. But Eric's high treble rang out true and clear.

Monica stole a glance at Lyn, and could see he was almost bursting with pride. As the carols were sung and the old story was again portrayed by children who believed, Monica reached over to her father and touched his hand.

He nodded, and her heart warmed. There would always be Christmas.

As if to remind them that it was a time to celebrate, the pageant ended with rollicking happy songs: "Deck the Halls" and "We Wish You a Merry Christmas."

Then, like a signal for the holidays to begin, lockers banged, doors closed and goodbyes were exchanged as students and staff departed to spend the Christmas holidays with families and friends.

For Monica it was the beginning of a new way to celebrate the season. During the years at Pueblo Beach where they knew few people and when her mother was alive, Christmas had been a happy but private family affair. Now, though fond memories of that time remained, Monica found she was looking forward to enjoying the holiday with all her new friends. Friendships formed, she thought, because of a little boy named Eric.

Oh, yes, she'd been pretty burned up when she'd learned how Eric had been tossed from one place to another after his grandparents' death. But if he hadn't been there, a sullen unhappy child...if Dave hadn't appeared in the false guise of Eric's father...

Dave. Oh, sure, she'd been furious. But even then, even before she knew what a truly wonderful caring person he was, something in the way he'd looked at her had drawn her in. As it did now. He only had to glance at her, that expression in his eyes, and she was in his arms.

Still, tiny doubts remained. Was it the way he looked at *her*—or at anyone? Did Val feel special when he looked at her, too?

Monica gave herself a shake. She had to stop thinking that way. Wasn't it enough that she'd have a happy Christmas now with Dave and Lisa, and the friends she'd made through Dave—Vicky, Duke and Lyn? Having a group of good friends around you was like being enclosed in a circle of love. Didn't someone say that love was the only real Christmas gift?

She smiled. Eric again. It was Eric who'd said that. Something he heard somebody say at Lisa's discussion group. That child registered everything. Now he was all excited about the Christmas Eve candlelight service. He assured everyone they'd all get their fortunes. She chuckled. Yes, they'd all be there. Wouldn't miss it.

Maybe, she thought, she'd have everyone come to the house before the service for eggnog and treats. Lisa thought it was a great idea.

"Tell everyone to dress casually," Lisa told her. "It's that kind of church. Anything goes. As Lyn says, we pray to 'whom it may concern.'"

"You *do* celebrate Christmas, though...."

"Definitely. But we *are* ecumenical."

It seemed to Monica that their house was particularly festive and welcoming that night. Herb had even found a place on one of the corner tables for the nativity scene with all the artifacts Mom had purchased so long ago. Holly and pinecones graced the mantel, and mistletoe hung from every doorway. Strategically placed candles flickered, reflecting the glow of tiny white lights on the tree. The sweet aroma of something baking lingered, mingling with the pungent pine scent of the Christmas tree.

Everyone arrived at once, all in a festive mood, and all dressed casually in sweaters and slacks. But Lisa's red sweater, sparkling with sequins, and Vicky's white cashmere, with its stunning rhinestone collar, added touches of elegance. Monica did her part by draping her mother's pearls over her green sweater.

When everyone was settled on chairs, sofa and floor, helping themselves to shrimp, tiny sandwiches and buttery shortbread, Monica passed around cups of her homemade eggnog. Eric and his friend, Bert, meanwhile, with the curiosity of young boys, began poking among the gifts piled under the tree.

Lyn told them that no gifts were to be opened until morning, "after Santa's come and gone," he added with a smile. But Herb, giving in to the boy's moans, said they could open the one marked "Eric and Bert." It proved to be a Nintendo game, and the boys immediately retreated with Herb to try it out on his bedroom television.

Monica, sitting beside Dave on the floor, was captivated by anecdotes about baseball, business mergers, past lives and past Christmases of those around her. She was enjoying her own party so much she was dismayed when Eric rushed back into the room to warn them that it was time to go. "Come on, you don't wanna miss it!"

Monica saw that the others were as reluctant to leave as she was. But it was nearing time, and Eric was so excited. He kept reminding them of their promise to go, asking, "Don't you want to get your fortunes? Don't you want to know what's going to happen next year?"

LISA WAS RIGHT about casual, Monica thought, as the congregation filed in and she saw silk dresses and tailored suits alongside shorts and sneakers. Like peasants mingling with kings in the old old story.

Even the old old story was told in a different way. Oh, a Christmas tree stood on one corner of the podium, the Christmas songs were sung, and a short scripture read about the birth of the Christ child. But the focus was on one single word...*love*. The minister ended his short sermon with the admonition, "God so loved the world that he gave his only begotten son. To teach us how to love one another!"

The little candles were passed out, the lights shut off and the candles lit one by one in the darkened sanctuary. Monica felt strangely moved as Dave touched the flame of his candle to hers, and she turned to light her father's. When all the candles were lit, each person raised his candle high, and together they proclaimed, "Let there be love and peace on earth and let it begin with me."

She felt calm, serene. As if it could really happen. As if each little flame could light a way to love one another, a way to end all petty squabbles, big dissensions...even wars.

A simple but powerful message. *Love.*

It followed them into the night, affected each in a different way. Each person holding the candle with his own personal message wrapped tightly around it, each with his own doubts and needs, each seeking an answer. The words rang in each ear...*let it begin with me.*

As they climbed the steps to their bedroom together, Duke said to Vicky, "I want you to throw away those stupid birth control pills."

She grinned at him. "Oh! That's because you want a boy like Eric!"

Yes, he thought. But something else he couldn't bring himself to talk about. All he said was, "My boy better have brown eyes!" He stopped on the steps and turned her to him. "And I want my girl to have your silky black hair, your eyes that slant just a little, and I want my children to laugh and love." He pulled her close and whispered in her ear, "We have so much, Vicky. Let's pass it on."

He couldn't tell her. Not yet. He was still trying to believe it himself. But honest to God, it was like Mom had been there, looking over his shoulder. He had come in from the garage, slipped his keys into his pocket and felt the candle. He took it out, un-folded the message, and read...

God's love has come to me. I ought to pass it on.

His mother's words. She had said them so many times that it was like she was saying them now.

Okay, Mom, I hear you. And I promise. All the love, all the luck, all the wonderful things I have been given...I'll pass them on.

Vicky, feeling his arms about her, glowed with happiness. It was coming true, everything she had ever wanted. A real home, Duke, children. And it hadn't been because she had nagged him into it. It had come of his own volition...from somewhere. God?

Well, wasn't that what her message had said...*Let go, let God.*

Thank you, she silently whispered.

IT WAS CRAZY, Lyn thought, the way he was begin-ning to accept as gospel anything Eric said. Like tonight. Okay, church was a good thing and maybe he ought to go more often. But the rest..."Get your fortune...don't tell anybody else..." Crap! Probably didn't want you to tell because almost everybody was getting the same fortune.

Crap, huh? So why did you linger in the vestibule to sneak a private look?

Eric. He believes. And I'm stupid. Two words.

What kind of message is that? Probably whoever wrote the damn messages got tired and...

It was no good. The two words were so powerful, so important, that even while the boys were waiting in the car, he lingered in the doorway of Lisa's apartment. Two words. Powerful words... *Try again.*

"Remember that so-called vision you had?" he asked her. "About me and Eric and horses?"

"Mmm-hmm." She looked at him expectantly.

"Well, I didn't tell you then, but the place you described was familiar to me."

"Oh?"

He nodded. "The lettering under the prancing horse reads 'Greenlea Stables.'"

Her eyes grew round. "Oh, Lyn, then maybe it really *was* a message."

"Seems it was. Eric's grandfather's will was probated last week. He left the place to Eric, in trust to me."

"How perfectly wonderful! Eric loves it so. He must be beside himself."

Lyn smiled. "I haven't told him yet. I'm saving it for tomorrow. A Christmas gift. With love from his grandfather, in lieu of the horse he promised."

"Oh, yes! That'll mean so much to him. The greatest gift he could ever receive."

"Right." Lyn stirred uneasily. "What I want to know is...that dream...vision...whatever you call it. Were you there?"

"Me?" She looked puzzled. "I don't know. I think... Well, it was like I was watching, I guess."

"I hope so."

She looked at him, trying to fathom his meaning.

"I'm thinking of cutting back on travel. Not so much need now, what with computers, fax machines, telephone conferences. A guy can conduct lots of business right at home. And a boy needs a home."

"What exactly are you saying, Lyn?"

"I'm saying Greenlea is where Eric and I will be. I'd like you to be there too."

Her mouth twisted ruefully. "You mentioned electronics. Said a boy needs a home. I didn't hear the word 'love.'"

"Love is easy to say. I've said it many times." He hesitated. "I can't put the way I feel about you into words, Lisa. It's too big. It's a certainty, a knowing... You're the only woman in the world for me."

She looked doubtful. "I don't marriage hop, either."

"Good. A guy gets tired of hopping." He kissed her lightly on the lips. "Sleep on it. We'll talk in the morning." He left before she could say more. Hopeful. At least she hadn't said no.

From her window, Lisa watched him get into the car, drive away. A lump rose in her throat. As if he was driving out of her life forever.

Because she couldn't take the risk. She had promised herself that she would never marry a man like Tup. And Lyndon Archer was Tup all over again. An exciting, charming, caring man. But a man with so much love in his heart that he couldn't help but spread it around.

Tup had loved her mother, and had made her happy. But Lisa remembered that there'd also been times when she was hurt.

She thought about Lyn, admitted that she loved him, knew without a doubt that he was a man she would love all her life.

But...marry him?

She shook her head. She couldn't take the risk. She didn't want to be hurt.

Tears stung her eyes, and to distract her thoughts from Lyn, she fumbled at the paper wrapped around the candle. Silly. But still she wondered. What message, what fortune, where did she go from here?

The words jumped out at her.

If in your fear, you would seek only love's pleasure, you will laugh, but not all of your laughter, and you will weep, but not all of your tears.

She stared, reading it over and over again. This message just for her? To remind her that her mother's life had been, and still was, more filled with happiness than hurt.

To let her know that without Lyn Archer, her own life would be empty. She needed him. Only with him would all the laughter spill over, all the tears. All the happiness.

She picked up the phone. Yes, she would say. Yes. She saw herself laughing with him and Eric.

Yes, she had been in the dream she had when Eric was lost. It had made her so happy. She was sure she was laughing as she watched him, and Eric, and the horse in front of the Greenlea stable.

How COULD SHE ever have dreaded Christmas, Monica thought as once again she sat with Dave on the floor beside her Christmas tree. Alone this time. The guests had departed, Eric's candlelight service was over, and Herb had gone to bed. Dave leaned against the sofa and she curled up in his arms, right where she wanted to be. This was the happiest Christmas ever!

The thought came unbidden.

This isn't enough!

She stirred in the comfort of his arms and tried to brush the thought away.

It persisted. *Not enough.*

What was the matter with her? Why did she feel so dissatisfied, so unfulfilled?

Was it the message she had read when she stopped to hang up their jackets?

Today I am born anew, to a fresh, bright, glorious day, filled with unlimited opportunities.

It had actually startled her. Ridiculous to think, as Eric said, that the message was special for her.

But...unlimited opportunities.

Something, someone, was telling her not to settle for less. That she deserved more. That Dave deserved more. If she were to be true to him... To herself.

"I love you, Dave."

His arms tightened around her. "My love."

"Do you love me?"

"Do I...? Sure. Of course."

"You've never said so."

"Yes, I—"

"No, you haven't. You've called me your love, you've said I was special. But you never, not once, said you love me."

"But I do. Monica, I—"

"Yes, I think you do." She reached up to caress his cheek, kissed him lightly. "I think you're just afraid to say it."

"Oh, come now. Why should I be afraid to say it? I love you, I love you. There."

"I know. Everything you do tells me so. And maybe it's not the words that scare you. Maybe you're afraid of commitment."

He started to speak, but she put her fingers over his mouth. "Wait...hear me out. I think both you and Lyn have been greatly affected by what your parents have. The perfect communion, the great love for each other. I don't want to say you're envious. It's more like an obsession to have what they have. Both of you are desperately searching for it."

"That's utter nonsense. Lyn falls in love, gets married at the drop of a hat. That's not me."

"No. You're afraid to make a real commitment. It may not live up to what you expect."

"Is that what you think?"

"I know you're scared." She paused, bit her lip. The thought of the message gave her courage. She looked up at him. "I'm not. I believe that...nothing ventured, nothing gained."

"What are you saying?"

"I'm saying I want more than this. I want it all. I want commitment, tradition." Her words poured out in rapid succession, trying to keep pace with her thoughts. "I want Christmases at *our* house...with dolls and a tricycle under the tree. I want a little boy with eyes like yours. I want to share lots of Christmas trees with you, the decorations changing year after year...the crooked ornaments made by Cub Scouts, the tattered angel the baby chewed on. Tokens of love that will change as love grows."

"Oh, my darling love." He held her so close she could hardly breathe. "Yes, my love. I accept."

"What?"

A dry chuckle sounded from his throat. "That was a proposal, wasn't it?"

"Oh, God!" She had proposed! Those few words, wrapped around a candle had made her so brazen that... "I...I was just thinking...saying...what I want."

He bent his head, trying to hide his smile. "I know. And I thank you for the honor, and accept with pleasure your—"

"Oh, shut up!" Her fists beat a light tattoo on his chest.

He caught her hands, laughing. "All I'm saying is that I want it too and I'm not afraid to take the risk. Let me show you something." He pulled from his pocket a traditional little box.

She gasped when he opened it. The ring was of

yellow gold and the big diamond solitaire seemed
to sparkle with a promise that warmed her heart.

"Oh, Dave, it's beautiful. It's…" She looked up
at him, stunned by the realization. "You were going
to—"

He nodded. "Of course. Didn't you think I'd
know when I found that special someone?"

"Oh, Dave!" She threw her arms around him and
kissed him over and over again. "Yes! Yes! I'll
marry you! That is, if you promise to forget that I
asked you first."

She nestled in his arms and smiled to herself.
He'd been going to ask her anyway. Still, it was a
good message that she would always treasure. She
looked up at him. "Dave, did you read your fortune?"

"Fortune?"

"You know. The candle you got in church. Eric
said the message wrapped around it would be your
fortune. Did you read it?"

He shook his head. "Didn't need to. I have my
fortune. Right here in my arms."

"Oh, yes. Yes." She laughed in the joy and wonder. A wonderful fortune. A happy beginning of
many happy Christmases to come.

YOU WEREN'T SUPPOSED to let anyone else see your
fortune. Eric waited until he was sure Bert was
asleep in the other bed. Then he turned on the bedside lamp and unwrapped the paper from his candle.

He read: *And a little child shall lead them.*

That wasn't a fortune! It wasn't even a message.
Dumb.

Every month there's another title from one
of your favorite authors!

October 1997
Romeo in the Rain by Kasey Michaels
When Courtney Blackmun's daughter brought home Mr. Tall,
Dark and Handsome, Courtney wanted to send the young
matchmaker to her room! Of course, that meant the single
New Jersey mom would be left alone with the irresistibly
attractive Adam Richardson....

November 1997
Intrusive Man by Lass Small
Indiana's Hannah Calhoun had enough on her hands taking
care of her young son, and the last thing she needed was a
man complicating things—especially Max Simmons, the
gorgeous cop who had eased himself right into her little boy's
heart...and was making his way into hers.

December 1997
Crazy Like a Fox by Anne Stuart
Moving in with her deceased husband's—*eccentric*—family
in Louisiana meant a whole new life for Margaret Jaffrey and
her nine-year-old daughter. But the beautiful young widow
soon finds herself seduced by the slower pace and the much-
too-attractive cousin-in-law, Peter Andrew Jaffrey....

**BORN IN THE USA: Love, marriage—
and the pursuit of family!**

Available at your favorite retail outlet!

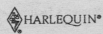

A showgirl, a minister—
and an unsolved murder.

EASY VIRTUE

Eight years ago Mary Margaret's father was
convicted of a violent murder she knew he
didn't commit—and she vowed to clear his
name. With her father serving a life sentence,
Mary Margaret is working as a showgirl in Reno
when Reverend Dane Barrett shows up with
information about her father's case. Working to
expose the real killer, the unlikely pair also
proceed to expose themselves to an unknown
enemy who is intent on keeping the past buried.

**From the bestselling author of
LAST NIGHT IN RIO**

**JANICE
KAISER**

Available in December 1997
at your favorite retail outlet.

MIRA
BOOKS

The Brightest Stars in Women's Fiction.™

DECEPTION (#773)
by Morgan Hayes

Shelby Beaumont is madly in love with homicide detective
Johnny Spencer. They've been living together for the past
year, and they've just become engaged. And though Johnny
doesn't know it yet, Shelby's pregnant with his child.

But Johnny's been investigating a possible case of police
corruption. And someone on the force has found out....

Then a bomb is rigged on Johnny's boat. And Johnny's on it....

Find out what happens next in
Deception by Morgan Hayes.

Available January 1998 wherever Harlequin books
are sold.

WELCOME TO *Love Inspired* ™

A brand-new series of contemporary inspirational love stories.

Join men and women as they learn valuable lessons about facing the challenges of today's world and about life, love and faith.

Look for:

Christmas Rose
by Lacey Springer

A Matter of Trust
by Cheryl Wolverton

The Wedding Quilt
by Lenora Worth

Available in retail outlets
in November 1997.

LIFT YOUR SPIRITS AND GLADDEN YOUR HEART with *Love Inspired* ™!

Steeple
Hill™

LI1297